Praise for Allan Leverone

"Allan Leverone's *Parallax View* is a sure-footed, masterful thriller with a breakneck pace that never lets up...Tracie Tanner is one for the ages. I loved this book!"

—J Carson Black, New York Times bestselling author of *The Shop* and *Icon*

"Parallax View...is a powerhouse full-throttle spy thriller...that leads readers down the shadowy back allies of international intrigue...a taut and thoughtful journey back to the dying days of the Cold War...it will keep you up, and on the edge of your chair, long into the night."

—*Nashua* (NH) *Sunday Telegraph*

"...Allan Leverone is a literary genius. His ability to write quality literature within multiple genres is dynamic. This book took off from page one and didn't stop..."

—A Book and a Review

"Suspenseful and well-written, *The Lonely Mile* shows how far a father will go to save his child."

—Debbi Mack, New York Times bestselling author of *Identity Crisis* and *Least Wanted*

"Written with edge-of-your-seat suspense and precise detail...The successor to Michael Crichton has landed. And his name is Allan Leverone."

—Vincent Zandri, Amazon bestselling author of *The Innocent* and the Dick Moonlight thriller series

"Allan Leverone delivers a taut crime drama full of twists and conspiracy. A serial killer thriller with a heart."

—Scott Nicholson, Amazon bestselling author of *Liquid Fear* and *The Red Church*

"Allan Leverone raises the stakes with every turn of the page…"

—Sophie Littlefield, Anthony Award-winning author of *A Bad Day for Sorry*

"Thriller fans will enjoy Allan Leverone's new book, *The Lonely Mile,* which will carry readers along…"

—Dave Zeltserman, critically acclaimed author of *Monster* and the Man Out of Prison series

"A dark and creepy chiller!"

—Ron Malfi, Bram Stoker Award-nominated author of *Floating Staircase* and *Snow*

"Fast-paced and eerily seductive, *Darkness Falls* is a well-told and atmospheric tale of loss and obsession, of madness and revenge. Allan Leverone is a terrific writer with a bright future…"

—Mark Edward Hall, author of *Apocalypse Island* and *The Lost Village*

"I was floored by the great writing…this book is a must for anyone that is a fan of a good crime thriller."

—Book Sake

"...a chillingly realistic suspense thriller that will have you holding on for the ride of your life."

—Life in Review

"...this story drew me in and grabbed my attention and wouldn't let go until the very surprising and climactic ending...one hell of a roller coaster ride..."

—Café of Dreams Book Reviews

"...the suspense never stops...an intense thriller..."

—Martha's Bookshelf

"...a must-have for anyone looking for a great page-turner with mystery and mayhem."

—Community Bookstop

"If you enjoy thrillers...this is a great option. It's a fast-moving storyline...and you'll find you care about the characters..."

—My Book Retreat

"...feels like I'm watching an episode of *24*. There is not a dull moment, and absolutely no lag time...The characters are well-developed, and I find the plot easily believable and very easy to get absorbed in."

—Southern Fiber Reads

"...a high suspense thrill ride..."

—Derry (NH) News

"...keeps you on the edge of your seat, turning pages as fast as you can...I highly recommend that you read this book...you will not be disappointed."

—Two Ends of the Pen

"...absolutely fantastic...The story moves along at a good pace, dripping with atmosphere...The frights come at you hard and fast..."

—Literary Mayhem

"...the storyline was haunting and creepy...I would recommend *Darkness Falls* to anyone who enjoys a really nightmarish tale."

—Horrornews.net Book Reviews

Books by Allan Leverone

Parallax View

The Lonely Mile

Paskagankee

Revenant

Novellas by Allan Leverone

Darkness Falls

Heartless

The Becoming

Story Collections

Postcards from the Apocalypse

Uncle Brick and the Four Novelettes

For my beautiful wife, Sue, who, luckily for me, took that whole "for better or worse" thing to heart, who has believed in me every step of the way, and who is my best friend.

FOR MARSHA —
WITH FRIENDSHIP
AND BEST WISHES!

FINAL VECTOR

ALLAN
LEVERONE

Cover design by Scott Carpenter

Print edition formatting by Robert Shane Wilson

I

"Hello?"

"Uh…hello…is this—?"

"No names! You know damn well who this is, and you know you are prohibited from calling this number except in an emergency."

"I know, I know, but this *is* an emergency."

Silence.

"Well, get on with it, then. What is the emergency?"

"She…uh…she knows."

"How much does she know?"

"I'm not sure. Maybe everything."

"She doesn't know everything, you idiot. If she knew everything, you would be in jail right now, and I would be residing in Guantanamo. The place isn't closed yet, you know."

"Nevertheless, she knows enough, I'm certain of it. I tried to gain us some time, though. I told her it was all a misunderstanding and that I could explain everything. I begged her not to turn me in to her superiors until I had the opportunity to do so."

"Okay. How much time did she give you?"

"Until Monday."

"This coming Monday? That's all?"

"Yes. I…I'm sorry…"

"You're sorry. Right. Of course you are. I'll take care of it, you untrustworthy fool."

"Are…are we…still on?"

"Of course we're still on. Nothing has changed. And don't call this number again."

"But…"

The line went dead.

2

"Boston Approach Control, this is Atlas 317. We've, uh, we've got a bit of a problem here."

Nick Jensen swore lightly under his breath. "Great," he mumbled to no one in particular. "A problem. Just what I need to hear when I've got airplanes out the ass."

It was Thursday night in the BCT—the Boston Consolidated Tracon—in Merrimack, New Hampshire, and the weather had been steadily deteriorating all afternoon. A massive low-pressure area was sweeping up the East Coast, carrying moist, unstable air and bringing high winds and heavy rain along for the ride.

The dark room hummed with the murmured voices of eight air traffic controllers sitting side by side facing eight separate radar scopes. Each controller was working a piece of the airspace immediately surrounding Boston's Logan International Airport, with each responsible for maintaining a safe and orderly flow of the airborne traffic transiting his or her sector.

Nick was working Boston's Final Vector position, so he was responsible for sequencing and spacing all of Logan's arrival traffic, being fed to him by the surrounding sectors. For the hour and a half or so that he would be assigned to the position, his job was literally to get all his ducks in a row. Using altitude separation, speed control, and unique headings assigned to each pilot, called radar vectors, Nick was systematically turning each arrival onto the ILS—Instrument Landing System—that served Runway 4 Right at Logan. The Final Vector controller was tasked with maintaining the minimum separation legally permissible, but absolutely no less than that, in order to get all the traffic on the ground with the least possible overall delays.

With the low overcast ceilings and reduced visibility caused by the wind-driven rain, every arrival into Logan as well as all the arrivals into the smaller airports in Boston's airspace were being vectored for the precision approach guidance provided by the ILS system. At the moment a dozen airplanes clogged Nick's tiny chunk of airspace, and the last thing he wanted to hear was that one of those planes was experiencing some difficulty. The strained urgency in the voice of the Atlas Airlines pilot, though, told him this wasn't your garden-variety equipment issue—this might be serious.

Nick pushed the foot pedal to the floor, keying the mike on his headset allowing him to speak to all the airplanes on the discrete radio frequency assigned to his sector. "Atlas 317, go ahead. What's the nature of your problem?"

"Ah, we've got smoke in the cabin." The pilot's voice came back professional but clearly tense. "And it's getting thick in here very quickly. We are either on fire or are experiencing a serious electrical problem. We need to get this crate on the ground. *Now.*"

Nick half turned in his wheeled swivel chair and yelled across the room to the watch supervisor, Earl Washington, seated at a desk behind the row of controllers manning the radar scopes. "Hey, Earl, I've got an emergency here, and I think it might be a bad one."

He pressed the foot pedal again. "Roger, Atlas 317. We'll get you right in. Descend and maintain three thousand, and turn right heading three-one-zero." He was turning the Atlas Airlines Boeing 757 directly at Logan's final approach course and would be forced to break out at least two other airplanes already established on the final, which at the moment extended nearly thirty miles to the southwest of Logan Airport.

As Earl coordinated with the supervisor on duty in the Logan control tower—the facility located right on the airfield responsible for separating the traffic on the surface of the airport—Nick rapidly issued a series of turns to all of the airplanes affected by the unexpected emergency, taking them off the final approach course and explaining the situation as he went. Time was a valuable commodity if the Atlas flight really was on fire. "Rapid Air 400, cancel your approach clearance, turn left heading two-seven-zero and climb *immediately* to maintain four thousand. I'm giving your spot to an aircraft inbound with an emergency."

"Rapid 400, roger. Left to two-seventy and hurry on up to four thousand."

"North American 28, cancel your approach clearance and maintain three thousand. Turn left heading two-seven-zero. This is a vector off the final for inbound emergency traffic."

"North American 28, roger. Left to west and we'll maintain three thousand."

By now Earl had positioned himself directly behind Nick's chair. The normally chaotic buzz of voices in the TRACON—Terminal Radar Approach Control—had dropped to an almost reverential, churchlike quiet as the other controllers in the room recognized that a serious situation had developed on the Final Vector position. The sectors feeding arrivals to Nick immediately began "spinning" their airplanes, turning them away from Nick's airspace and holding them in their own sectors. They knew Nick was juggling far too much traffic now to take any more until the emergency situation was resolved.

Earl bent down and spoke quietly in Nick's ear. "When you can get it, we're going to need"—

"I know," Nick replied. "Souls on board and amount of fuel remaining. I'm getting to that." Standard emergency protocol dictated that the number of people on board the aircraft and the amount of fuel remaining in its tanks get passed to the emergency response personnel on the ground as soon as possible. The rescue crews needed to prepare for the potential worst-case scenario—a plane crash at the airport.

Nick keyed his mike. Despite the skyrocketing stress level and the chaotic situation unfolding on the radar scope in front of him, he maintained a calm demeanor on the frequency. Sounding in control meant being in control. "Atlas 317, you're only about eight miles from the ILS final approach fix. Will you be able to get down from there?" Turning the plane toward the airport too soon and then finding out the pilot would not be able to descend rapidly enough to land would be the worst thing Nick could do.

"We're doing our best," came the answer. "It's getting really hard to see the instruments in here with all the smoke. Yeah, we'll make the descent because we have to."

"Atlas 317, roger. Turn right heading zero-two-zero and intercept the Runway 4 Right localizer. I know you're very busy up there, but when you can get to it, we need souls on board and fuel remaining."

"Zero-two-zero to join the localizer, and we have . . . let's see . . . one hundred seventeen people with a little over two hours of fuel."

"Roger that, Atlas 317. You're doing great with the descent. Your position is five miles from the final approach fix. Descend and maintain two thousand until established on the localizer, cleared ILS Runway 4 Right approach."

Nick inclined his head slightly toward Earl without taking his eyes off the scope. "One hundred seventeen people and two hours of fuel."

He didn't wait for a response from the supervisor; he was already busy formulating a plan to deal with the other arrivals, all of which were now completely out of position thanks to the emergency. Hopefully Atlas Air 317 would be safely on the ground soon, but Nick's work was just beginning. "Liberty Air 5, you're now going to follow a Boeing 757 on final. Caution for wake turbulence."

"Liberty 5, roger, we'll be careful."

"North American 28, continue your left turn heading two-three-zero. I'll get you right back in as soon as I can."

"North American 28, left to two-thirty. We understand."

"Swift 400, you can also turn left heading two-three-zero. Thanks a lot for the fast climb to four thousand feet."

"Left to two-three-zero. You're welcome."

"Atlas 317, how are you doing, sir?"

"We're struggling, but I think we'll be able to make it."

"Okay, Atlas 317, contact Boston Tower now on frequency 123.7. Good luck to you."

"Tower on twenty-three-seven. Thanks a lot for the help."

Behind him, Earl said, "Nice job, Nick."

Nick didn't answer; he had already turned his attention to the mess he had yet to sort out—the nearly one dozen airplanes whose sequences had been disrupted by the sudden emergency and who were now nowhere near where they should be in Nick's airspace. There was a lot of catching up to do.

Nick took a deep breath and started barking out commands as the control tower supervisor called on a landline to tell Earl that Atlas 317 had landed safely and the aircraft was being evacuated on a taxiway.

The traffic kept coming. The controllers kept talking. The Thursday night shift continued.

3

Lisa Jensen blinked rapidly, attempting without any measurable level of success to maintain her concentration as she navigated the rain-slicked highway. Alone and overtired, she had already tried every trick she could think of for remaining alert while traveling late at night, including cranking her music up to earsplitting levels and rolling her window down. She was fading fast, though.

Rain slanted at a forty-five degree angle out of the coal black sky, pelting the area as it had been doing virtually nonstop since Lisa had left D.C. The headlights of the passing traffic cast the landscape surrounding Interstate 95 in a shimmering, almost surreal muted glow. Hours ago, she had reached the conclusion that the sensible decision would have been to stay the night in the city and drive back to New Hampshire tomorrow morning after the storm passed through the area. But her time with Nick was already limited enough, and Lisa couldn't stand the thought of spending even one more night away from her husband. *Hell,* she thought, *we don't see enough of each other as it is.*

Lisa gazed longingly at the Styrofoam coffee cup perched in the holder directly in front of her Toyota's gearshift, its emptiness taunting her, and blinked again, hard. Her scratchy and bloodshot eyes began to water. She forced herself to sing along with the radio.

A fully loaded eighteen-wheel automobile carrier passed her in the left lane, moving much too fast for the conditions, rocking her little car on its springs and spraying a solid sheet of water onto the windshield in its wake. The Toyota's overmatched wipers worked at clearing it all away, the rapid *whup-whup-whup* of the wiper blades trying to lull Lisa back into the state of intense drowsiness she was trying so hard to avoid

Lisa's gaze snapped immediately into focus as her car plunged into a long, deep, and nearly invisible pool of black water stretching into the travel lane. Instantly the car began to hydroplane. She wrenched the wheel to the left as the Toyota slewed out of control toward the guardrail, water splashing in massive fountain-like arcs outward from both sides of the vehicle.

She knew enough not to hit the brakes, although the temptation to stomp on them was almost overwhelming. Instead, she concentrated on steering out of the slide, allowing the car's momentum to slow on its own. She held her breath as the guardrail crept closer and closer. After seconds that felt like hours, the Toyota was back under control, and Lisa gradually began to increase her speed. She checked her mirrors and then angled out of the breakdown lane.

Chuckling nervously and breathing hard, Lisa muttered, "Well, at least now I'll be wide awake for a while. Nothing like the occasional near-death experience to give you a jolt of adrenaline!"

She was no longer drowsy but still longed to be home with Nick, couldn't wait to be in his arms. A Pentagon auditor, Lisa spent every Monday through Thursday in Washington away from her husband, who was forced to stay alone at the couple's Merrimack, New Hampshire, house. Nick was employed as an air traffic controller at one of the busiest airports in the country, unable to relocate to a city nearly five hundred miles away.

At the close of administrative hours at the Pentagon

every Thursday, Lisa's standard routine was to eat dinner in a small café a few blocks from the mammoth office building and wait for the Beltway area traffic congestion to ease. Then she would hit the road in her trusty Toyota, which was only three years old but which had already racked up well over 150,000 miles. She would work her way up Interstate 95 to New England, then zigzag various interstate highways to Route 3 into New Hampshire, eventually reuniting with the other half of her tiny family. Lisa's ten-hour workdays Monday through Thursday allowed her to spend a couple of full days every weekend with Nick.

It certainly wasn't the perfect arrangement. Making a marriage work was enough of a strain for a husband and wife who were together every day, but the challenges faced by a couple forced to spend nearly three quarters of their lives apart sometimes seemed insurmountable.

The Jensens had been enduring exactly that situation, though, for most of their married life, and the plan was to continue in a similar fashion for several more years. By then they estimated they would have enough money set aside for Lisa to quit her job and stay at home to raise a family full-time. That was the theory, anyway. At moments like this, she wondered about the wisdom of The Plan, but the prospect of that happy family, complete with two or three children running around their home, was the carrot dangling on the end of the stick that kept her going even when things were the most difficult.

As she drove, Lisa's mind wandered inexorably back to the mess she had somehow gotten mixed up in at work, to the intrigue that seemed to reverberate within the dozens of miles of passageways running through the Pentagon. She wished she could discuss it with Nick. She hated deceiving him, but knew in her heart it was best to keep him in the dark, even though he was a valuable sounding board and never failed to give her good advice when she asked for it—and sometimes even when she didn't.

She wondered what a relationship expert would say

about the fact that she was how hiding things from her husband, the person with whom she was supposed to have a closer relationship than anyone else in the world. After all, everyone knew honesty was the foundation of a good marriage. Lisa chewed on her lower lip, a habit she had developed as a youngster when confronted with stress. Hiding things from Nick. She detested the idea and considered what it said about her.

Ensuring Nick's safety was paramount, though, and Lisa's work situation was potentially explosive, even when compared with the enormity of some of the other secrets held inside the walls of the massive Pentagon building.

As hard as it was for her to believe, there seemed to be the very real possibility of people getting hurt or even killed because of her discovery. Hell, killing seemed to be the whole *point* of it, and she was determined not to do or say anything that might put Nick's life at risk. Lisa pursed her lips and shook her head firmly as she drove, trying to bury the small nugget of guilt eating away at her insides.

This afternoon Lisa had come to the conclusion that it was time to involve her supervisor. She had been dealing with the situation on her own for the last two weeks, quietly digging, searching for evidence of a serious—perhaps even treasonous—criminal conspiracy.

Against her better judgment, Lisa had agreed to allow Nelson W. Michaels, one of the men she suspected of heavy involvement in the activity, an opportunity to explain himself when she returned to D.C. next week. The evidence she had uncovered against Michaels was so damaging that it could ruin Nelson's life. She knew she would never be able to look herself in the mirror every day if she allowed a man's career to be destroyed without first giving him the chance to prove his innocence.

But there was a *lot* of evidence. Some of it was tucked securely away in the hard drive of her laptop, the one she was careful to keep in her possession at all times when she was at work. The rest was stowed safely in the back of the walk-in closet of their home in Merrimack. Lisa had stacked it all behind a pile of sweaters and parkas. Attempting to safeguard the evidence in her office at the Pentagon would be foolhardy, even if it were kept under lock and key, and the same thing went for trying to hide it in the studio apartment she rented outside D.C. There simply wasn't any place to secure enough to conceal the papers in the three tiny rooms.

She didn't like the idea of storing potentially dangerous material in their home, but she reasoned that it would be there for only a few more days. Besides, what was the likelihood that anyone searching for the evidence would even know she had a husband and a home in New Hampshire, anyway?

Lisa sighed. She couldn't wait for Monday, when she could haul everything back down to D.C. and dump it all into her boss's lap. She would leave it up to him to figure out how to pursue the investigation. The implications of her discovery, if correct, were far above her pay grade. She decided to schedule a consultation with her supervisor immediately following her planned meeting with Nelson Michaels Monday morning. If by some miracle Nelson was able to convince her that her concerns were groundless, she would simply cancel the meeting and appear silly in her boss's eyes. She wouldn't mind that in the least.

By now Lisa had nearly completed the long drive home. It was almost three o'clock in the morning, and she had been so wrapped up in the consideration of her work situation that the miles had flown by. She knew Nick would be waiting up for her, a cup of steaming tea in one hand and some sexy lingerie he had picked out for her in the other. "To get to know each other again," he would say with a mischievous smile, in what had become a part of their weekly routine they both looked forward to.

Lisa smiled at the picture in her head and accelerated through the traffic light at the end of the long, winding off-ramp leading from the highway to the surface streets of Merrimack. It was still pouring; to Lisa's amazement the rain had gotten heavier over the course of the last eight hours as the storm moved up the East Coast and gained in intensity. She stopped at the red light, even though it was ludicrous to think that any other cars would be out at this late hour, especially in such miserable weather.

She pulled through the intersection when the traffic light flashed green, planning to make a left turn toward her home. As she did, her side window was filled with the bright white headlights of an eighteen-wheel semi hauling beer from the Budweiser brewery that was one of the town's biggest employers. The massive rig had run the red light, its driver obviously thinking exactly what Lisa had been thinking just seconds before—that no one would be out in Merrimack this late.

The huge vehicle lost traction on the slick road, its driver locking up the brakes in a desperate attempt to avoid running down the little car. The truck barely slowed, its own momentum and the water-covered pavement combining to thwart the efforts of the frantic driver.

Lisa hesitated, then jammed the accelerator to the floor, praying that she could shoot across the street in front of the semi; it was her only option. For a second, it appeared that it might even work. Maybe on a dry road it would have.

But the road wasn't dry, and her tires spun, and the drive wheels stuttered for purchase. Lisa watched through the side window in utter helpless horror as the massive truck smashed her Toyota broadside.

4

The occupant of the nondescript blue sedan that had been tailing Lisa Jensen's car since leaving Washington—known in the United States as Tony Andretti, although that was not his real name—watched in amazement as the eighteen-wheeled behemoth lost traction on the wet road, sliding out of control and running over the Toyota, the mass of the truck virtually enveloping the much smaller car. Tony could not believe his good fortune. This unexpected but welcome development would make his job even simpler than it already was.

The force of the violent impact drove the young woman's car – splattered all over the truck's grille like a bug – across the road, straight through the deserted oncoming traffic lane, and directly into a huge maple tree.

Fire erupted from somewhere underneath the car, which was instantly mangled beyond recognition and buried under several tons of beer-laden tractor-trailer. Moments later the truck's driver, apparently injured but only superficially so, tumbled out of the cab and limped to the front of the vehicle, obviously hoping to be able to pull the other driver out of the wreckage. Tony sat in the blue sedan and watched closely through narrowed eyes as the man skidded to a halt next to the tree and shook his head. For all intents and purposes, the car had vanished, compacted to a fraction of its original size.

Tony eased his vehicle behind the beer truck and flicked on his emergency blinkers. It would be the worst sort of cosmic irony to have his car rear-ended by some damned fool motorist driving along in the middle of the night not paying attention to what he was doing.

He put on a light jacket and stepped into the heavy rain. The deluge instantly plastered his clothing to his skin, but he didn't care. He walked alongside the jackknifed trailer toward the cab in time to see the weeping driver of the beer truck flop down on his hands and knees on the pavement and crawl under his rig. The man still hadn't noticed him.

Tony sighed deeply and squatted as well, peering under the truck's frame. Thick black smoke poured out of and around the engine compartment, issuing from where he assumed the car must now be, as flames licked their way around the fenders on both sides of the cab. He could see the beer truck's driver, outlined by the rapidly expanding fire against the twisted metal now barely recognizable as a car. "Are you okay? Hello? Is anybody there?" the frantic man shouted in the direction of the ruined Toyota.

Tony listened for any sound that might indicate someone was alive in the wreckage. There was nothing. All he could hear was the crackling of the spreading fire, greedy and grasping, consuming everything it could reach and still searching for more. He began to smell the unmistakably sharp odor of gasoline and considered the possibility of explosion. He knew it was unlikely, something that happened a lot more in the movies and on television than at accident scenes in the real world, but he also was well aware that it was not unheard of, especially when the fuel tank of one of the vehicles was nearly empty. The fumes, not the actual gasoline, were the truly explosive component, and a tank with very little gas left in it was by definition filled with potentially deadly fumes.

Tony had been following this car since D.C., and he knew it had been hours since Lisa Jensen had stopped to refuel, meaning it was critical he finish this now before he became part of the tragedy.

He stood and strode along the muddy shoulder to the maple tree. The battered car, now flickering in the eerie glow of the expanding fire, had been crushed up against it. The driving rain slicked his curly black hair flat against his skull, and he gagged from the stench of burning rubber as he clambered up the hood of the Toyota, careful not to slice his skin open on a razor-sharp edge of crumpled sheet metal. It was an easy climb; the entire front section of the car had been compressed down to about a four-foot square.

The impact of the crash had smashed the vehicle's windshield, and Tony nodded appreciatively. The shatterproof safety glass had come completely dislodged from the frame, allowing easy access to what was left of the cabin, which was not much. Lisa Jensen lay motionless, pushed by the devastating impact mostly into the passenger's side of her car. Her eyes were closed and she was covered in blood. Tony wondered whether he could possibly be so lucky as to discover she was already dead.

Then she moaned, the sound thin and quavery. Her eyes remained closed, so Tony knew she was unconscious, but there was no longer any question about whether she was alive or dead. Tony shook his head and sighed again. Nothing in life was ever easy.

He had to admit, though, that the car wreck was an incredibly lucky break. It would take the authorities some time to discover that Lisa Jensen had not actually been killed in this horrendous accident; she had been murdered. And by the time they pieced it together, it would no longer matter, at least not to Tony. This unexpected bit of good fortune had saved him from following the Jensen bitch to her home and killing her there, which had been the original plan.

This was better.

He fumbled in the pocket of his Windbreaker—it was woefully inadequate against this weather—for his switchblade, finally wrapping his fingers around it and yanking it out. He was beginning to shiver heavily but tried to ignore the chill. This would be over soon, and then he would climb back into the toasty warmth of his idling car, where he would have hours to dry off while driving back to D.C.

The switchblade snapped open with a snick. Tony reached into the passenger compartment, moving carefully, supporting himself with his right hand on the crushed windshield frame. With a practiced flick of his wrist, Tony deftly sliced Lisa Jensen's throat, opening a gash that ran from the right side of her jawbone to the left.

Blood spurted. It was not the cleanest kill Tony had ever made, but under the circumstances he was satisfied with the result. Dead was dead, after all. Following the initial burst of bright crimson arterial spray that added more of Lisa Jensen's blood to the interior of a car already soaked with it, the volume rapidly slowed, then ended entirely.

Within ninety seconds Lisa Jensen was dead, and Tony no longer had to worry about this particular loose end—he had tied it up into a very nice, neat bow.

5

The driver of the beer truck was named Bud Willingham—a never-ending source of amusement to his fellow drivers, who thought it the funniest thing in the world that a guy named Bud was driving a truck filled with Bud—and he was crying hard now. He crawled out from under the wreckage of the car he had rammed and struggled back to the cab of his truck. He was soaking wet and freezing and certain he was about to lose his job.

Oh yeah, and he had probably just killed someone.

Looking at the scene from the inside of his truck, lit by the flickering yellow glow of the fire, Bud thought you would never know there had just been a horrible car accident were it not for the smells of burning cloth and rubber. The amount of damage his rig had sustained was minimal and the Toyota was mostly invisible from this vantage point.

Bud grabbed his cell phone from where he kept it clipped to his sun visor and punched in 911, giving his location to the emergency dispatcher. The operator asked him to stay on the line until the emergency responders arrived, but he disconnected the call. Then he removed the portable fire extinguisher from the back wall of the cab and leapt back down to the wet road. He landed in a puddle and didn't notice. He began spraying the base of the fire in wide arcs around the carcass of the smashed car.

He sprayed the fire-retardant foam until the canister was empty and then threw it to the pavement in frustration where it bounced once and skittered to the side of the road. He had made virtually no dent in the still expanding blaze. Helpless to do anything now but wait, Bud trudged to the side of the deserted road and waited for the emergency vehicles to arrive, something he fervently hoped would happen soon. He blinked in surprise when he noticed a dark sedan drive slowly away from the scene toward the interstate's southbound ramp.

Bud had assumed he was alone except for the poor victim trapped inside the car, but it was obvious from the position of the departing sedan that it had been parked right behind his truck. How long the sedan had been there and what its driver had seen Bud had no idea, but the occupant was a witness to a major automobile accident. Bud knew the driver of the other car should not be leaving and yet there he went, motoring into the darkness, swallowed up by the rain.

He shook his head, spraying water in all directions, trying to comprehend what could possibly have compelled the anonymous witness to stop at the scene of a car wreck and then drive away without offering any help.

Then he forgot all about this strange occurrence until much later as his attention was drawn to a string of emergency vehicles speeding toward the accident site from the direction of Merrimack proper. Within seconds they began screeching to a halt, their strobes jaggedly slicing the 3:00 a.m. darkness in brilliant flashes of red, white and blue.

6

Lady Bird Johnson Memorial Park was unseasonably warm for mid-May as bright sunlight flooded the Washington, D.C. area following the massive overnight storm. Now, with the rainfall just a memory, people crowded into the park, eager to enjoy the early taste of summer.

Young mothers pushed baby strollers along walking paths, stopping and chatting and admiring each other's infants. Joggers of all ages pounded the paths, weaving around old folks leaning on canes and walkers as they shared the same routes. College students tossed Frisbees back and forth, running and leaping and shouting.

Tucked into the southeast corner of the park, backed snugly against a row of neatly trimmed ficus bushes, was a wrought-iron bench. On this bench sat Nelson W. Michaels, middle-aged, balding, dressed in a rumpled blue suit—not expensive but not cheap—with a maroon rep tie loosened to enable him to unfasten the top button of his off-white dress shirt. A briefcase rested on the ground next to his nervously tapping left foot. He was a good thirty pounds overweight, the extra baggage making him appear at least a decade older than his thirty-eight years. He was sweating heavily.

Nelson hoped he looked just like any other anonymous government bureaucrat passing the time on his lunch hour by ogling the throngs of sexy young women in the park. He pretended to read the newspaper, which he had opened randomly to the sports section. The Washington Nationals, widely considered the worst team in baseball, had just won their seventh consecutive game, leading fans to begin hoping the team might actually be competitive after all.

Nelson raised his face to the sun and tried to slow his racing heartbeat through sheer force of will. He was just one of dozens of guys in the park – hundreds really – plain and invisible. There was no reason to work himself up to a stroke over an illicit lunch hour rendezvous, for Chrissakes. What he was doing had been going on in the capitol since the days of Washington and Jefferson.

Without warning, a man dropped onto the other side of the bench, legs splayed, sweat glistening on his olive skin. He seemed to have materialized out of nowhere and Nelson gasped in surprise.

The man looked younger than Nelson by a decade. He had a full head of thick, wavy black hair that he wore slicked back from his high forehead. He was dressed in stonewashed jeans and an Oxford shirt with the top two buttons unfastened and the long sleeves rolled up to his elbows. He carried a brown leather briefcase, virtually an exact replica of Nelson's.

The new arrival leaned forward and placed his briefcase on the ground to his right, then sat without moving, saying nothing and staring unabashedly at the steady stream of young women walking and running past the bench. Many of them looked barely half his age. He made no effort to hide his interest in their forms, especially the ones outlined nicely in tight-fitting T-shirts and Lycra running shorts.

Nelson felt his stomach clench in an unwitting visceral response to the man's arrival, and he tried to examine his newspaper with renewed interest. He read the same sentence about the Nationals three times but absorbed nothing. He knew the man sitting to his left was the one he was scheduled to meet today, although he had never seen him before and had no idea what he looked like. Obviously it was impossible to get a sense of the man's appearance from a few emails and a whispered phone call or two.

Nelson began to sweat even more profusely and wanted nothing more than to get this meeting over with. He had never felt more exposed in his entire life. It was as if the word *traitor* was emblazoned on his chest, like the scarlet letter in the classic Nathaniel Hawthorne novel he had been forced to suffer through in high school.

Now, though, he knew exactly how poor Hester Prynne must have felt. It seemed to Nelson that everyone was staring suspiciously at him. He knew that wasn't really the case; in fact, no one was paying him the slightest bit of attention. The exposed feeling was just his overactive imagination playing games with his nerves, but knowing it logically and accepting it emotionally were two completely separate issues.

After ten long, silent minutes, Nelson picked up his contact's briefcase. He had been given very precise instructions, and had been told he must follow the instructions to the letter when making the exchange. There had been no *or else* attached to the instructions, but none had been necessary. Nelson had no idea who he was dealing with, nor did he care. But he knew they didn't play by the same rules as everyone else, and was fully aware that if he expected to see the sun rise tomorrow morning, he had best do exactly as he was told.

Nelson risked a glance at the man's face. His companion looked completely at ease. He never even returned Nelson's glance, just continued sitting with his legs stretched out, watching the girls pass by as if he could spend the rest of the day enjoying the sunshine and doing absolutely nothing else. Nelson figured maybe he could.

With the new briefcase clenched in his sweating hand, all Nelson wanted to do was sprint to his car—and although he realized his sprinting days were long past, it was *still* what he wanted to do—and race back to his office. The urge to escape was almost overwhelming. Somehow, though, he forced himself to stand and walk through the park at the leisurely pace that had been demanded of him by the stranger.

After an eternity, Nelson reached the safety of his car. He didn't think he had ever been as relieved to slide into the stained and torn cloth driver's seat as he was right now. He fired up the engine, avoiding even a single look into Lady Bird Johnson Memorial Park as he drove out of the lot, and then continued the short distance to the Pentagon.

Nelson had not eaten lunch and normally would be starving by now, but he had never felt less like eating in his life. He was queasy, and he could feel acidic bile rising into his throat. A headache, the seeds of which had been threatening to bloom all day, continued to worsen and showed signs of morphing into a full-blown migraine. All he could think about was getting back to his office.

Nelson W. Michaels, traitor.

He could not get that sickening thought out of his head, and it made him feel weak and shaky, even though he was confident his malfeasance would never be discovered. He had been extremely careful in the correspondence he conducted with his shadowy contact and believed strongly that no one knew he had just sold classified information to a group he knew nothing about. He justified his actions by telling himself that he had only sold a transportation schedule and a map depicting a delivery route.

That was all. It wasn't like he had trafficked in nuclear weapons or anything truly dangerous.

Nelson was feeling better, if only marginally so, by the time he finally arrived at his office. He entered quickly and closed the door behind him, realizing with some surprise that he had absolutely no recollection of the past ten minutes. He had been so lost in his paranoia that the last thing he remembered was walking through the wrought-iron front gate of the park and crossing the pavement to his car.

He tossed the briefcase onto his desk, where it landed with a thump, then sank into his well-worn chair in the corner of the office, listening to the air aahing out of the faux leather seat as it was displaced by his body weight.

Nelson was miserable.

7

Tony sat on the park bench watching the fat fuck waddle away and couldn't make up his mind whether he should laugh his damn fool head off or spit in disgust. Getting the information he wanted had been so easy that if he actually gave a crap about his adopted country he would have been appalled.

All it had taken to select his mark was a little judicious Internet research into the personal lives of a few of the most likely Pentagon candidates. It was amazing how much of people's private lives was available on the information superhighway just waiting to be discovered if you were willing to take the time to look for it. And inside of two days, he had narrowed the list of potentials to three, eventually settling on Nelson W. Michaels as his stooge.

Tony had learned that Michaels spent an inordinate amount of time at Pimlico, so he arranged a "chance" meeting, where they commiserated over gambling debts. That orchestrated meeting was followed up with a few innocuous emails and within weeks Tony had the man dangling expertly on his hook.

Nelson was valuable to Tony because as an acquisitions specialist at the Pentagon, he had unfettered access to the information Tony needed. The information had seemed harmless enough to the midlevel bureaucrat that he had agreed to part with it for a measly ten thousand dollars. Tony had been prepared to go much higher if necessary. He didn't really care either way. It wasn't his money.

Nelson's briefcase rested on the ground next to Tony's feet, exactly where the Pentagon staffer had left it. Tony passed the time observing the pretty American girls, all of whom appeared self-absorbed and shallow, pressed from the same Western mold. He watched with the emotionless dead eyes of a shark and chuckled thinking about the just completed rendezvous. To say Nelson had been nervous would be an understatement. The fact of the matter was that Nelson had been about ready to shit his pants in terror and had done a lousy job of hiding it.

For a few minutes, Tony had thought that maybe the frightened amateur was going to stroke out right there on the bench. He pictured Michaels holed up somewhere counting his unmarked bills, thanking his lucky stars for the good fortune of meeting a man who had been willing to pay him so much money for such harmless information, and he smiled.

He wondered if Nelson had heard the news yet that his coworker Lisa Jensen was dead; he supposed he must have by now. Even in an office the size of the Pentagon, an employee dying in a tragic auto accident surely didn't happen every day. It had to be the talk of the building.

Tony chuckled again, and when he did, an overweight middle-aged woman in too-short shorts and a tight T-shirt shot him a half-fearful look as she race-walked past. He watched her with amusement and decided it was time to go.

Tony Andretti, formerly of Syria and Afghanistan and now living in the United States of America, picked up the battered brown leather briefcase without bothering to look inside it—he had no doubt whatsoever that the information he had paid for was safely tucked inside because Michaels did not have the balls to screw him over—and strolled through the park in a direction opposite the one Michaels had used when he left a few minutes ago.

It was a picture-perfect afternoon, and Tony took his

time walking because his workday had just ended.

8

The artificial cool of the Pentagon's climate-controlled interior was ordinarily a welcome relief to Nelson on humid days, of which there were plenty in Washington, D.C. Today, however, the air-conditioning was doing little to control his heavy perspiration, which ran in rivulets down his face and neck. It trickled under the collar of his shirt and spread in an ever-expanding arc under each armpit.

Nelson tended to perspire a lot anyway, but after the extreme stress of the illicit meeting with . . . well, whoever the guy was, he felt as though he had been through the wringer. So he continued to sweat. A lot.

After breathing a sigh of relief and sinking into his chair, Nelson had tossed the briefcase onto his desk, preferring to get his pounding heart and racing pulse under control before examining the inside of the case to verify that the agreed upon ten thousand dollars was actually even in there.

Nelson laid his head on the cool surface of the government-issue desk, instantly turning it slick with his sweat. Still breathing heavily, he tried to force himself to relax, clear his mind, enjoy in the fact that he had actually gotten away with it.

He only now realized that he had half expected a bunch of grim-faced FBI agents or military police to surround him as he exited the park. They would force him spread-eagled onto the pavement while they patted him down for weapons, then perp-walk him in front of dozens of television cameras and newspaper reporters to a waiting police car before whisking him off to jail.

He felt completely drained. Between the physical exertion and the stress, Nelson wanted nothing more than to drive home, toss his jacket and tie over the back of a kitchen chair and go straight to bed. Unfortunately, it was only one o'clock in the afternoon, and guys on the lower rungs of the mid-level management ladder didn't just take an afternoon off, even if they *had* successfully completed a very busy lunch hour filled with treason and ill-gotten monetary gains.

Finally he raised his head, feeling the tension headache building in the base of his skull. Rising slowly—*God I'm sore, could I really be that out of shape? Of course I could*—Nelson shuffled to his closed office door and thumbed the button on the knob, locking it from the inside.

He knew he was probably overdoing the cloak-and-dagger stuff a bit. Not many people had occasion to visit Nelson Michaels in his cramped little office. Most of his communication was conducted via telephone or email, so it was rare for anyone just to walk in on him. And it wasn't like he had a steady stream of friends dropping by to shoot the breeze. In fact, now that he thought about it, it wasn't like he had many friends at all, either at work or outside of it.

Still, you could never be too careful. It wouldn't do for a coworker to waltz in and find Nelson hip deep in wads of unmarked bills like some overweight bureaucratic version of Scrooge McDuck in his counting house. Even the most dim-witted government drone would realize something was amiss in that little scenario, so Nelson wasn't taking any chances.

Settling back into his overstuffed vinyl-covered imitation leather chair—this wasn't your typical institutional metal and plastic worker bee's chair, but Nelson had figured when you spent all day sitting on your ass you should at least be comfortable, so he had paid for the thing out of his own salary—he took a deep breath and held it for a moment, dizzily certain he would pop open the briefcase only to discover it was empty. Then he exhaled nervously and popped the brass clasps and lifted the top of the case.

And broke into a satisfied treasonous smile.

Piled neatly inside, rubber bands holding them snugly together, were stacks and stacks of non-sequential bills in small denominations, exactly as promised. The rich green tint of all the tens, twenties and fifties provided a dazzling contrast to the faded red felt of the briefcase's interior. He didn't stop to count the money, not right here at his desk inside the Pentagon—Nelson may have been a traitor, but he wasn't an idiot—but judging by the size and number of stacks, the full ten thousand dollars had been delivered.

The sense of relief Nelson felt at not being stiffed was palpable. He still couldn't figure out how he had gotten so incredibly lucky, managing to bamboozle that olive-skinned idiot from the park into trading a boatload of untraceable cash for a small amount of trivial information regarding the transportation of a small amount of military hardware and the route the delivery truck was going to take.

Now he would be able to replace a large portion of the money he had gambled away at the track and other venues in the past year or so. He had been withdrawing cash from his retirement nest egg for quite some time while conveniently forgetting to mention that fact to his wife. Nelson had been on a losing streak for months, and every good gambler knew that the time to start betting heavily was when you were losing: nobody loses forever, and every loss meant a win was now that much closer to reality, statistically speaking.

That was Nelson's theory, and he was still convinced it was a good one, though it had yet to work in his favor. But he was certain Joy would disagree, especially given the results. The couple had had several knock-down-drag-outs over the years on the subject of Nelson's gambling, and he knew Joy would be more than a little pissed off if she discovered he had siphoned thousands of dollars of retirement money into unsuccessful wagers.

Joy just didn't understand. He *knew* he was on the verge of hitting it big; he just had to stick to his guns a little longer.

But even a full-fledged optimist like Nelson had started to get nervous when the losses continued to mount and the IRA totals continued to dwindle. Sooner or later the little woman was going to find out. How long could he reasonably expect her to go without checking the balance of the damned thing? Now, through an incredible stroke of dumb luck followed by some shrewd negotiating, Nelson had managed to recoup enough of his losses in one day that even if Joy discovered he had been gambling with their future, she wouldn't be able to complain too much.

Feeling much better now about his situation and about life in general, and sufficiently relaxed that he had nearly stopped sweating, Nelson stuffed the stacks of twenties and fifties he had been admiring back into the briefcase and then snapped it closed. The exhaustion he had felt just a few minutes earlier had magically been replaced by an almost narcotic-like state of euphoria.

He walked across his office with a spring in his step and unlocked the door, opening it again to the world, or at least to the dreary corridor with the institutional green vinyl floor tiles, then returned to his desk revitalized, ready to finish out the workday.

9

Tony pushed open the door to a large but anonymous private garage located on a large but anonymous private lot in suburban Washington. He had purchased the property for a song several years ago because, not to put too fine a point on it, the lot wasn't in one of D.C.'s most desirable neighborhoods.

In fact, at the time Tony made the cash purchase (another reason the price had been so low), the garage was in the middle of a ten square block area the local authorities had virtually given up on as unsalvageable. Crime was rampant; gangs and drugs and prostitution were everywhere.

Tony didn't care about any of that. He wasn't in the business of urban redevelopment, but he *was* in the business of protecting his assets. So after closing on the property, Tony Andretti undertook the process of introducing himself to the local underground entrepreneurs, the ones trading in the guns, the drugs, and the prostitution, and convincing them it was in their best interest to leave him the hell alone.

After a fashion—and a brutal weeding-out process that involved the disappearance or the very public execution of a few of the entrepreneurs—an uneasy truce was reached. The local gangs would be permitted to continue trading in their areas of specialization provided they gave Tony's property a wide berth while they did so. In exchange for leaving his property undisturbed, Tony would allow the gang members to live.

Once the bloody details had been ironed out, the arrangement was one that worked more or less to everyone's satisfaction. The exceptions, of course, were the young men who had died during the negotiating process.

Tony walked through a reinforced metal door featuring a blacked-out Plexiglas window. The door was located between the double bays of the ancient two-car garage that served as his organization's workspace, and he found himself staring into the gaping double barrels of a Mossberg twelve-gauge. Holding the weapon was Brian Waterhouse, a blond twenty-five year old, who sat at the far end of the cement-block structure on a high, hard-backed stool.

When Brian saw who had entered, he lowered his weapon. Giving Tony a sheepish grin, he said, "Sorry about that, boss."

"No apology necessary. That was perfect. Unless and until you know exactly who is coming through that door, you should always be prepared to blow them straight to hell. As long as you don't jump the gun." Tony smiled thinly and crossed the garage. He placed the briefcase on a battered gunmetal-grey desk and lowered his bulk with a satisfied sigh onto a metal folding chair behind it.

Although it was still midafternoon on a sunny spring day, row after row of fluorescent lamps hung suspended from the ceiling, casting the interior in a harsh, almost antiseptic, artificial brilliance.

Weapons of all types littered the makeshift office. There were semiautomatic rifles and pistols, most altered to full auto. There were revolvers, and even some single-shot rifles and shotguns like the big Mossberg that had been aimed at Tony when he had entered. The weaponry took up one entire wall.

A locker filled with hunting and tactical combat knives was angled into one corner, and next to it a row of shelves held an array of grenades and other explosive devices. An impressive assortment of Tasers and nightsticks occupied another row of shelves.

Stored along the wall directly opposite these weapons were racks of electronic equipment: military grade GPS units, walkie-talkies, police scanners, cell phones, and shortwave radios.

The back wall was home to a mountain of tools, including welding equipment and automobile batteries, tires, and spare parts. The garage, in addition to serving as an office and staging area for Tony's team, was exactly what it appeared to be: a mini supply depot for a deadly paramilitary organization.

Tony surveyed the room with a critical eye. Three of the five men who comprised his organization were present.

Brian asked, "So . . . how did it go?"

"I haven't looked inside the briefcase yet," Tony answered with a smile, "but I'm confident it contains everything I specified during negotiations. When I showed up at the meeting place, our Pentagon contact was so frightened that I was afraid he might actually suffer a stroke right on the spot. Anyway, he probably assumes that if he stiffs me, he will get carved up like a turkey on your Thanksgiving holiday. Now that I think about it, he seemed pretty perceptive, at least on that point."

The group shared a laugh and the men went back to doing the chores they had been occupied with when Tony arrived: cleaning and organizing weapons or just lounging around on lawn chairs like the garage was some sort of low-rent social club.

Tony stared at the case lying on his desk for a few minutes without making any move to open it. Despite his outward nonchalance, he felt a tug of tension in his gut. He was so close now to having compiled everything he needed to complete his mission that he felt like a child waking up on the morning of his birthday. The anticipation was so strong he could almost taste it, and he wanted to savor that feeling for just a little longer.

Finally, with an impatient sigh, Tony grabbed the briefcase by the handle. He snapped the latches and lifted the top. He examined the contents, then looked up to see everyone in the garage staring at him expectantly.

Tony smiled. "We are in business, gentlemen."

10

Nelson loved summer. When it was muggy and hot and everyone else was driving around with their windows closed tightly and the artificial chill of their air-conditioning keeping them comfortable, Nelson would lower the top on his Chrysler Sebring convertible and enjoy the commute to and from his office. He loved the way the hot breeze ruffled what was left of his thinning hair; he loved to feel the heat and humidity.

Today didn't feature the broiling heat he loved so much, but the temperature was about as warm as it ever got in the Mid-Atlantic region in May, and Nelson was taking full advantage of the unexpectedly balmy conditions on his drive home.

The adrenaline rush that had followed his noontime meeting gradually leached away over the course of the afternoon, but Nelson was still able to accomplish more work in the four-hour stretch before quitting time today than he had in any one-day period for as long as he could remember. Who would have guessed the way to increase organizational productivity would be to sell a briefcase full of classified material? He imagined himself developing a motivational speech based on that concept and smiled wryly.

Nelson was amazed at how the thought of all that cold, hard cash had enabled him to power through his jitters and beyond his exhaustion. Now, with the top down, the warm air rushing by, and Vivaldi playing much too loudly on his stereo, he felt damned near invincible. A briefcase full of untraceable cash lay on the seat next to him, and against all odds, he was suddenly out of the financial hole hi gambling jones had dropped him into.

While he drove, Nelson wondered if maybe it wouldn't be prudent to parlay his good fortune into an even bigger score with a quick detour to the track on his way home. There was no question his luck had turned, and as the old saying went, "Strike while the iron's hot." Nelson had no idea what that expression meant if you examined it literally, but he figured it was damned good advice anyway. *When you're on a roll, don't stop for anything. Keep right on going until your luck starts to change, then stop. Ya gotta know when to hold 'em and know when to fold 'em.* And all the rest of that happy horseshit.

The breeze began to cool noticeably as the sun sank in the mostly cloudless western sky, and Nelson reluctantly concluded it would be in his best interest to continue straight home. He was excited about his newfound windfall and was looking forward to celebrating with Joy.

Of course, she was blissfully ignorant of the financial gymnastics he'd gone through to replace the retirement money she didn't even know was missing; thus she would have no idea what they were celebrating. But Nelson was certain that when he walked through the door, buoyant and cheerful for a change, she would join him in a little impromptu party anyway.

Behind him on the winding country road that let to Nelson's home in rural Virginia, a vehicle rapidly closed the distance between itself and Nelson's Sebring. He watched as it grew in size in the rear view mirror. He swore quietly under his breath. *Christ, that idiot must be going eighty!* On this two-lane road that twisted and turned like a drunken serpent, driving at that breakneck speed was practically suicidal.

Nelson leaned forward in the driver's seat and peered into the mirror, his attention so taken with the lunatic approaching that he nearly drove off the road. The damned fool was going to kill somebody and Nelson didn't want it to be him. He eased off the gas and flicked on his right turn signal, letting the nitwit behind him know that he was getting as far out of the way as was possible without actually leaving the road.

He could see quite clearly now that it was a Ford F-150 that was endangering his life. The pickup was maybe ten or twelve years old, with dents and dings all over the front bumper and grille and a right quarter panel that was a markedly different color than the rest of the truck. It was one ugly piece of shit.

Nelson gasped as the rattletrap truck picked up speed, its body shaking and shimmying, barely under control. An oily blue cloud belched out behind the rustbucket, trailing the truck like smoke behind a skywriting airplane.

The vehicle veered sharply left, almost as if the driver had just now seen Nelson's car, which was of course impossible. The truck was now *right behind* the Sebring, and Stevie Wonder would have to be driving to not see the Chrysler convertible dead ahead. Nelson breathed a shaky sigh of relief as the truck swerved into the thankfully empty oncoming traffic lane to pass him. He began increasing his own speed in anticipation of the truck roaring by.

As the truck blew noisily past, Nelson risked a glance into the cab and was surprised to see a blond-haired, surfer-looking dude of maybe twenty-five years old looking intently at him from the passenger seat. The kid had no reason to be angry with Nelson, but he seemed to be glaring at him.

Nelson caught a glimpse of the driver and felt a strange, disorienting stab of recognition. *Who the hell is that guy and how do I know him?* he thought.

And then all at once it hit him, like a piano falling on a cartoon character. The maniac driving the truck on this secluded road in the middle of nowhere was the same man he had met in the park today on his lunch hour.

Confused, Nelson turned his attention back to the winding road, and as he did, the truck suddenly whipped back to the right, slamming into the left front of the Chrysler and sending it careening directly toward a stand of trees just off the shoulder. Nelson registered a loud *bang* as his left front tire blew out and the steering wheel began shimmying violently. The car lifted onto its right two wheels, and the panicked Nelson jerked the wheel left, overcorrecting and nearly sending the vehicle tumbling end over end into the woods.

For one crazy second Nelson thought he might get the badly damaged Chrysler under control and coast to a stop along the side of the road. Then the pickup nudged his left front quarter panel again, just kissing it, touching it so lightly it seemed the vehicles might not even swap paint this time. But the contact was enough to eliminate any illusion of control Nelson may have felt he retained over the car. The Sebring started a long, slow slide to the right and into the thick forest.

He had just enough time to think *They did that on purpose!* before the car rocketed into a tree, the sound of the crash much shorter and more abrupt than Nelson would have expected based on a lifetime of watching action movies with the drawn-out car crash scenes Hollywood was so fond of. A quick explosion of grinding metal and shattering safety glass, a painfully bone-jarring deceleration inside the vehicle, the rag-doll-like feeling of his body being held in place by the safety belt—thank God for the safety belt—and then darkness overtaking everything.

Nelson felt the coppery taste of blood burst into his mouth with frightening force, and then consciousness disappeared.

II

One hundred yards from the crash scene, just shy of another hairpin curve, the F-150 idled loudly on the road's thin, sandy shoulder. Time was critical; there was no telling how long it would take before someone encountered the wreckage. If that happened, Tony and Brian would be forced to eliminate more people, something Tony wanted to avoid if at all possible. It wasn't that he minded wasting another worthless civilian or two, but he didn't want or need the added attention from the authorities that killing more people would inevitably bring.

Still, they sat for a little longer, biding their time, carefully watching where Nelson W. Michaels's car had entered the woods and smashed through a small line of scrub brush and into a stand of trees roughly thirty feet into the forest. Tony wanted to see if the guy would be able to escape his damaged car. If so, he would come stumbling out onto the road any minute now, and they could simply drive back and pick him up. It didn't seem a very likely scenario given how fast the guy had been going when he impacted the trees, but you never could tell.

Another minute went by, and still no sign of Michaels. Tony shifted the creaky automatic transmission into reverse, and the truck chugged slowly back to the spot where the victim's car had slid into the woods. A thick black slash on the road from the screeching tires made the location impossible to miss. It had been close to three minutes now since the collision, and still no other vehicles had passed the scene. Michaels really did live in the middle of nowhere; the feeling of isolation was completely at odds with the knowledge of how close they were to Washington, D.C.

The two men looked at each other inside the cab of the F-150, and Tony nodded. Without a word, they stepped down to the ground and picked their way into the woods, heading toward the wrecked Chrysler, walking slowly and carefully but at the same time confident they had nothing to fear. Each man drew his weapon, identical Glock semiautomatic pistols—undoubtedly overkill, pun definitely intended, against an injured and disoriented middle-aged lifelong government bureaucrat—but Tony Andretti was not one to take unnecessary chances, especially since he was now so close to achieving his goal.

12

Everything felt hazy and fuzzy and a little unreal. Nelson was angry with Joy for waking him up when he was so goddamned tired, especially considering how she did it: lying across the foot of the bed, the full weight of her body covering his legs. He struggled to kick them free, to pull them out from under her, but he hadn't realized how much weight she must have gained recently because he couldn't move his lower body at all. He kicked again, hard, and was rewarded for his efforts with lightning bolts firing up each shin all the way to the knee.

The bright, throbbing pain in his legs dragged Nelson fully back to reality from his haze of semi-consciousness. He wasn't at home in bed at all; he remembered now that he had just been involved in a very serious automobile accident after being forced off the road by his contact from earlier in the day, the man whose name he didn't even know and furthermore didn't *want* to know. His legs were pinned in the wreckage between the car's dashboard and firewall, which had slammed together like pincers from the force of the impact and trapped his shins in their viselike grip.

Nelson knew he was in big trouble. His legs were shattered, and blood was flowing freely down the side of his face. His head pounded with what felt like the world's worst migraine—concussion, anyone?—and he was having considerable difficulty breathing. He wondered about internal injuries and felt the first real stab of panic.

How far into the woods had the car gone before smashing into the trees? Was the wreckage even visible to anyone who might be driving by on the road? If not, Nelson knew there was a good chance he might die right here before ever being discovered. This road was remote, but it wasn't so far out in the sticks that no one would come by for hours on end. Nelson felt confident that if his car were visible to motorists driving past, help would come along relatively quickly.

And if it wasn't, well, he didn't want to consider that possibility.

The sounds of cracking branches, of people working their way steadily through the heavy underbrush penetrated Nelson's consciousness, and even in his state of panicked confusion and pain, he knew the best-case scenario had already occurred. Someone had seen the wreck and called for help or perhaps stopped on the side of the road to investigate before calling the authorities.

Nelson wondered how long he had been trapped in his car and realized he had no way of knowing. But it didn't matter. The main thing—the only thing, really—was that help had arrived and he was going to survive.

"Help me!" he tried to scream, succeeding only in issuing a soft breathless croak. This frightened Nelson more than everything else combined—more than seeing the guy from the park driving the truck that had forced him off the road, more than crashing into the trees in the forest, more even than the utter certainty that both his legs were broken and he was quite possibly suffering from life-threatening injuries.

And the pain was worsening. Rapidly. Nelson tried to take a full breath and could only manage to force a short little bubbling gasp through his windpipe. Where the hell were the people he had heard approaching through the woods? Didn't they realize they had to hurry? He peered out what was left of the smashed driver's side window, and his heart leapt as he saw what looked like two fuzzy, indistinct shadows approaching. They seemed to be moving with frustrating slowness.

Finally the shadow people made it to the door and wrenched it open. A loud screech told Nelson that there had been significant damage to that side of the vehicle—he was lucky they were able to get the door open at all. A chunk of shattered safety glass fell to the ground. He tried once again to tell his rescuers to hurry but succeeded only in rasping out something unintelligible, even to him.

"You okay, buddy?" one of the men asked.

It seemed like a stupid question to Nelson, who shook his head. "Need help," he croaked. The coppery taste of blood in his mouth was getting more pronounced, and he could feel the torrent of blood running down the side of his face like a small stream. And he was freezing.

"No problem. That's why we're here," the guy answered.

Nelson smiled in gratitude and forced himself to focus on the faces of the Good Samaritans, and when he did, he felt his bowels clench instinctively in fear. It was the men from the truck, the men who had intentionally forced him off the road in the first place.

The olive-skinned man from Lady Bird Johnson Memorial Park grinned when he saw the recognition dawning in Nelson's eyes. He pulled the door open a little wider and reached into the car with both hands.

13

They approached the Chrysler cautiously. The car was canted at an angle and wedged up against a tree. Tony and Brian could see that Michaels was alive but he was trapped inside and clearly in bad shape. He was dazed, moving slowly and clumsily, sliding into shock.

Michaels smiled out the window in misplaced gratitude; his eyes were glazed over from pain and it was obvious he did not yet recognize them.

Tony managed to pull open the damaged door. Broken glass littered the car's interior, and a steady pulse of blood washed down the side of the man's face. It wasn't exactly streaming, but it was flowing steadily, and in addition, both of his legs seemed to have been swallowed up by the car. He looked exactly like a helpless bug being devoured by a Venus flytrap.

The injured man mumbled something Tony couldn't make out. His breathing was labored and he seemed to be fading fast. As long as their luck held for a few more minutes and no nosy passing motorists stopped to investigate the scene, he and Brian would soon be out of the woods—literally—and on their way home.

Tony glanced at Brian and nodded slightly, and the younger man slipped behind the vehicle to approach it from the other side. Meanwhile, Tony hefted a half-full bottle of cheap whiskey in his right hand and splashed liberal doses of the amber liquid over the seats, the dashboard, the floor, and, of course, over Michaels. The crash victim was slipping in and out of consciousness and didn't seem to notice what was happening.

As the sharp smell of whiskey filled the car's smashed interior, Tony roughly pulled Michaels's head back by his hair and poured some down the man's gullet. He choked as he reflexively swallowed. Whiskey and spittle flew from his mouth in a fine mist, spraying Tony and everything else in its path. Michaels's eyes flew wide with fear and panic, but in his weakened state he was utterly unable to defend himself.

The bottle now nearly empty, Tony pitched it hard against the dashboard. It smashed into a thousand glittering pieces, razor-sharp missiles shredding the air, and the brown glass from the liquor bottle mixed with the opaque greenish automobile safety glass scattered throughout the car.

***

On the other side of the ruined Sebring, Brian located the briefcase full of cash Tony had given Michaels earlier today. The case had flown off the seat with the force of the accident and gotten wedged under the ruined dashboard, much like Michaels's legs, and Brian tugged it back and forth before it finally popped free, its battered leather shell ripping on an exposed jagged iron support bracket. He pulled the case out of the Sebring just as Tony smashed the whiskey bottle, peppering him with shards of glass. He wanted to tell the crazy bastard to be more careful but didn't dare.

***

Tony studied the inside of the car thoughtfully, like an artist stepping back from his easel to get a better perspective on the canvas. Time was of the essence, but he wanted to be sure this was done properly. Satisfied, he nodded and returned to the driver's side door for one last time. The whiskey stench was overwhelming and nearly made him gag.

Wrinkling his nose in disgust at the smell, Tony leaned

inside and gently, almost reverently, placed two gloved hands around Michaels's flabby neck. The man had regained consciousness and was clearly terrified, but he gave Tony a look that was almost indignant, as if he couldn't wrap his brain around the fact that he was being double-crossed.

"Don't take it so hard," Tony said with a brief smile, leaning into the wrecked car and putting his mouth next to Michaels's ear so he was sure to be heard. "It's nothing personal. This is just business. I'm sure you understand." With that he began choking what little life remained out of Nelson Michaels, who tried to thrash and resist but was unable to do much of anything but shake his head like he disagreed with Tony's plan, which undoubtedly he did.

Within seconds Michaels was gone. He had been breathing only with extreme difficulty anyway, and even in the short time Tony and Brian had been working at the car, his respiration had become noticeably more labored.

Tony again examined the inside of the car with a critical eye, pulling off his latex gloves and stuffing them into the back pocket of his trousers. Blood and glass were everywhere, giving the scene the look of some twisted surrealistic painting. Michaels was slumped in the driver's seat, his indignant expression still framing his lifeless features.

"What do you think?" Brian asked, handing Tony the briefcase with the slashed leather front and removing his own gloves with a snap. "Does it look believable? Will the cops buy the idea that our guy croaked as a result of the accident?"

"Well, that whiskey I splashed all over the place will lead the investigators to believe he was drinking on his way home from work and lost control of the vehicle. And his legs being trapped under the smashed dashboard is very helpful to us. The investigators will initially assume he was alive after the accident but couldn't move and died before help arrived.

"Of course, once the autopsy is performed, it will become clear that virtually none of the liquor actually made it to his stomach. The authorities will thus learn he wasn't really drunk, and they will discover fine traces of powder from the latex gloves around his neck. They will piece it together and eventually reach the obvious and correct conclusion—that Mr. Michaels was murdered. But by the time they do, it will be irrelevant. At least to us."

The two men had by now hiked almost all the way back to the truck. They peered out at the road through the thick brush. It would not do to be seen exiting the woods by a car driving past.

But there was nothing.

Tony and Brian clambered out of the woods and hurried back up the lonely road to the stolen F-150 in silence. The sun had sunk beneath the trees, and there was a very good possibility that Michaels wouldn't be found until morning, which would suit their purposes perfectly. Placing the damaged briefcase on the bench seat between them, Tony slid into the beat-up Ford and fired up the truck's tired engine. Then they chugged slowly away from the site of the ambush.

14

Nick was exhausted. He had never realized until now just how much effort, both physical and emotional, went into burying a loved one. He had been to plenty of funerals before, but putting a grandparent in the ground after eighty-five years of life was a lot different than saying goodbye to your wife, especially when she had been just twenty-nine years old when she died, and had been taken from you without warning in a single violent instant.

"Honey, you need to get some rest." His mother brushed his shaggy hair from his eyes, something she had been doing since he was a little kid and something he had always hated. "Lisa wouldn't have wanted you to wear yourself down and get sick, I'm sure of that."

"Yeah, I know." Nick breathed deeply and looked at his watch. Two hours until he had to drive his parents to Logan Airport to catch their flight back to Dayton. Everyone else who had gathered to bury Lisa was already gone, and Nick was anxious to be alone so he could grieve the way he badly needed to. He was touched by the support of the throngs of friends and relatives, both his and Lisa's, but Nick had not truly been alone since those first few horrible hours after the police officers had shown up five days ago with the news that his wife was gone. Irrevocably and permanently gone.

With everyone using his house as a staging area—people

coming and going at all hours for days, and his parents staying with him—Nick felt as though his entire focus had been on remaining strong for everyone else, on keeping up some ridiculous charade where he tried to convince the onlookers who were watching him so closely that he was doing just fine.

The fact of the matter was that he was doing the opposite of just fine, whatever that might be. Just shitty? Just stunned? Just lost and rudderless and totally numb? He hadn't yet had a chance to contemplate how he was going to continue without Lisa or whether he really wanted to, for that matter.

It wasn't like he was contemplating suicide; he knew Lisa would never forgive him if he were to take his own life. But since the very first day he had met Lisa Harrison, way back in high school, Nick had never given one solitary thought to the possibility that he might *not* spend the rest of his life with her. Now that she was gone, Nick hadn't the slightest idea what to do next.

"Listen, Mom, maybe getting some rest is a good idea. I think I will take a short nap. I'll make sure I'm up in plenty of time to drive you and Dad to the airport. Don't worry."

"That's fine," she said, gliding out of the bedroom and pulling the door softly closed behind her. Moments later Nick heard the whine of the vacuum cleaner running at the other end of the house as his mother finished getting the home in tip-top shape before departing for Ohio.

Sleeping was out of the question, of course; Nick had simply used that excuse as a convenient way to carve out some time to himself. He felt a pang of guilt, knowing his parents were leaving soon and he wouldn't see them again for months, but he needed to be alone. He rose and paced, walking from the bedroom door to the dresser filled with his dead wife's clothes, behind the foot of their bed to the window, then back to the bedroom door, starting the cycle all over again. He couldn't remember ever having been this wound up.

Nick threw a stick of gum into his mouth and wandered

into the massive walk-in closet. Lisa had loved that closet. In fact, it had played a major role in their choosing this house over several others.

He stood quietly in the middle of the closet, inhaling Lisa's scent. He wasn't a guy who paid much attention to what he considered "girlie stuff," so he hadn't the slightest clue what she wore for perfume, but whatever it was, he could smell it here—something cinnamony—and it made his heart ache. He wondered how long it would take for the scent simply to fade away and then was gone forever, and he felt the tenuous control he had kept over his emotions beginning to crack.

Hanging in a far corner of the big closet was Lisa's wedding gown, which had belonged to her great-grandmother. Lisa had absolutely adored it. She had been planning to put it in storage to save for her own children in case one of them wanted to get married in it but had never gotten around to accomplishing that task. The gown hung inside a clear plastic garment bag to protect the delicate silk and lace.

Nick walked over and slid the surrounding clothes out of the way. Lisa had owned a lot of stuff, and the heavy mass of clothing hanging on the rod moved slowly, reluctantly. He lifted the gown off the rod, planning to place it on the bed for no particular reason other than to run his hand over the smooth silk and think about Lisa.

When he lifted the dress, a bright blue notebook binder caught his eye. The binder was big, at least three inches thick, and had been placed behind the gown on the closet floor, wedged up against the back wall. It would have remained out of sight indefinitely had Nick not moved the dress. He stared at it in wonder. What the hell would a binder be doing amongst Lisa's clothes? It looked new, too; it was completely free of dust. Nick had never seen it before.

He placed Lisa's wedding gown back on the rod in the closet and lifted the binder off the floor, turning it over in his hands, as if he could learn its secrets through osmosis. When that didn't work, he carried it over to their bed—his bed now—and sat down to examine it more closely.

15

The harsh white light generated by the fluorescent lamps shone down on Tony's men as they worked. Tony was seated in his customary spot behind the battered desk. He couldn't stop smiling. Not so much as one twenty dollar bill was missing out of the ten thousand in cash he had given Michaels in exchange for the map and personnel roster. Now he had not just the information he needed, but all the money it had cost him to procure—the best-case scenario as far as he was concerned.

Dimitrios Stavros, who despite the Greek-sounding name had been born and raised in the United States and was another of the American citizens working with Tony, saw him smiling and asked, "Why did we need to kill the guy? He gave you what you wanted."

Tony shot Stavros a scornful look. "Why? Two reasons." He held up a finger. "One, that idiot was a cog in the machinery of the corrupt United States government, a government I have devoted my life to destroying, and which, I remind you, every one of you in this room has committed to destroying as well. There was absolutely no good reason to allow him to live and continue making his small contribution to the oppression of my people in the Middle East when we had the means and the opportunity to rectify the situation.

"Two"—he held up another finger. "Even though ten

thousand dollars is a small amount of money in the grand scheme of things, why should I allow it to go to an American and to the pigs I am trying to destroy when *we* could better use it to purchase more equipment and weaponry? In this manner, we can use the Americans' own money not once but twice to contribute to their downfall. It is an unintended but not unappreciated bonus.

"Now . . ." Tony paused, searching the eyes of each of his soldiers in turn. "Does that make sense to you, or do we have a problem we need to iron out? If anyone here does not see the wisdom in what I am saying or disagrees with the direction our operation has taken, now would be the appropriate time to mention that fact. In order for us to be successful, we must all be on the same page, as you Americans like to say."

He waited. The silence in the garage spoke volumes. "Well?"

No one answered. Each man averted his eyes when the laser gaze of Tony Andretti fell upon him. There was no doubt as to who was in charge. The only member of the team not an American citizen was Tony, a Syrian by birth. The others had graduated from an intense indoctrination program held in a remote training camp located deep in the mountains of Afghanistan. Run by resurgent Taliban and financed by various Middle Eastern governments through dummy organizations and generous individual donations, the camp specialized in training disaffected Westerners. They worked mostly with young white American males, teaching them guerilla tactics and warfare as well as providing an introduction to radical Muslim theology.

The days of using Middle Eastern men to fly airplanes into buildings were over. Forward-thinking terror organizations like the one Tony represented now recognized the value of employing homegrown citizens, who could blend seamlessly into the cultural landscape of the West, to accomplish their goals.

Although born and raised in the West, the graduates of

this particular training camp were men who had developed a burning hatred of their countries, usually the United States or Great Britain, and to the guerillas providing the training, that was good enough. Being a true believer in radical Islam would be nice, but was not necessary. All that mattered was that the recruits be willing to sacrifice themselves to their leaders' bidding at the time and place of their choosing.

The four men currently wilting under Tony's smoldering glare had been recruited for the Afghanistan program from diverse locations all over the United States. Brian was a native Southern Californian who had attended Stanford University briefly before dropping out, unable to reconcile his anti-American beliefs with the benefits of an elite education.

Jackie Corrigan was a high school dropout and former gangbanger from Brooklyn. Dimitrios Stavros was a second-generation American from Las Vegas who had been born into casino wealth but wanted none of it. And Joe-Bob Warren was ex-military, out of Frankfurt, Kentucky, the recipient of a dishonorable discharge from the United States Army when he was busted for purchasing child pornography while stationed at Fort Hood, Texas.

All of the men were in their twenties, none possessed any loyalty to the ideals of the United States of America, and all had passed the Afghanistan training course with flying colors. They had been sent back to the States more than six months ago with instructions to report to Tony and live their lives in the D.C. area quietly and unobtrusively while awaiting their assignment.

That assignment had come just a few weeks ago, and with the information acquired yesterday from Michaels, the team was ready to proceed.

Tony snapped the briefcase containing the ten thousand dollars shut and smiled. "No one has a problem with my leadership. Very good. I will assume we are all rowing this boat in the same direction. Now, let us discuss the specifics of this operation."

16

Nick hugged his mother tightly and shook his father's hand as they said their good-byes at the departure gate. Logan Airport was crowded as usual, and Nick was surprised to see that his parents' plane was scheduled to depart on time. He knew he should be sorry to see them go, but he was still emotionally raw and wrung out.

After watching his mother and father disappear into the boarding area, Nick made his way to one of the airport lounges and ordered a scotch and soda. He knew having a drink before hitting the road for the hour-long drive back to his depressingly empty home wasn't the best idea, but there wasn't any point in being careful any more, was there? Nobody was left alive to worry about him. He was alone. Totally alone. That realization shook him more than he had realized until just now.

In a couple of hours, Nick was going to walk through the front door of their little Cape-style home, and Lisa would not be there to carp at him when he tossed his jacket over the kitchen chair or when he kicked off his sneakers and left them lying on the living room floor in front of the television. Sure, she had been gone four days every week during most of their marriage, but the absence had only served to make them appreciate each other that much more when they were together.

Now they never would be again. Nick didn't know how he would be able to stand it.

He took a sip of his drink, savoring the warm bite of the scotch as it burned down his throat and splashed into his stomach, and let his mind wander to the strange discovery he had made in their walk-in closet. In *his* walk-in closet, he reminded himself. It was now his alone, not his and Lisa's.

The blue binder had to have been stuffed behind the wedding gown intentionally; it wasn't the sort of place the thing could have fallen by accident. Clearly it contained information Lisa had not wanted Nick to see.

But what information? Nick knew the binder had to be related somehow to Lisa's auditing job at the Pentagon, as it contained names and dates and places, all of which seemed random and meant nothing to Nick. But Lisa had always been forthcoming about her work; as far as he knew, she had never kept anything from him. Most of the time—hell, just about all the time—the investigations she found herself involved in at the giant office building had been straightforward. Boring, even.

He remembered one instance she related to him last year where a very well-respected—and well-compensated—high-level bureaucrat had been caught stealing toilet paper from a Pentagon men's room. For years the man had been taking a roll every couple of days, stuffing it inside his briefcase and bringing it home with him. The guy had nearly been fired. Over *toilet paper!* As it was, he had earned a three-day suspension without pay and been put on probation. The United States government apparently took their lavatory responsibilities very seriously, Lisa had told him with a straight face, before breaking into hysterical laughter.

The recollection made Nick smile briefly, then it occurred to him he would never again share in his wife's infectious sense of humor. He finished his drink with one deep swallow and chewed on an ice cube. So why did she hide the blue binder? And why hide it from *him,* of all people? It made no sense.

After finding the binder so cleverly hidden, Nick had expected to find some earth-shattering revelation hidden inside, perhaps somehow involving him, but in reality it hadn't contained much. There were a list of names and a notation written in block letters that said "*Tucson Bliss?*" Written below that, also in block letters that were barely readable because they had been smudged before the ink was dry, was another notation that might have said *"Stringers"* or *"Stingers"* or maybe even *"Singers."*

The binder contained copies of emails that had obviously been taken off someone's hard drive, presumably someone who worked at the Pentagon. The emails went back and forth between a guy named Michaels and an unnamed person in a coy, roundabout manner, eventually culminating in an agreement to meet last week at a park in Washington. The name of the park hadn't been specified in any of the emails, but Nick guessed it would be easy for someone familiar with the area to deduce the location. He had been to Washington only a few times, none recently, so it was all a mystery to him.

And that was it. That was the sum total of the binder's contents. Nick couldn't begin to guess what Tucson Bliss might mean or what sort of singers (or maybe stingers or stringers) had been involved in Lisa's investigation. To the best of his knowledge, Lisa had never been to Tucson in her entire life and would not have considered it blissful even if she had. She hated extreme heat, and for that reason alone Nick couldn't imagine her ever using the words *Tucson* and *bliss* together in the same sentence.

All of which brought him back to his original question: Why hide the material from him? It was not like he could decipher the meaning of any of it. Besides, what difference could any cloak-and-dagger stuff going on in D.C. possibly make to an air traffic controller living and working in Merrimack, New Hampshire?

Was it possible Lisa had been involved in something illegal? Instead of the binder's material being part of an investigation she had been working on at the time of her death, could it be that she had hidden the binder in their home, away from his prying eyes and everyone else's because it contained evidence of her own malfeasance?

Nick felt a ball of unease forming in the pit of his stomach. His beautiful wife of five years, the only woman he had ever really loved, was dead less than a week, and he was entertaining a possibility he would have considered ludicrous before he had discovered the existence of the binder. Guilt gnawed at him for even thinking it. He knew Lisa better than that.

But still, why else would she have hidden it, and in such a perfect spot? Had she not been run down by that goddamned beer truck, he would never have found the material in the first place. He wished to hell he hadn't.

He laid a ten-dollar bill on the tiny circular table and walked out of the bar and through the terminal, paying little attention to the throngs of travelers jostling him on all sides. It was time to face the long drive back to his empty house. Nick walked slowly to Logan Airport's Central Parking garage and slid into his car, his mind hundreds of miles away at a Pentagon building he had never set foot inside.

17

"It is time to discuss the next step." Tony gazed into the faces of his men, using his intense dark stare to capture and maintain their full attention. "We have been training and preparing for months—years, even decades, in the case of some of us—to ensure our readiness for this moment.

"No doubt you are all wondering what was inside this briefcase that was so important we spent ten thousand dollars of our valuable resources to purchase it." Tony didn't bother mentioning the obvious—that he had then murdered the seller and stolen their money back. "I am sure you are familiar with the expression, 'information is power.' If that is the case, then the information inside this briefcase has increased our power exponentially."

He pulled a simple road map out of the case with a flourish and spread it out on the desk in front of them. "What do we have here, Mr. Waterhouse?"

Brian glanced at it. "It's a map of a driving route between Tucson, Arizona and Fort Bliss, Texas."

"Exactly. Thank you. Can you tell me what significance Tucson has to us?"

No one answered, so Tony continued. "Tucson is the home base of the company that is contracted with the United States government to produce Stinger shoulder-fired missiles for the U.S. military. These missiles are manufactured at a plant in Tucson, then delivered to bases all over the world, including Fort Bliss, Texas. Currently the missiles are undergoing minor software modifications requested by the U.S. Army. Thursday night a small shipment of these modified Stingers will leave Tucson in an unmarked Army cargo truck, to be delivered to Fort Bliss for inspection and approval before the full-scale manufacturing process resumes.

"Thanks to my contact—excuse me, my now-deceased *ex*-contact—at the Pentagon, Mr. Nelson W. Michaels, we now have in our possession all the information we need to allow us to intercept this delivery. We know when the missiles are being shipped to the base in Texas. We know the exact route to be driven by the truck transporting the missiles. We know how many men will be handling the delivery. We even know their names and ranks and exactly what they look like."

Tony traced with one finger an area outlined on the map in red marker and trained his intense stare on Joe-Bob Walton. "What are we looking at here?"

Walton returned Andretti's stare unblinkingly. "Well, unless I miss my guess, that's where we're going to take the Stingers away from the army and make them our own."

Tony smiled and nodded, and as he did, Dimitrios cleared his throat.

"What is it?" Tony asked.

"Ah, I'm sure you would have considered this," Dimitrios stammered, "but don't they deliver those missiles in separate shipments? We might be able to hijack portions of the Stingers Thursday night, but won't they be useless without all of the pieces?"

"Normally, yes, that is true," Tony answered, appreciating the question. His men were sharp for soft, spoiled Westerners. "It is rare for Stingers to be shipped intact in one vehicle. In this case, though, the missiles are being delivered in one nearly complete package. This particular transport vehicle will contain everything necessary to fire Stinger missiles with the exception of the guidance system, without which the missiles are useless."

Dimitiros rubbed the back of his neck and shook his head. "So my question remains the same: What good will they be to us if we have *almost* everything we need?"

Tony chuckled softly. "I said the missiles are useless without the guidance system. I didn't say we don't *have* the guidance system. A couple of years ago a similar military transport vehicle was hijacked while driving a similar route between Arizona and Texas. Would anyone care to speculate as to what that truck was carrying?"

A buzz of anticipation filled the room.

"We have the guidance system for the Stinger missiles already," Joe-Bon said wonderingly.

"Bingo, as you Americans like to say."

Jackie piped up, his normally high-pitched voice rising a couple of octaves. "So we're going to use Stinger missiles to shoot down an airplane?"

"That is exactly correct," Tony answered. "But not just any airplane. The president is flying into Logan International Airport in Boston very early next Sunday morning. We will be removing him from office. Permanently."

"The president? The president of what?"

"What do you think?"

Stunned silence filled the room as the significance of Tony's statement began to sink in.

"The President of the United States?" Joe-Bob whispered. "We're going to shoot down Air Force One?"

Tony's eyes glittered like hard black diamonds as he turned his cool smile on his small band of revolutionaries—the group that would soon change the course of history. "That is correct. President Cartwright is scheduled to celebrate the reopening of a historic church in Boston, which has been closed for renovations. I have learned that he will be flying into the airport around 5:00 a.m. next Sunday in order to arrive at the church in time to attend a sunrise service. He is then scheduled to lunch in the city with some of his major political contributors before flying back to Washington in early afternoon.

"Of course, as we now know, he will do none of those things, because he will be dead, blown to pieces, lying at the bottom of a smoking hole in the ground just shy of Logan Airport. With a little bit of luck, perhaps people in the city will be killed as well, but that remains to be seen and would only be a bonus."

Chaos erupted and then died down immediately when Tony help up a hand to silence his men.

Brian shook his head. "But how will we know where the plane is going to be, and when to fire the missile? It's a big sky up there."

Tony smiled again. "We'll know because we're going to tell the pilot where we want him to go."

18

The full moon shone brightly in the crystal-clear night sky, casting an eerie glow over the scrub brush littering the desert floor. The Arizona landscape was illuminated starkly by the pale moonlight, and although it was past midnight, visibility was close to that of daytime. The Tucson city limits were only few miles northwest, but out here the landscape appeared alien, almost lunar in nature.

Vehicular travel over this portion of the two-lane country road was sparse; most people traveling at this time of night preferred the wide lanes and higher speed limits of the interstate highway following a more or less parallel course just a few miles away.

On this deserted highway, heavy black smoke poured from the scene of a recent automobile accident. Two late-model sedans had collided precisely in the middle of the road, with both cars slewed sideways, apparently from their desperate and unsuccessful last-second attempt at avoiding each other. Now the road was almost completely blocked, with little more than a narrow passageway available on either side.

Two miles east, moving slowly in the direction of the accident, an olive-green military transport truck with a large cargo bed covered by heavy-gauge camouflage canvas lumbered past a roadside billboard advertising *Joanne's*

Diner—Bottomless Cup of Coffee with Trucker's Breakfast Special! Immediately after the truck rumbled past, two men emerged from behind the sign, walking quickly through the moonlit semidarkness to the center of the highway.

One of the men carried over his shoulder a large Road Closed sign bordered with reflective tape. He placed it in the center of the road, facing east, while the other man carried an armful of orange rubber traffic cones and placed one every six feet along the pavement, moving outward from the large sign in both directions until the entire highway surface was blocked off.

The men worked quickly and efficiently, and inside of forty-five seconds, they had eliminated vehicular access to the crash scene. To the west of the staged auto accident, identical signage had already been erected, complete with rubber cones, blocking access to the four-mile stretch of highway in between.

Their task complete, one of the men pulled a radio from his back pocket and spoke quietly into it. He advised the person on the other end of the call that the transport truck would be arriving at the scene momentarily and that the road was now clear. The entire operation took just over one minute.

The men disappeared into the night behind the billboard.

19

"I'm tellin' ya, the Cubbies are never going to win a World Series." Private First Class Eric Young pounded his fist on the truck's steering wheel to emphasize his point to the man in the passenger seat, Private First Class Milt Stanley, who seemed utterly uninterested in the fortunes of the Chicago Cubs, or in anything else Young had to say, for that matter.

"Yeah well," Stanley said in his distinctive Alabama drawl, "baseball's a pussy sport, anyway. Who gives a shit about the Cubs? You wanna talk sports, let's talk Crimson Tide football. Nick Saban's brought that program back to where they belong, which is on top of the heap in the SEC. They might just be better right now than they have been at any time since the Bear." He referenced the late, great coach of the University of Alabama football team, Bear Bryant, the way a devout Catholic might discuss the Pope, with awed reverence and maybe a hint of fear.

"You know," he continued, "I could have played for the Tide if I hadn't blowed out my knee my senior year of high school."

Young snorted. "Christ, Milton, you couldn't have gotten into 'Bama on the best day you ever had, even considering the virtually nonexistent admissions standards they have for football players, you dumb fuck. I'll bet you can't even spell 'football.'"

Stanley's expressive black face took on an aggrieved look. "I can spell 'kick your ass,'" he answered without any real conviction, his attention diverted by what looked like a serious car accident a few hundred yards ahead on the lonely road.

Young slowed the truck as the glare of the headlights brought the scene into focus. There had definitely been a two-car wreck, and it looked as though it must have occurred just moments ago, as acrid black smoke hung thickly in the desert air. It billowed heavily from beneath one or both of the damaged cars.

Standing in front of the accident scene were two men, clearly the drivers of the vehicles that had been involved in the wreck. They were trading punches, completely oblivious to the camouflaged U.S. Army transport truck slowing to a stop a few yards away.

"Just go around these two dumb motherfuckers," Stanley drawled. "Let them beat the crap out of each other. What the hell do we care?"

"I don't think I can make it without going off the road and into the desert," Young answered, "and I don't really want to take the chance of getting stuck in that sand. If that happens, we're screwed."

At that moment, the confrontation between the two men escalated. One caught the other with a roundhouse right and knocked him to the pavement. That man immediately leapt back to his feet, swinging from the heels.

Young reluctantly stopped the truck a few feet away from them. He opened his door, leaving the truck idling, its big diesel engine rumbling softly in the desert night. "What the fuck are you doing?" asked Stanley.

"What does it look like I'm doing? We can't get around these idiots, so we're going to have to break up this fight and help them push their cars to the side of the road. It's either that or be stuck here until one of them kills the other. I like watching mixed martial arts as much as the next guy, but we don't have time for this."

Stanley grunted noncommittally.

"You stay here and I'll be right back," Young told him, following protocol, which dictated that at least one soldier remain with the vehicle to safeguard its contents at all times. He climbed down out of the cab and approached the two men, barking authoritatively, "Hey!" to get their attention.

It didn't work, as they continued pounding on each other as if he were not even there.

Young hesitated, placing his hand on his sidearm but leaving it holstered. There was no way on God's green earth he was going to draw down on two unarmed civilians, especially on two men who didn't pose any kind of threat, at least not to him. His military training had included nothing even remotely resembling instruction on how to deal with the situation he found himself facing now, and he was unsure how to proceed.

On one hand, this truck and its contents were expected at Fort Bliss, Texas, first thing tomorrow morning, and if it was late getting there, they would catch hell. The circumstances contributing to the late arrival would not be given much consideration, if any.

But on the other hand, getting involved in a fistfight between two civilian motorists would likely be viewed as a mistake in hindsight, especially if he were to injure one of them while trying to break up the fight. And what if one or both of them became belligerent and refused to move their damaged vehicles? What then?

All these considerations ran through Young's head as he cautiously approached the pair. He considered calling the base for guidance, but finally decided the best thing to do would be to take decisive action and get moving again. It was late, he was tired, and he had no desire to get his ass hauled into the woodshed when he got back to Bliss because he couldn't decide how to handle a freaking traffic accident.

The problem was these two guys were really going at it. He had mentioned mixed martial arts to Milt and an MMA bout on Pay-Per-View was exactly what the scene resembled. Fists were flying. Now that he was up close, Young could see that both guys were pretty good-sized dudes. Young reluctantly waved Stanley down from the cab to help him subdue the two guys, since it was patently obvious he couldn't take them both himself, at least not without drawing his weapon, which he had already determined would be a very bad career move.

With Stanley's help, though, these two clowns would be disabled in a matter of seconds—his partner was six foot six and two hundred eighty pounds of sculpted muscle. Young had no idea whether Stanley had actually received a scholarship offer from Alabama or not, but he was definitely big enough to have been one hell of a football player.

Scowling, Stanley climbed down from the truck's cab. "Goddamn it, let's get the fuck out of here," he complained. As he strode up next to Young, both of them roughly five feet from the fighting motorists, the two men suddenly stopped trading haymakers and pulled semiautomatic pistols from behind their backs, turning in unison and facing the two young Army privates.

In that instant Young knew he had made a very serious mistake.

20

When the radio call had come in from Dimitrios, telling them that the Army transport truck carrying the Stinger missiles had passed the billboard located two miles east and would arrive at their position in approximately two minutes, Jackie and Joe-Bob started their vehicles simultaneously and pulled them together nose-to-nose over the double yellow line separating the opposing lanes of traffic. The cars were positioned perpendicular to the yellow stripes so as to take up as much available road space as possible.

They shut down their engines and leapt out in unison, Joe-Bob carrying a smoke bomb, which he ignited with a Bic lighter and placed in the road under the two front bumpers. Instantly, thick black smoke began billowing into the air, creating the illusion that the vehicles had sustained serious damage.

It took no more than a few seconds for the front ends of both cars to become obscured by the heavy black shroud, and as the smoke continued to accumulate, the men checked their weapons one final time. Each placed his Glock 9mm semiautomatic pistol under the waistband of his trousers, snug against the small of his back, covered by his untucked shirt.

In the distance the transport truck lumbered over a shallow rise and into view. It was still too far away to make out any detail, but they knew it was the right truck. It had to be, since there was now no one else traveling on this closed-off section of highway.

Joe-Bob looked at Jackie, a smirk crossing his face and then disappearing. "Let's dance," he said, shoving the other man hard. The two began exchanging blows, hesitantly at first, then with increasing gusto as each connected with the other and adrenaline and instinct took over.

Jackie and Joe-Bob had been selected to run this portion of the operation due to both men's advanced fighting skills – Joe-Bob's having been perfected in the military, and Jackie's learning to scrap and fight on the streets of the Bronx, running with some of the most brutal gangs in New York from the time he was eight.

They heard the truck pull up behind them, its headlights washing them in a bright white glare as they traded haymakers. By now they were actually fighting; there was no chance the truck's occupants might suspect the whole thing was being staged for their benefit. The brakes on the big vehicle squealed long and loud as it slowed to a stop.

Blood mixed with sweat flew off the bodies of the sparring terrorists in great arcing droplets, illuminated in the truck's headlights. They grunted and strained and paid no attention to the Army vehicle idling just a few feet away. A couple of minutes that felt like much longer passed. Then a door opened and a young soldier stepped down from the truck and crossed the pavement warily. He stood, ignored by Jackie and Joe-Bob. A few seconds later, the door on the far side of the truck opened and the other occupant climbed down as well.

This was what they had been waiting for.

The two Army privates moved forward unwittingly, and when they reached a point approximately five feet away, Jackie growled, "Now!" They dropped their fists simultaneously, each man pulling his weapon from behind his back and leveling it in the stunned face of the soldier closest to him.

Shock—and an instant later understanding—etched itself onto the faces of the soldiers.

Jackie and Joe-Bob squeezed their triggers, their moves choreographed with the same split-second timing they had displayed in their fight, and two human heads exploded in a spray of blood and pulverized silver-grey bone. Milt Stanley and Eric Young dropped instantly to the ground, dead before their bodies hit the pavement.

Still breathing heavily from the staged fight, Jackie and Joe-Bob shoved their guns back into their waistbands and grabbed the ankles of their lifeless victims. They dragged the men off the road and into the scrub brush dotting the side of the highway, leaving two wide swaths of blood on the pavement. There the trail disappeared, the blood soaking into the sandy terrain.

The terrorists jumped into their cars and fired up the engines. Tony, who had been sitting motionless in the back seat of Jackie's sedan, had already clambered into the Army transport truck, which was still idling in the middle of the road. The three vehicles moved out, traveling in a single-file convoy east for two miles, where they retrieved their compatriots waiting behind the big billboard and then continued into the night. They encountered no cars traveling in either direction.

Back at the scene of the staged auto accident, the black smoke bomb smoldered a little longer and then extinguished itself. The desert grew quiet and still.

21

The vast desolation of the Arizona desert was pockmarked by clumps of scrawny scrub brush sprouting randomly from the ground, casting skeletal shadows from the washed-out light of the full moon. Thousands of stars glittered in the cold sky. The few buildings visible were spaced far apart, appearing delicate and insubstantial. Three vehicles—a nondescript sedan in the lead, followed by an olive-drab U.S. Army truck with a canvas-covered cargo box, and another sedan trailing behind—approached a massive parking lot.

As they turned into the property, three sets of headlights flashed across a mammoth sign: *Welcome to Southwest RV Center—Arizona's Largest!* Below, in only slightly less enthusiastic letters, it proclaimed, *RVs, Campers, Motor Homes of all sizes for Sale or Rent, Long- or Short-Term! All Price Ranges!* The three vehicles snaked around the campers and motor homes. In less than a minute the convoy had arrived at the back of the lot.

They parked neatly in a row next to a plain white panel truck. One by one, the drivers shut down their engines. The truck they had parked next to was obviously a recent addition to the RV center's lot and clearly did not belong. It had been stolen the day before in Tucson and would be used to transport the Stinger missiles Tony's group had successfully acquired. The Army transport truck was much too conspicuous for Tony's taste, and he knew it was imperative they lose it immediately. Once the bodies of the two murdered soldiers were discovered, the authorities would seal off the entire area like a drum, and they would risk being apprehended if they hadn't moved the Stingers to another truck.

The men piled out of their vehicles and stepped onto the tarmac, stretching their backs and yawning. Southwest RV Center may have been Arizona's largest, as the sign proclaimed, but the facility's owners hadn't spent much of their income over the last few years on pavement maintenance. The acres of blacktop were cracked and rutted from exposure to the relentless desert heat, with sandy potholes forming dangerous and randomly located landmines all over the lot. To step in one meant the possibility of a turned ankle or worse. An injury now was something the group could not afford.

Tony pulled out a Maglite and examined the area immediately surrounding the four vehicles until he was satisfied there was no possibility of injury to himself or one of his men. Shining the light represented risk, but it was minimal. This portion of the lot was mostly invisible from the road, with dozens of bulky campers and RV's forming a very effective screen, and vehicular traffic was virtually nonexistent this time of night anyway.

His men stood next to the vehicles smoking cigarettes and mumbling quietly to each other until he was ready. After a few seconds, Tony swung the rear gate of the transport truck down and said, "Let's get this done." He left the rest of the crew to do the heavy lifting and strolled toward the front of the deserted facility, semiautomatic rifle slung over his shoulder and toothpick hanging out the corner of his mouth.

The men set to work unloading the crates containing the precious cargo from the Army vehicle and moving it onto into the stolen panel truck. There were no markings of any kind on the truck; it was completely anonymous and would blend nicely into the landscape as the team moved west to east across the United States until arriving back home outside Washington. There they would go to ground and prepare for the next step in the operation.

First things first, though. They needed to put as many miles between the dead soldiers and themselves as possible before morning. The U.S. Army didn't take kindly to its soldiers being murdered, particularly on American soil, and the search for the killers would be more intense even than the search for the thieves who had taken the Stinger missiles. The weapons were useless without the appropriate guidance system, and the government had no way of knowing the group that had taken the Stingers was also in possession of that critical component as well.

They would find out soon enough.

The four men worked quickly and efficiently at their backbreaking task. Dimitrios knelt in the back of the Army truck sliding the Stinger crates along the floor of the cargo bed to the open tailgate, where Joe-Bob and Jackie trundled them the short distance to the waiting panel truck. There, they dropped the crates on the cargo bed with a thud. Then Brian slid the crates along the wooden floor, moving each crate as close to the front of the cargo box as possible, securing each with bungee cords to ensure there would be no shifting of the material.

They were breathing heavily but moving at a brisk pace, a light sheen of sweat coating each man's body in the cool desert air. Their breath crystallized and then disappeared. Conversation was kept to a minimum, with each man concentrating on his own role in securing the heavy crates so the group could get back on the road as soon as possible and disappear.

The reinforced wooden boxes contained two Stingers apiece, each weighing about thirty-five pounds. With the pallet-like crates added into the equation, each one weighed in at close to eighty pounds. Even the heavily muscled young men began to tire as the job approached completion.

Joe-Bob and Jackie were precisely halfway between

vehicles, duck-stepping one of the heavy crates toward the back of the panel truck, when a bright spotlight blazed on, bleaching the scene in its glare.

From beyond the light source, a tense voice grated, "Tucson Police! You all stay right where you are and keep your hands where I can see them!" The thin, dry air amplified the cop's voice, making it sound loud and intimidating.

The team had been so involved in their work, so intent upon getting the crates secured in the panel truck, that no one had noticed the Tucson PD cruiser gliding through the parking lot, lights off, the deep rumble of its Police Interceptor engine lost in the stillness of the night.

Now everything stopped and time stood still. Jackie and Joe-Bob were completely neutralized, trapped in the spotlight's unblinking eye holding an eighty pound box filled with stolen military hardware. Dimitrios stood helplessly in the back of the Army truck, hands held out at his sides, while Brian crouched on his knees in the panel truck with his hands on top of the crate he had been pushing toward the front of the cargo box.

22

The doorbell rang, and Nick walked across the living room, wiping his hands on a dishtowel. He had just finished washing and drying the few dishes generated by his solitary dinner—it struck Nick as unnecessary and maybe even a little pathetic to use the dishwasher to clean one plate, one glass, one fork and one knife. He glanced at the clock hanging in the living room as he approached the front door. Nine o'clock exactly. Right on time. He wasn't sure why, but Nick had expected the FBI agents to be late.

He swung the door open and saw a man and a woman standing on the small stoop outside and almost laughed out loud. The two agents looked like polar opposites. The man was tall and wide like a football player, with thick dark hair and a serious look on his face. The woman was petite and slim, with blonde hair pulled back into a ponytail and a disarming smile lighting up her delicate features. The agent reminded Nick of an Olympic gymnast he had seen on TV as a kid. Her name escaped him, but she had possessed a similar smile that the television cameras loved.

They haven't even met me yet, he thought, *and already they're doing the good-cop/bad-cop thing.* He smiled politely and said, "Hi, I'm Nick Jensen, and you must be the FBI agents I was told to expect. The Merrimack Police said you would be coming at nine."

"Yes, sir. I'm Special Agent Kristin Cunningham and this is my partner, Special Agent Frank Delaney." They flashed their government ID's at exactly the same time in a move that had to have been choreographed. "We were advised by the Merrimack Police Department that you were in possession of information possibly relating to national security. Is that true, Mr. Jensen?

"Not exactly," Nick answered. "Honestly, I'm not really sure what I have, if anything, but I assume the police must have called you for a reason. Anyway, thank you for stopping by. Please come in, and I'll let you determine for yourselves if what I've found is of any significance or not."

After going back and forth on the matter for a couple of days, Nick had finally decided to call the police and tell them about the mysterious blue binder and its contents. What he had found was probably nothing, but for Lisa to have stashed away evidence related to an ongoing investigation at the Pentagon—if, in fact, that was what the binder represented—was so unlike her that the discovery gave Nick serious concern.

No sooner had he read the words, *Tucson, Bliss* and *Stingers* to the Merrimack cop on the telephone than the whole tone of the conversation had changed. The cop instantly dropped the casual, almost bored tone he had affected in the beginning and had asked a few more perfunctory questions before telling Nick that he could expect a call from the FBI regarding his unusual discovery. That call had come less than thirty minutes later, and tonight's meeting had been hastily arranged.

He showed the two agents into the small living room, where they sat side by side on the couch. Nick eased into a stuffed recliner Lisa had placed at an angle facing a wooden coffee table directly across from the couch. She had claimed that the positioning of the furniture increased the "intimacy" of the room—feng shui or some such shit—and promoted good conversation. Nick supposed he was about to find out if that was true.

"Can I get you something to drink? Coffee? Tea? A glass of water?"

"Thank you, but we're fine," Agent Cunningham said. She appeared to be the designated talker of the pair, which was okay with Nick because the guy didn't seem to have much personality at all.

"Okay, then." He picked up the bright blue binder he had placed on the coffee table prior to the arrival of the agents. "I guess we should get right to it. My wife worked at the Pentagon as a civilian auditor prior to her death - "

"We know," Agent Cunningham replied softly. "We're very sorry for your loss."

Nick sat back, surprised. "Thank you, but how do you know about my wife?"

She smiled. "Just a little quick research before visiting, Mr. Jensen. We like to be prepared."

"Oh, yeah, of course. And it's Nick."

"Nick, then."

"Anyway," he said, taking a deep breath, "I found this material very well hidden in a closet after Lisa's death. I'm assuming it's something she was working on before she died, but I can't make heads or tails out of any of it."

"Okay," Agent Cunningham answered. "But why call the police?"

"You have to understand something about my wife. She was one of the most straightforward people you could ever hope to meet. Deception wasn't her thing. If she was stashing this stuff here, I can only assume she was afraid someone in Washington would find it. And if she was being that careful, then that tells me she felt she had stumbled onto something very big, something potentially dangerous, and she was trying to decide what to do with the information. While she made up her mind, she wanted to safeguard the material the only way she could, by hiding it here, hundreds of miles from the Pentagon."

The two agents shared an uneasy glance that was not lost on Nick. Again Agent Cunningham spoke. "We can't divulge too much information to you, Mr. Jensen..."

"Nick."

"Sorry, Nick. We can't tell you too much other than this: There has been the growing suspicion in Washington that someone inside the Pentagon has been selling classified information regarding United States weaponry to known terrorist organizations, both inside and outside this country. If so, it wouldn't be the first time this has happened, as I'm sure you are well aware. Aldrich Ames is a good example. He sold secrets to the former Soviet Union for nearly ten years before his eventual arrest in 1994. Any time you combine human beings subject to temptation with knowledge of sensitive material and a willingness to profit illegally off that knowledge, the potential exists for treasonous activity. The lure of easy money becomes too much for some people to resist.

"The word *Stingers* mentioned inside this binder refers to a type of weaponry belonging to the U.S. military. It appears your wife uncovered evidence potentially implicating one or more persons inside the Pentagon in the sale of classified information regarding Stinger shoulder-fired missiles, and the FBI—not to mention the Department of Homeland Security and all law enforcement agencies—takes this very seriously."

Nick whistled softly. "What happens now?" he asked.

"We will have to seize this binder as well as all the other material you've collected. We'll share it with Homeland Security in an attempt to determine whether your wife may have discovered the identity of the person or persons leaking information from inside the Pentagon. Based on what I see here, it would appear as though she had."

Nick's blood ran cold. He wasn't sure he wanted to know the answer to his next question but couldn't stop himself from asking. "Earlier this evening I was informed by a homicide detective form the Merrimack Police Department that my wife wasn't killed in a car accident as had been previously assumed. He told me the autopsy showed she probably survived the crash but may have been murdered as she lay helpless in her car. Did she die because of the material inside this binder?"

Agent Cunningham hesitated. She shook her head. "Not necessarily. To my knowledge, the police have not yet developed any working theories regarding your wife's death. It may well have been unrelated to this information. That assessment could change, of course, pending results of their investigation. But what doesn't change is the fact that she was working on something with potentially critical implications for national security.

"I have to ask if you would permit us to take your wife's laptop back to the office for forensic analysis as well. It's entirely possible, likely even, that there is more information on her computer that could help us discover the identity of the Pentagon leak. We can't force you to release the computer to us tonight, but it could be crucial to our investigation, and realistically, we'll be back tomorrow with a warrant anyway. We will provide you with a receipt for it, of course, and will return it to you as soon as we can after it has been examined."

"Of course you can take it," Nick said, getting up to retrieve the computer. He wasn't buying the bullshit story that Lisa's death had been unrelated to her work at the Pentagon. It would be a coincidence of monumental proportion if that was the case, and Nick wasn't a big believer in coincidences.

Ultimately, though, it didn't really matter to Nick. Lisa was dead and she wasn't coming back. Nothing changed that. The FBI could have her computer forever if they wanted it. They could return it or not; he didn't care. He certainly wasn't about to use it or even look at what was on it. At least not now, and maybe not ever. It was just too painful.

Nick excused himself and walked into the master bedroom to retrieve the laptop. He handed it to the two agents, who gathered up everything on the coffee table and headed toward the front door.

Agent Delaney had still not said more than one or two

words during the entire interview. Nick decided maybe they weren't playing good-cop/bad-cop at all, but rather Agent Cunningham was the one with the brains in the partnership, and the man knew it. Better to keep your mouth shut and be thought a fool than to open it and remove all doubt.

The pair paused at the front door. "We'll get everything back to you as soon as we can," Agent Cunningham said again, almost apologetically. "Thank you for making that call to the police. You did the right thing. Hopefully we can use this information to help avert a serious tragedy before it occurs."

The FBI agents stepped through the door and into the night.

Nick could hear the lonely sound of crickets chirping in the front yard, and a lump rose in his throat. He was thankful his visitors were on their way out.

"Thanks again, and enjoy the rest of your evening, Mr. Jensen."

He almost reminded her to call him Nick but didn't bother. He watched them walk to their unmarked Bureau car, then closed the door and prepared to face another night alone. Enjoying his evening was out of the question. Nick's goal was simply to get through it.

23

The Tucson police officer crouched behind the open door of his vehicle, bracing his weapon in the crease between the hinges and the cruiser's frame, keeping it trained on the men trapped in the glare of the spotlight. Nothing happened for what seemed like minutes, although it was undoubtedly only a few seconds. Then the cop eased the door fully open and stepped slowly and cautiously around it, eyeing the surreal scene in front of him. "Let's all just take it nice and easy, and nobody gets hurt, all right, boys?"

As he finished the upward inflection on the word *boys* and took one step away from the patrol car toward the men, a burst of automatic weapons fire erupted from behind him.

***

Tony's weapon roared and bright orange fire flashed from the muzzle as he strafed the cruiser and swung his barrel slightly to the left, cutting down the officer.

The cop's body stuttered forward from the impact of the gunfire, twisting and writhing before falling to the ground. He thudded to the pavement with the slightly hollow, moist squishing sound of a pumpkin being smashed in the street on Halloween night. He died without uttering a sound.

The sharp smell of gunpowder filled the air, the sudden quiet disorienting after the AK's throaty roar. Nobody moved.

Finally Tony spoke casually, almost lazily. "Well, what are you waiting for? Let's wrap this thing up and get out of here. Undoubtedly that cop radioed his location to his dispatchers and advised them he was checking out a possible breaking and entering. When he doesn't report back within a few minutes, they will send more police out here to investigate. Maybe they already have. It would seem to be in our best interest to get as far away from this place as possible before they arrive, so let's pick up the pace."

While the men hurriedly finished transferring the last few crates and lashing them securely into the cargo box of the panel truck, Tony bent down and put both hands under the armpits of the fallen officer. With a grunt, he muscled the man's still-bleeding body into the back of his own cruiser. Blood immediately began pooling on the vinyl bench seat beneath the corpse.

Tony then slipped behind the wheel and put the idling Crown Vic in gear, moving it the short distance from the scene of the massacre to the chain-link fence at the very back of the dealership. He nosed in behind the rusting hulk of a decades-old used Airstream trailer, hoping the cruiser's semi-concealment behind the big rig might buy the team a few more minutes before the authorities became aware of the murder. It was their third in the last two hours, and Tony knew they were tempting fate as the bodies piled up.

He shut down the engine and jumped out of the patrol car. He thought for a moment about taking the dead cop's riot gun—after all, he reasoned, the cop certainly didn't need it anymore, and you could never have too many weapons, especially high-quality ones like the Remington 870—but ultimately decided that it might be detrimental to his freedom if he were to get pulled over with a murdered police officer's weapon lying on the front seat of his vehicle.

Tony had no doubt he could shoot his way out of any confrontation if necessary, but it was important to keep his eyes on the big picture, on his sacred destiny. Getting into a shootout with the police during the drive back to D.C. was a distraction he didn't need when he had been given the honor of ridding the world of the President of the United States, the oppressor of so many of his people half a globe away, Robert Cartwright.

Tony slammed the door of the cruiser, sealing the dead cop inside with a satisfying clunk, then jumped when Brian, standing right behind him, announced, "We're all done and ready to roll."

He decided he must be extremely tired. There was no way any of these American pseudo-terrorists, despite graduating from the rigorous Afghanistan training program, should have been able to approach from behind without him being aware of it.

He closed his eyes and centered himself, focusing on the steps he needed to accomplish to achieve his goal. Right now that meant getting the Stinger missiles out of here and as far away from Tucson as possible before daybreak. Sleep would have to wait.

"Thank you," he said to Brian, forcing himself to remain calm and doing his best to keep the annoyance out of his voice. He hated for these nonbelievers to see him at anything less than his best, although he doubted Brian or any of the others would even notice.

A quick inspection of the back of the panel truck convinced Tony that the missile crates were well secured with bungee cords and completely covered with wool blankets. Anyone looking into the back of the truck would see only piles of unidentifiable material. A closer examination would reveal the true nature of the truck's cargo, but Tony would ensure no one made that examination. Anyone attempting to do so would suffer a fate identical to that of the cop lying dead in his own vehicle just a couple of dozen feet away.

The team climbed into the two cars that had been used to stage the accident, while Tony slid behind the wheel of the panel truck. The military transport vehicle they left parked in the rear of the lot. There was no way to hide it effectively, and it would be discovered soon enough in any event.

The three-vehicle caravan snaked its way along the rutted tarmac to the front of the Southwest RV Center. It was now nearly four o'clock in the morning, and the horizon to the east would begin lightening soon. Already the sky in that direction looked a little lighter than it had a few minutes ago.

The team pulled onto the road, moving west toward Interstate 10. The plan was to take the highway north, hoping to lose any initial pursuit in the urban sprawl of the Phoenix/Glendale/Scottsdale metropolitan complex, before continuing on to Flagstaff and then turning east on I-40 to begin the long drive back to their home base in Washington, D.C.

A few cars were beginning to populate the roads, early risers getting a jump start on the workday or perhaps a few heading home after a long night of drinking and partying. The team observed no law enforcement activity between the RV center and the highway. They hit the interstate and accelerated to an invisible sixty-five miles per hour and drove for ten hours straight, stopping only for food and fuel. Things were right on schedule.

24

Nick had taken just a week off from work following Lisa's death, but as he walked through the double doors into the Boston Consolidated TRACON operations room to begin his workweek, he felt as though nothing and everything had changed. He flashed his key card at the scanner mounted outside the door and flinched like always as the annoying, high-pitched beep sounded, signifying the reader had recognized the chip embedded inside his ID card and he was permitted to enter.

The door swung open noiselessly, and Nick stepped into the massive room. Built in 2004 to house four separate radar approach control facilities, the building was currently home to just two—the controllers formerly quartered at Logan International Airport in Boston, and those from Manchester-Boston Regional Airport in Manchester, New Hampshire. This meant that the majority of the radar scopes placed side by side around the outside of the room—shaped more or less in a fair approximation of a giant Roller Derby rink—were unmanned, giving it the look of an air traffic control ghost town of sorts.

Glancing to the right as he entered, Nick saw the controllers in the Manchester Area, at the moment operating with three radar sectors plus a flight data position. Each controller sitting at a scope was responsible for his or her own sector within the Manchester airspace; that is, a slice of the airspace "pie" belonging to Manchester was delegated to each position.

The flight data controller answered landline calls, handled coordination for the radar sectors when they were too busy to do it themselves, and took care of routine paperwork. Fully certified controllers rotated among positions and most tried their best to avoid flight data, which was almost universally considered boring.

Nick walked toward his own area of specialization: the Boston Area, located in the rear of the operations room. At the moment it was running with five radar sectors plus one flight data position.

Within the giant oval of the operations room was what controllers referred to as the inner ring—a console built approximately ten feet inside the room, running in a complete circuit around the oval like the radar scopes but with five openings, each roughly four feet in width, allowing people access into and through the ring.

The inner ring was where management tended to congregate when in the ops room. The workspace for each area's supervisor was inside the inner ring, and the Traffic Management Coordinators—tasked with the responsibility of ensuring a smooth flow of traffic into and out of the facility's airspace—worked inside it as well.

The history of FAA air traffic control was filled with decades of animosity between controllers—who often considered themselves the only ones who did any real work in the FAA's Air Traffic Division—and management, many of who were viewed by controllers as "weak sticks" who couldn't handle the constant unrelenting pressure of separating airplanes and had moved on to positions with more authority but fewer challenges than live air traffic control.

For their part, many in management—especially those above the level of first-line supervisors who worked next the controllers in the ops room and faced many of the same pressures the controllers did—considered air traffic controllers independent, overpaid prima donnas, to be kept in line by any means necessary, up to and including management by fiat and the imposition of strict disciplinary measures for minor, non-safety related infractions.

From the disastrous PATCO strike of 1981, when nearly all of America's air traffic controllers participating in an illegal job action against the government were summarily fired by President Reagan and replaced with an entirely new workforce, to the rancorous contract negotiations of 2005 and 2006, when management finally broke off talks and simply imposed their own set of work rules on controllers in an attempt to break their union, now known as NATCA, controllers and management were often at odds. In the eyes of controllers, management was often arrogant and militaristic, while to management, controllers were often arrogant and disrespectful of their authority.

This historically adversarial working relationship eventually led to a situation where controllers often tried their hardest to avoid anything more than a purely professional relationship with representatives of FAA management and vice versa, even though most of the personnel populating management ranks were made up of people who had, at one time or another, done the very same job the controllers were doing now.

The inner ring at the BCT was a perfect example of this fundamental disconnect. Management considered it their province within the ops room, and controllers tended to stay outside it.

As Nick walked toward the back of the ops room, skirting the inner ring, he glanced at the giant plasma screens placed high on the walls above the radar scopes encircling the room. Displayed on one screen was a depiction of the equipment monitoring the status of all the approach aids serving both major airports in the airspace, Manchester and Boston. Another featured a real-time display of all the traffic inbound to each airport from across the country and overseas, and still another screen showed the status board indicating which runway configurations were in use at each airport.

To the uninitiated, the darkened ops room looked impressive and intimidating, with its electronic equipment and flashing lights and buzzers and alarms. Even to people who moved thousands of airplanes through a congested chunk of airspace every day, it was pretty impressive when they actually stopped and thought about it, which controllers rarely had the time or the inclination to do. The ops room was just where they went to work and did their thing. Another day at the office.

Nick trudged through the dimly lit room, approaching the Boston Area slowly and with some trepidation. Air traffic controllers tended to be strong-willed, decisive people, with take-charge personalities and irreverent senses of humor, given to regarding virtually any situation as fodder for a joke. Nick supposed it was a natural coping mechanism in a job where you held more lives in your hands every single day than a brain surgeon did in his entire career.

Today, though, Nick wondered how he would be received. Losing a spouse, especially at such a young age, was no joking matter, and he felt nervous, on edge, and reluctant to face his coworkers. It was almost as if he thought people would view him with suspicion, like he had done something wrong, which, of course, he hadn't. His wife had been killed, for crying out loud, murdered; it wasn't like he had something to be ashamed of.

He needn't have worried. No sooner did the controllers spot him in the gloom of the low TRACON lighting than a shout went up from John Donaldson working the Bedford sector. "Futz, welcome back, my man. We've missed you! It's been boring as hell around here. There's nobody as much fun to heckle while they're running their airplanes together on Final Vector as you!"

Nick grinned in spite of himself. The nickname Futz had been bestowed on him by someone—he couldn't remember who—when he had first arrived at the facility as a wet-behind-the-ears trainee years ago. It was short for Fucking Nuts, which had been his style when working Final Vector. He would aim everybody at the same point in space, then at the last minute begin to sort them out. As an operating technique, it was not the sort of thing you would ever train someone to do, but from his earliest days as a controller Nick had possessed an uncanny ability to visualize the sequence of arrivals developing well before anyone else could, so what appeared random and accidental to the uninitiated was in reality a well-choreographed aerial ballet.

"Hey, John, thanks a lot. I'd like to say it's good to see you too, but I still find your hideousness repulsive, even in the dark."

"Jeez, now you're starting to sound like my wife," Donaldson shot back. "Of course, she would say, '*especially* in the dark,' if you get my meaning."

By now, everyone along the line of scopes had turned their attention away from their sectors long enough to add their own welcome-back message to John's.

Even Larry Fitzgerald, working the intense Final Vector position, took a second to shout, "Hey, Futz, enough with the hearts and flowers. Make yourself useful for a change, and come give me a break," before turning back to his scope and leaning so close to it his nose practically scraped the screen.

Final Vector was generally considered the busiest and most pressure-filled position because the goal was to get the airplanes as close together as legally possible and keep them that way, all the way to touchdown on the landing runway. Often that meant taking a steady stream of arrivals from four or more different directions and running them almost directly at each other—a task requiring intense concentration and nerves of steel, and one not to be undertaken by the faint of heart.

The watch supervisor, Dean Winters, leaned his head around the opening to the inner ring and said, "Okay, everybody, the comedy act's over; let's keep it down, shall we?"

As the controllers working the operational positions once again began transmitting to the airplanes inside their sectors, Dean beckoned Nick into the inner ring and to his desk. When he had moved inside, Dean told him, "Take a seat. We need to talk."

Nick rolled a chair over to the supe's desk and sat down. He had expected to be grilled by someone in management upon his return and had figured it wouldn't take long. He didn't blame them—his wife had just died, and the FAA would want to make absolutely certain he was in the proper frame of mind before assigning him to work a sector where one wrong move could spell disaster. Generally speaking, CYA was the rule of the day in FAA management, and no one would want to be known as the guy who sent the controller with the dead wife back to working airplanes if he then fucked up and ran two of those planes together. It would be a real career ender for the supervisor who made *that* decision.

"Nick, I'm really sorry about Lisa. How are you holding up?"

"Thanks. I'm okay, I guess. I've never had a wife up and die on me before, so I don't really know how I'm supposed to react. I don't know whether I'm behaving typically or not. I'll tell you this, though: as much as I appreciate the well-intentioned gestures of support from everyone, I really need to get back to some semblance of normalcy; you know what I'm saying?"

"I can understand that," Dean replied, nodding, "but are you sure you're ready to come back to all this? After all, you took only a week off; that's not very much time to grieve."

"Oh, I'm sure. I need this. I need to start working airplanes again, if for no other reason than it will help take my mind off what happened. If I were to wait until I was done grieving, you'd probably never see me again, because I don't think I'll ever *be* done."

"I don't know . . ."

"Listen, sitting around my empty house with the ghost of

my wife, waiting for her to come walking through the front door when it's never going to happen, is not doing me any good. Accomplishing something positive and contributing even a little bit to the operation of this facility will go a long way toward helping me get back on my feet, believe me."

Dean searched his eyes for a moment and then sighed. "I understand. If you want to ease back into it and work a slow position every now and then, just let me know. But I think I would look at things just the way you do if anything were to happen to Cheryl. Anyway, welcome back."

"Thanks a lot. I appreciate it, probably more than you know. Is there anything else, or can I get to work?"

"Actually," Dean said, "there is one more thing. You're scheduled to work the midnight shift this Saturday night with Fitzgerald. I need to go over a couple of things with you before then."

"What things?"

"President Cartwright is flying into Logan early Sunday morning."

"Okay, well, you said I have the mid shift on Saturday night. Shouldn't you be having this conversation with the Sunday day shift guys?"

"No, by early Sunday morning, I mean like 5:00 a.m. when you and Larry are still going to be the only Boston controllers here."

Nick shrugged. "That's fine; I've worked Air Force One before plenty of times. So has Larry. It won't be a problem."

"I know that. But someone in charge has to plug in and monitor the controller whenever he's working the president's plane."

"That's not a problem, either. Who's been designated as CIC on that shift?" Controller in Charge was the designation given to the air traffic controller assigned the responsibility of running the watch when a supervisor wasn't available, and supervisors were never assigned midnight shifts at the BCT.

"You're CIC Saturday night on the mid."

"Well, then, I'll plug in behind Larry when he's working

the president's plane. End of problem."

"I know you could do it, but Don Trent wants to be here just in case. He wants me here, too."

"Just in case? Just in case what?"

Dean sighed again. "I don't know. But Don is the operations manager, and if he says we need to be here, then we need to be here."

"So let me get this straight. Larry and I are good enough to handle the airplanes that don't matter—you know, the ones with several hundred *regular* people on board—but when it comes to the president of the United States, we need the assistance of two guys who haven't done the job in twenty years?"

Dean's face tightened in annoyance. "It's not like that. I know you and Larry would be fine here by yourselves and so does Don. But he wants us to be here, so we're going to be here, whether you like it or not. Work your midnight shift as normal, but be ready for Don and me to walk in a little before five."

"Fine. Whatever. That it?"

"That's it."

"Then what do you want me to do now?"

"Go get Fitz out of Final Vector. He's backing up the whole East Coast."

25

The garage was cool and quiet in the middle of the night, which was exactly the way Tony liked it. He had been out of the Middle East so long now that he wasn't sure whether he would be able to withstand the relentless baking heat when he was finally able to return. He was anxious to find out, though, and thrilled to know that day was rapidly approaching, after many long years of waiting and doubting he would ever go home again.

Tony had been living legally in the United States for nearly a full decade. In the beginning it had been difficult. At times during the first long, lonely years, he questioned the judgment of those who had given him this assignment, even though he had been well trained and thoroughly prepared for his insertion into the U.S. as the leader of a Jihadist sleeper cell.

For that initial period, Tony did nothing but live quietly in the community, scrupulously learning the customs, working hard to obey all the laws of his adopted country, and avoiding any activity that might suggest he was anything other than a hardworking immigrant, anxious to make a new life for himself in this alleged land of opportunity. He reported to his superiors via secure satellite phone once a month, but otherwise, to anyone paying attention, Tony Andretti could have been the poster boy for the American dream, post-9/11 melting pot edition.

He worked long hours at his job, provided by an anonymous patron sympathetic to his organization overseas and its revolutionary cause. Driving a delivery truck for a uniform services company gave Tony ample opportunity to insinuate himself into multiple different law enforcement and military agencies. After years of seeing the same quiet, respectful man come and go, serving them with all their uniform needs, many within these organizations came to view Tony as one of their own.

When Tony had established a standing in the community, he expanded his activities, using the Internet and the connections he had painstakingly developed in his job to identify and begin recruiting potential additions to his team. He also began stockpiling the impressive array of weapons and gear that was now practically overflowing the garage in which he now sat. He accomplished all this while never knowing precisely what his assignment would be or even when it would come.

Before Tony had arrived in America, he wondered whether his hatred for all things Western would begin to diminish as he fell into a routine and made a life for himself. After all, he would be forced to do the acting job of a lifetime: to convince everyone around him that he was not disgusted by the very sight of them. Perhaps at some point he would lose his edge and feel some empathy for these people and their twisted and heretical culture.

It never happened. In fact, the opposite was true. The longer Tony lived away from his true home, the more he missed it and the more he despised these strange people for their silly religions and their materialistic lifestyles and especially for the sexually suggestive way they permitted their whorish women to dress while advancing the ridiculous notion that women were the equals of men.

Several years into his mission, Tony received more specific direction regarding his eventual assignment, and he was able to finalize the recruitment of the men who now made up his team. He enticed them with promises of wealth and power in another country upon completion of one simple task.

Now, sitting alone in the cool semidarkness of his D.C. base of operations, hours after he had sent his men home, Tony waited patiently for the sat phone to make the connection. When it had been established and his contact had been called to the phone, Tony wasted no time on small talk or pleasantries. Those things were pointless. "We're ready," he announced amiably into the handset.

"You have succeeded in acquiring everything you will need?"

"Yes."

"Good. You already know the president's itinerary. All that remains is for us to discuss your team's extraction once the mission is complete. There is an abandoned grass landing strip in northern Massachusetts roughly halfway between the two locations where you and your men will be operating. I sent you the GPS coordinates of this airfield last week. I assume you have familiarized yourself with it?"

"Of course."

"Good. That is where we will have a small aircraft waiting to transport you and your team to a freighter, which will depart out of Newport News, Virginia, immediately upon completion of your assignment to bring you home at last. Assuming you suffer no casualties, you will need a plane big enough for the pilot plus a five-man team; is that correct?"

"No."

"Excuse me?"

"No, that is not correct."

"You mean to tell me I have been misinformed as to the size of your team?"

Tony chuckled. "No, I mean to tell you that you have been misinformed as to the likelihood of the potential casualties that will be sustained by my team."

"Meaning?"

"Meaning there will be some. Four, to be precise."

There was a pause. Then the man thousands of miles away on the other end of the satellite connection chuckled, too. His voice took on a hard edge. "Am I correct in assuming you will not be one of them?"

"I certainly hope so."

"So, you . . ."

"That's right. If all my men survive this mission, I will ensure none of them survive this mission."

Tony's contact paused again. The seconds ticked away in silence. Finally he asked the question Tony had been expecting. "Why? These men are going to help us achieve our greatest triumph, greater even than the success of September 11, 2001."

"True," Tony conceded. "But the answer is quite simple. For all their technical proficiency, these men are still nothing more than filthy infidels. They know nothing of our culture and religion; care nothing of them, either. They are greedy, unclean pigs, and I will not be responsible for infecting the sacred land of my country with the likes of them. They will help us accomplish our goal, and then they will be executed. A two-seater plane will be sufficient for the flight to Virginia."

Tony broke the connection and placed the bulky satellite phone inside the bottom drawer of his desk, locking it securely. He lit a cigarette and took a long drag, exhaling slowly, watching as the smoke drifted away on the invisible currents of air circulating through the drafty garage.

26

Special Agent Kristin Cunningham reviewed all the material the FBI had removed from Nick Jensen's home for about the thousandth time in the last several days. To Kristin and Frank, it had been instantly clear that the information could mean only one thing: some nameless and faceless group had planned to hijack Raytheon-made Stinger shoulder-fired missiles somewhere between the company's home base in Tucson and the ultimate destination of the weapons, in this case Fort Bliss.

Their assumption had been right on target, too, although Kristin felt no satisfaction being right. Last week, on the very same evening that Kristin and Frank sat in Nick Jensen's living room discussing the strange collection of information his dead wife had hidden inside their closet, that nameless and faceless terrorist group had indeed hijacked an Army transport truck, murdering the two soldiers assigned to the delivery and dumping their bodies by the side of the road in the desert.

The killers had then driven twenty miles to an RV sales center on the outskirts of Tucson, where they exchanged vehicles, abandoned the Army truck, and disappeared into the night, but not before killing one more person, a Tucson police officer who stumbled onto the exchange during a routine patrol.

There were no witnesses, at least none who had survived, and by now the missiles could be anywhere in the country—or possibly even overseas—under the control of a terrorist organization that had already murdered four people, if you included Nelson W. Michaels, the midlevel Pentagon staffer who sold the information to the group. Michaels had originally been presumed killed in an auto accident while driving home from work on the same day he had made the trade, but it was later determined that he had been murdered in his car following the wreck. It was the second time someone connected to the case had been killed in this manner.

Over the last several days, Kristin had been in almost constant contact with officials from the Department of Homeland Security. Their working theory was that the stolen Stinger missiles were hidden somewhere inside the United States and had been hijacked with a specific domestic target in mind. The murder of Michaels was executed cleanly and professionally, but no serious effort had been made to mask the killing. To Homeland Security, this indicated the group in possession of the Stingers was planning on using them soon.

The theft had triggered red flags throughout both the law enforcement and intelligence communities, because the stolen missiles were almost completely intact. In most cases, Stingers were delivered in several separate pieces to guard against an occurrence like the one that had just taken place. In this case, however, time-sensitive critical software modifications had been made, necessitating the shipment of missiles that were virtually complete. The only thing missing was the guidance system, which, if added, would give whoever possessed the shoulder-fired Stingers the ability to wreak untold havoc and kill potentially many thousands of people in a disaster that could rival the September 11, 2001 attacks.

The likelihood that the group which had stolen the weapons was actually in possession of the software needed to accurately control them was slim, but still, law enforcement agencies at all levels around the country had been put on the highest alert status. This would remain the case until the missiles had been safely recovered.

Kristin stifled a surge of annoyance that Nick Jensen had waited a couple of days after discovering the notes and other materials before alerting the authorities. Had he done so even one day sooner, DHS and the FBI could have set up a sting operation, driving a decoy truck along the mapped-out route that night with nothing inside it but a few empty crates. They could have taken down the terrorist organization that had purchased the information, and today there would be one less group of murderous fanatics out there bent on the destruction of the United States or some other Western country.

Of course, Kristin couldn't really blame Nick. The poor guy had just lost his wife in a terrible accident and didn't have any idea what he had stumbled upon when he found it hidden in the back of a closet. Plenty of people would never even have bothered to contact anyone. They would have tossed the binder in the trash and gone on with their lives, never giving it a second thought.

It was hard to blame Nick's wife, either. Lisa was employed as an auditor at the Pentagon, and her work had been mostly limited to staffers stealing pens and surfing inappropriate websites. She had clearly known she was dealing with something big, but had been too hesitant in informing her superiors. Hell, maybe she had been concerned that a supervisor was involved and hadn't known who she could trust with the discovery. Ultimately, Lisa Jensen had been involved in something much bigger than she was prepared to handle, and it had cost her her life.

Kristin found her mind wandering back to her meeting a few nights ago with Nick, and she was embarrassed to admit that she felt a tug of attraction. The man had just lost his wife, for God's sake. Still, she couldn't help how she felt, and even though his face had been pale and drawn from sorrow and lack of sleep, there was something about him that she found alluring. He wasn't football-star handsome, had probably never dated the prom queen in high school, but still, he seemed honest, with an easy smile and natural charm…

Jesus, she thought, *what's wrong with me? There's a group of homicidal maniacs running around with a stolen truckload of lethal weapons, and I'm daydreaming like some love-struck junior high girl about a guy whose wife is barely in the ground.*

She shook her head, disgusted with herself, and got back to work.

27

An eight-foot-high chain-link fence encircled the outer perimeter of the large plot of land housing the Boston Consolidated TRACON. The upper eighteen inches of fencing consisted of four strands of tightly wound barbed wire angled outward forty-five-degrees. The fence was set back from the ugly mustard-colored brick building a minimum of fifty feet in all directions.

Ornamental trees, small and insignificant looking against the backdrop of the big building, dotted the landscaped property, but most of the area had been left open, presumably for security purposes. Anyone somehow managing to scale the fence without being incapacitated by the barbed wire strands—in addition to leaking copious amounts of blood—would be forced to cross a wide expanse of well-lit open ground before getting anywhere near the BCT building itself.

Closed-circuit cameras were mounted on all exterior corners of the building, providing three hundred sixty degrees of CCTV surveillance around the BCT, as well as in dozens of locations throughout the interior. The cameras were monitored twenty-four hours a day by armed security personnel quartered inside a brick guard shack, complete with bulletproof glass, located at the only entrance to the facility. A reinforced steel gate could be trundled across the entryway at the touch of a button, repelling access by any vehicle smaller than a tank.

Outside the fence, though, was a different story entirely. The land immediately behind the property was heavily populated with decades-old, maybe centuries-old, fir trees. They were big and ancient and provided excellent cover for anyone interested in observing the facility while keeping his presence a secret.

Sitting quietly in this thickly forested area were Tony, Brian, and Jackie. It was Sunday, just shy of 2:00 a.m., and United States President Robert Cartwright was scheduled to fly into Logan Airport on Air Force One in approximately three hours. Tony's goal was to ensure that it was the last time the president ever flew anywhere, except straight to hell where he belonged.

Clouds gathered overhead, thickening rapidly, effectively obscuring the quarter-full moon. Ambient light would not be a problem. The weather forecasters were calling for ceilings to continue to lower and eventually for a light but steady rain to begin falling across the region. If the conditions deteriorated too quickly, it would spell problems for the remaining two members of the team, who were hunkered down in a remote location outside Logan Airport with the stolen Stingers, but Tony wasn't worried. He had studied several different forecasts, and they were unanimous in their estimates that the worst of the conditions around Logan would not occur until much later in the day—long after their mission had been completed.

All his men needed in order to fire upon Air Force One as it hung in the sky over the airport—exposed like a fish in a barrel, just waiting to be blown to bits—were cloud bases of as low as a few hundred feet. Assuming the current forecast was accurate, in a few hours the president would be killed in a fiery plane crash. Once the job was done, the clouds could extend all the way down to the ground; it wouldn't matter to Tony in the least.

The faint sound of rubber-soled shoes scuffling on

pavement floated through the heavy air. Tony glanced at his watch. Two o'clock. Right on time. He and his men had staked out the BCT for several days now, and each morning at exactly the same time, one of the two security guards on duty clomped past on the paved walking path encircling the facility just inside the perimeter of the security fence.

Protocol, not to mention common sense, should have dictated that the guards vary the timing of the nightly sweeps, but it had become quite clear to Tony that security at this facility—located far off the beaten path in New Hampshire—was inexcusably lax; the guards had not varied their routine in the slightest from one evening to the next.

A damp breeze rustled the massive evergreens all around them, and the group held their positions, standing perfectly still in the shadows as the patrolling security guard materialized out of the darkness. He yawned, practically sleepwalking as he strolled the path, paying little attention to his surroundings and moving with the gait of someone who couldn't wait to get back to his favorite chair and take a load off.

***

Jackie lay prone on the cold carpet of moss and reddish brown fallen pine needles and watched the man pass. He was stationed just far enough into the pitch-black area behind the trees that he remained invisible to the security guard as he made his rounds.

He sighted down the barrel of a TCI M89SR sniper rifle, patiently tracking his prey. The compact semiautomatic weapon, originally manufactured for the Israeli Defense Forces and now in common use by the Special Forces units of numerous countries, was fitted with a sound suppressor and rested comfortably in a portable bipod, barrel angled upward. Jackie followed the ambling gait of the unwitting guard, making minute adjustments, keeping the man's body centered in the crosshairs.

Minutes earlier, Jackie had taken out the lone security camera monitoring the grounds behind the BCT building. The camera, mounted high on the back wall of the building, had been programmed for constant motion, continually scanning for anything out of the ordinary. Now, however, this area remained free of electronic surveillance, the camera currently resting in a thousand useless pieces scattered across the rear parking lot.

***

The possibility that the guard manning the security station might be alarmed by the lack of video surveillance in this area didn't concern Tony. There were so many cameras on this federal government property that it was unlikely the guard would even notice the blank screen for some time, and that was assuming he was even paying close attention to all the monitors in the guard shack rather than sleeping—an unlikely scenario given the late hour and general security laxness Tony had observed.

The patrolling guard wandered sleepily in front of Tony and his unmoving men, three pairs of eyes quietly marking his progress. When he reached a point almost directly in front of them, passing less than forty feet away on the other side of the chain-link fence, Jackie squeezed the trigger of the M89, and a soft *phht* sound was accompanied a second later by the sight of the guard tumbling to the ground. He executed a slow, almost balletic, pirouette before dropping gracefully to the pavement. He kicked his legs once and lay still.

Under the over of the trees, no one moved for nearly a full minute. When Jackie was finally satisfied the man was either dead or fully incapacitated, he took his finger off the trigger and began dismantling his equipment and repacking it into his bag.

***

Brian approached the fence carrying a small but powerful set of bolt cutters. He was covered by Tony, but the team anticipated no interruption from the other guard, who was undoubtedly still huddled in the security building and out of sight around a corner, unaware of what had befallen his partner. The two men never patrolled together.

When Brian reached the fence, he began snipping the tempered steel with the powerful jaws of the bolt cutter, steadily moving from the ground up in more or less a straight line, until he had created a jagged opening in the fence roughly six feet high and three feet wide that the group could squeeze through. For sixty seconds, the only sound was a muffled ting-ting-ting as he worked his way through the reinforced steel.

***

The sound of the links snapping was surprisingly clear, enough so that Tony wondered whether it would carry through the moist, still air all the way to the guard shack. He then decided it didn't really matter.

Even assuming the lone remaining guard was awake and heard the noise, he would take some time to try to figure out what the hell it was. By the time he decided to get off his ass and investigate, the sound would have long since stopped, and he would likely just shrug and forget about it. It was clear to Tony that these rent-a-cops didn't exactly represent the top of the law enforcement food chain.

***

When Brian finished creating an opening in the security fence big enough for the team to squeeze through, he pulled the chain links apart, and Jackie slipped through and entered the property. The fence creaked quietly and then fell silent as Brian maintained a steady tension on the links.

Jackie approached the fallen security guard cautiously, his Glock 9mm semiautomatic pistol with sound suppressor trained on the unmoving man. He reached the guard in a few steps and knelt beside him, running his fingers lightly along the side of the man's neck, feeling for a pulse. He shook his head in disbelief, then placed the gun at the guard's temple, turned his body, and squeezed off a single shot. He felt for a pulse again.

Now satisfied that the man was dead, Jackie jammed the

gun into the waistband of his jeans and grabbed the prostrate guard's ankles, dragging him back through the fence and into the relative darkness and safety of the thick stand of trees just outside the BCT property line. Brian eased the makeshift gate closed behind him and then retreated into the trees, too.

Shivering from the cool and damp air, Jackie began to undress.

28

Jim Shay was bone tired. Working two jobs—one of which required him to be alert between 12:00 and 8:00 a.m. while the rest of the world slumbered snugly in their beds—was a major pain in the ass. But with five kids and a wife who spent money like they had a printing press in their basement, he had no choice but to do what he was doing. "Keep on keepin' on," as the song lyrics went.

On the bright side, this BCT security gig was a piece of cake once you got past the shitty hours. He worked days as a Merrimack town cop, slept in the afternoon and early evening, then put on his generic security guard's uniform and drove to this out-of-the-way government facility to work the graveyard shift five nights a week. As the sun peeked over the evergreen trees in the morning, he would leave the BCT and drive straight to the Merrimack Police Department to begin the whole exhausting cycle all over again.

It was a tiring life, boring too, but the way Jim saw it, he had no real reason to bitch. The United States government paid damned good money to maintain a minimum staffing level of two armed guards at the BCT 24/7, and Jim was thankful he had been selected to fill one of the slots when the air traffic control facility opened five years ago. In this economy, when a lot of people were scrambling to keep one job, Jim wasn't going to complain about having two.

He leaned back in his rolling office chair and yawned. As tempting as it was to close his eyes and take a quick power nap, Jim was too conscientious to ever sleep on duty. It wouldn't be right. More to the point, if he got caught, he would definitely get fired, and what would he do then? Lucy was sure as hell not going to stop spending money, and there was no way he'd ever find another second job that paid the kind of scratch this one did.

At least he had someone to talk to; that little bonus helped pass the time. And although his night shift partner, Morris Stapleton, wasn't going to make anyone forget Albert Einstein and didn't exactly set the world on fire with his initiative, he had a pretty good sense of humor and loved to talk sports, so for the most part, the nights went by as quickly as Jim had any right to expect.

Thinking of Morris made Jim wonder what was taking him so long to return from his perimeter patrol. There were only three duties mandated by the government on the overnight shift: maintain a constant presence in the guard shack in order to screen traffic at the front gate; scan the bank of monitors showing the real-time video feed from the dozens of CCTV security cameras positioned inside and outside the BCT building; and patrol the perimeter of the property and the inside of the building several times a night.

In other words, do a little bit of law enforcement.

Over the course of their partnership, Jim and Morris had worked out an agreement whereby they would trade off perimeter patrol duties on alternating nights. Walking perimeter patrol was by far the most distasteful of the job's few requirements, since it involved exercise often conducted in weather conditions that were less than desirable.

Tonight was Morris's turn to "Walk the Line," as they called it, and he was pretty fortunate; the conditions weren't too bad. It was cool, and it was going to rain later. But for now the air was still, and although the atmosphere was saturated with moisture, the rain had thus far held off.

As Jim considered whether he should go look for

Morris—maybe the fat slob had suffered a heart attack and was even now lying face down and motionless behind the building—he noticed the vague shape of his partner coming into focus in the dim, hazy glow of the sodium vapor arc lights spaced at regular intervals around the property. Morris was still far off across the open empty expanse of field bordering the access road, ambling along like he always did. Jim often wondered if Morris even knew how to run. If he did, Jim had never seen any evidence of it.

Jim turned his attention toward a large imitation maple console that ran alongside the front interior wall of the guard shack. The console contained a series of small closed-circuit television monitors, each one countersunk into the surface so that only its viewing screen protruded. The guards had had a few close calls with spilling coffee onto the damned things, but so far, thank God, none of the accidents had fried any of the monitors.

He wondered how much money would be withheld from his paycheck to replace a monitor if he destroyed one and shuddered. They were just basic black-and-white CCTV monitors, five inches high by seven inches wide, but with the United States government doing the purchasing, undoubtedly the sky was the limit on the cost of the goddamned things. Each one probably priced out at upwards of a thousand bucks or something.

He glanced at the three rows of monitors, looking away and then doing a double take. Something was wrong with camera seventeen, the one mounted on a swivel high on the southeast corner of the BCT building. It provided the only video coverage of the grounds directly behind that portion of the building, and either the camera had just shit the bed, or else the monitor itself was on the fritz. All that was being displayed was interference, like the snow you used to get on the broadcast TV channels—in the Dark Ages before cable—in the middle of the night when the station was off the air.

Jim tried to remember whether that particular monitor had been working the last time he checked and was pretty sure it had been; he would have noticed if the screen had been grey and fuzzy like it was now. It wasn't all that unusual for the cameras to suffer glitches, though. He would have to ask Morris if he had noticed anything unusual in that area when he made it back to the shack. He had passed by there just a couple of minutes ago. Where was he? Christ, that guy was slow.

Finally the man's bulk filled the open doorway. Jim registered him entering in his peripheral vision but continued watching camera seventeen's monitor as if he could somehow will the piece of crap to begin operating normally again. It would certainly make life easier if he could.

"Check out this piece of shit," Jim said, glancing up at the man and immediately freezing in place, his blood running cold. He had no fucking idea who was standing inside the guard shack's bulletproof door dressed in Morris's ill-fitting uniform, but it certainly wasn't Morris. This guy was shorter than Morris, squat and powerfully built, with curly jet-black hair sticking out of his blue ball cap at odd angles, making it look as though he had a bunch of antennae coming out of his head. Kind of like Uncle Martin on *My Favorite Martian,* the old TV comedy he had loved when he was a kid.

But there was nothing funny about the gun the guy was pointing at Jim's chest. He held the weapon securely in a two-handed shooter's grip like he knew exactly what he was doing, and he appeared completely at ease. "Check out what piece of shit, my friend?" he said pleasantly in a high-pitched nasally voice tinged with traces of a Brooklyn accent.

"Who the fuck are you?"

"I would think you might try to take a more civil tone, considering I have absolute control over whether you live or die in the next few seconds."

Jim tried to get his breathing under control as he considered his options. There weren't many. He could try to draw his weapon on the man, but it was holstered at his hip, held in place by a thick leather strap. He would have to unsnap the strap, lift the gun, and shoot in one smooth motion before the guy squeezed the trigger on his own weapon, which he now recognized as a Glock very similar to his own. Odds of success: pretty fucking slim.

Other options? He couldn't think of any, except maybe to keep the guy talking. Slow things down a little. Maybe he would have the opportunity to get a jump on this character if he could draw things out and establish some control over the situation. Easier said than done, though, especially since this guy looked like a pro.

"Yeah, you're right. Sorry about that, dude. Let me try a different question: Where's my partner?"

"Partner? What partner? You had a partner?" The guy had a wiseass smirk on his face, and Jim realized he was playing with him. He also realized the guy said "*had* a partner," not "*have* a partner." He didn't like the choice of wording and didn't think it was accidental.

He pushed on. *Keep the guy talking. Wait for an opportunity.* What choice did he have? "Yeah, my partner, the man whose uniform you're now wearing. I gotta tell ya—he fills it out a lot better than you do."

"Not anymore he don't." The man's dark eyes had gone cold, and they glittered dangerously. He held the gun perfectly centered on Jim's chest. His hands looked relaxed and steady. This guy knew what he was doing. "He won't be filling any uniforms out anymore, good or bad."

Jim's heart sank. Unless the guy was playing with him again, and that seemed unlikely, he was making clear that Morris was dead. Matters suddenly became much more dire, if that was possible. Question: What could be worse than a man pointing a loaded gun at you from no more than seven feet away? Answer: A man who *had just killed another human being in cold blood* pointing a gun at you from no more than seven feet away.

If this crazy bastard really had murdered Morris, then clearly he had nothing to lose. He was already facing a lethal injection and would have zero reason to allow Jim to live and every reason in the world not to. Jim knew he should be shaking, should be shitting his pants actually, but he felt a strange sort of Zen calm envelope him. He had been in bad situations before, serving two tours with the Marine Corps in the Middle East, where there was virtually no respect for human life among many of the people; they just didn't place the same value on it that Westerners did.

He had survived confrontations with men who were twice as savage and cunning as this young man, and Jim was sure if he kept his wits about him that he could survive this, too. He just had to figure out how.

"So Morris is out of the picture. That's too bad, man, but we can still resolve things without anyone else dying. Especially me. That sound reasonable to you? What's your name?"

The guy coughed out a harsh laugh like the question was the funniest thing he had heard all night. His dead shark eyes narrowed. He probably knew exactly what Jim was trying to do. "Okay, I'll play along, seeing how we're becoming so close and all. My name's Jackie. Jackie Corrigan. It make you feel better knowing my name?"

"Not really, Jackie. Since we're being honest with each other, I have to tell you it makes me feel damned uncomfortable. It makes me feel like you've already decided what you're going to do with me, and I'm afraid it's something that I'm not going to like very much."

A genuine smile flitted across the man's face and disappeared. "I like you. You've got balls. In a different life we could have been friends. It's too bad I've got to do this. No hard feelings, okay?"

In that instant Jim knew what was coming and tried to fling himself backward. The guard shack was small and packed with equipment, and there was virtually no place to take cover, but Jim was a sitting duck in that chair, propped up right in front of the killer with the Glock. He pushed off with his feet and launched himself up and over the back of the chair just as the first shot came. The pistol roared, and fire spit out of the muzzle. Jim screamed, and against all odds he almost made that first shot miss.

Almost, but not quite.

The bullet caught Jim in the right wrist, and blood splattered all over the far wall. For a split second Jim wondered whether they would take the cost of repainting the building's interior out of his pay, and then the man fired again.

This time his aim was true. Jim had run out of room.

The bullet struck him in the center of the chest, opening up a ragged gaping hole and causing a gushing wave of blood to soak his uniform shirt.

Jim found himself crumpled on his back on the console, his uninjured left hand resting just inches from the telephone. He reached for it instinctively, but before he could punch a single button, a third bullet pierced his neck, and the curtain came down on his world as rapidly and as completely as the end of a Broadway show, except there would be no applause. His last aching thought was of Lucy, and then the world disappeared.

29

A rickety old Dodge Dakota pickup prowled slowly along Ocean Drive in Hull, Massachusetts. The road was mostly deserted at this hour. Abruptly Dimitrios extinguished his headlights and turned sharply left, leaving the road and striking out across the roughly three-quarters of a mile of empty marshland filling the space between the edge of the Atlantic Ocean and this portion of Ocean Drive.

Dimitrios shifted the Dakota into four-wheel drive to navigate the loose, spongy terrain. Mud and water sprayed in all directions, caking the outside of the truck in a matter of seconds. It was slow going as they moved relentlessly toward the Atlantic. The truck jounced and slid, its tires sinking into the soft ground before the force of the drivetrain pulled them back out again.

After ten minutes of muscling the pickup across the empty marshland, Dimitrios splashed to a stop roughly fifty feet from the water. He shut down the truck, and silence rushed in to fill the void left by the absence of the struggling engine's whine. Low waves lapped at the rocky shoreline.

The Dakota's nose faced the water. Across the three-mile inlet was the southernmost edge of General Edward Lawrence Logan International Airport, an ancient field by aviation standards that had come into existence in the 1920s as a single 1500-foot cinder runway. The airfield, known originally as Boston Airport, began offering passenger service between Boston and New York in 1927.

Expansion occurred on a regular basis over the decades, and now Logan's traffic count made it about the twelfth busiest airport in the United States. Logan was rather unique among major airports due to its close proximity to the metropolitan Boston area. Flying into the airport serving most major cities often meant another thirty- to sixty-minute cab ride to actually get to the city. With Logan, the drive might still take that long thanks to traffic congestion, but the airfield itself was less than two miles from downtown Boston.

The marshy area currently serving as a staging point for the Dodge was a small spit of land known as the Hull Peninsula, one of the main battlefronts in the long-running war between local community activists concerned about airport noise and aviation officials anxious to provide air service to the region. The peninsula sat just three miles across the water from the approach end of Logan's Runway 33 Left, which meant aircraft landing on that runway would pass almost directly overhead, just a few hundred feet above the ground.

At the moment, different runways were being utilized for Logan Airport's arrivals and departures, so all was calm in the airspace above the truck. From their vantage point inside the cab, Dimitrios and Joe-Bob could see the seemingly never-ending stream of lights from the airplanes landing and departing Logan. It looked like a line of bees arriving on one side of a hive, with another line of bees taking off from the other side. The airplane noise from this distance was nothing more than a nearly continuous low rumble.

Tony's plan called for Dimitrios and Joe-Bob to get into position nice and early. He hadn't wanted them to run into any unexpected difficulties and then not have enough time to set up. There would be only one chance to get this right.

Everything had gone smoothly, so now Dimitrios and Joe-Bob were hunkered down in position a couple of hours early and could relax for a while. They would begin setting up the equipment in the bed of the retrofitted truck in half an hour. That would give them roughly ninety minutes to prepare before Air Force One came floating out of the sky with its big fat belly hanging in the air above them, exposed and vulnerable and waiting to be blown to a million scorched pieces along with everyone inside.

Across the water, the bees continued to swarm, one long line of airplanes arriving, their yellow landing lights seemingly suspended in the air in complete defiance of the laws of gravity, and another line departing. The throaty roar of the departing engines floated across the water, shattering the stillness every couple of minutes like clockwork. Dimitrios and Joe-Bob smoked cigarettes and watched the aerial ballet in silence.

30

Nick glanced at the big clock hanging on the wall on the east end of the TRACON operations room. Amidst all the high-tech electronic gadgetry, the clock seemed anachronistic—a Flintstones timepiece in a Star Wars world. It was big and round, with clunky black hands fitted over an off-white face, an exact match to the clocks that used to hang in the classrooms of the Sydney Street Elementary School Nick had attended when he was a kid. He had always thought that a fancy digital display would have been much more appropriate to the air traffic control setting.

It was 2:15 a.m. Airborne traffic in and out of Logan had slowed to a trickle, and that would remain the case until flights began gearing up for the new day, normally at around 5:15 to 5:30. Today would not be a normal day, of course, with the anticipated arrival of President Cartwright at about 5:30. The ops manager and the day shift supervisor would be stumbling in all bleary-eyed around five o'clock or so to stand around and look important, and the Secret Service or FBI would also be represented.

Sitting alone at the Initial Departure scope, where the Boston area's sectors were typically combined for the midnight shift, was Larry Fitzgerald. He looked like a lost little kid, manning one scope while surrounded by all the others dutifully displaying their boundary maps and traffic, but with no controller sitting in front of any of them. There was no need for more than one sector to be open in either the Boston or the Manchester area on the overnight shift, given the lack of traffic.

Nick stood up from the supervisor's console, where he had been reading a book and trying, mostly unsuccessfully, to stay awake. He strolled over to Fitz's scope and saw one arrival in the entire Boston area airspace, an Atlas Airlines flight that had been delayed departing Tampa, thanks to a series of thunderstorms pummeling the west coast of Florida.

"Fitzy, I'm going to grab a bite to eat, then I'll be back to give you a break. Does that work for you?"

"That works for me, boss. I'm pretty sure I can handle this solitary airplane all by myself."

Nick laughed. "Don't kid yourself. You could have twenty airplanes, and I'd still be taking a break."

"Hah! Who needs you, anyway? Go ahead and abandon me. I'll face the onslaught alone."

"I'll be back in like twenty minutes. Do me a favor and try not to kill anybody in the meantime."

This was how it went between Fitz and Futz, two veteran controllers who had been hooking airplanes in the Boston area for years. They were forever denigrating each other's abilities, but both men knew that when push came to shove and the traffic was heavy and things were going to hell in the TRACON, they could trust each other implicitly. The bonds of shared experience were strong among air traffic controllers, and until you proved yourself time and time again under the intense pressure of busy traffic and poor weather conditions, you could look cool and sound sharp on the frequency and you would still garner little or no respect from your peers.

Nick and Larry had been there. Each man knew he could count on the other when it mattered.

31

The bodies of the two dead security guards lay side by side on the cold ground, tossed next to each other like trash piled on a curb awaiting collection.

Jackie had thrown the second guard's bleeding body over his shoulder and carried him to the security fence the team had breached just a few minutes before, where the rest of the small team huddled, waiting impatiently.

"Took ya long enough," Brian groused, stamping his feet to keep warm and lighting a cigarette. Tony had expressly forbidden smoking while both guards remained in play. Now, however, with the small security force eliminated, there was no reason not to light up. No residences or businesses populated the area immediately surrounding the BCT, meaning there would be no one to see the flare of a lighter or match. Even if a patrolling Merrimack town cop should happen to cruise past on the access road, he would see nothing, as the team had retreated into the relative safety of the thick stand of trees on the east side of the property.

Jackie glared at Brian. "Oh, really? I didn't ice this guy fast enough for you? Well, maybe next time you can do all the heavy lifting, and I'll hide back here in the friggin' forest and sit around complaining. How's that sound to you, pretty boy?"

"Shut your mouths and focus, both of you," Tony cut in. "We've got work to do, remember? Or would you rather just stand around arguing like spoiled children the rest of the night?"

The two men stared at each other for a moment. Finally they knelt next to Tony, who was busy rifling through the pockets of the guards. The most valuable item in each guard's possession was not his weapon or his radio or his money or any of his personal effects; it was the picture ID hanging on a lanyard around his neck.

Every BCT employee possessed a similar identification card, and embedded in each was a chip limiting BCT access to those portions of the property the employee had reason to use based on his or her job description. Electronic locks adorned the entrance to every sensitive area, but not every ID would provide access to every area of the building.

As security personnel charged with protecting both the interior and the exterior of the property, however, the chips embedded inside the guards' identification cards opened all locks and permitted access to every area within the BCT, and thus were keenly valuable to the terrorists. Tony took Morris Stapleton's ID and hung it around his neck like an Olympic athlete displaying his gold medal. He then removed Jim Shay's, lifting the dead man's upper body off the ground to slide it off before dropping his head with a muffled thud. He handed the ID to Jackie, who placed it around his neck.

They performed the same ritual with both men's two-way radios; Tony kept one and handed the other to Corrigan. The guards' weapons they ignored. The men were already heavily armed and had no use for more firepower. What they had brought with them would be more than enough to force compliance from the overnight skeleton crew of three air traffic controllers and one electronics technician, now unprotected inside the building for the next several hours.

Brian smoked his cigarette as he watched the two men. The air was heavy and damp, thick with the promise of approaching rain, which had thus far held off exactly as the weather forecasters had predicted. He burned it all the way down to the end, flicking the butt into the trees and holding his breath to keep in that last puff as long as possible.

"All right, let's go," Tony ordered.

Brian reluctantly blew out the smoke in a slow, steady breath.

The three men lined up and slid through the opening Brian had cut in the security fence. They made no particular effort to hide either the dead bodies lying on the ground or the damage that had been done to the chain-link fence. No one would make the gruesome discovery until a full complement of guards, controllers, and technicians began arriving for the day shift. By then it wouldn't matter.

32

Dimitrios awoke with a start, confused. It took him a moment to get his bearings—he was slouched in the front seat of the Dodge Dakota parked in a marsh, a couple of miles across the water from the approach end of Runway 33 Left at Logan Airport. Dimitrios squinted at his watch. It was 4:00 a.m. He realized he had been dozing, snoring lightly, and he turned angrily to Joe-Bob. "Jesus, why didn't you wake me up when I fell asleep?"

Joe-Bob shrugged. "Why should I? There was nothing to do for a while, anyway. It doesn't really require two of us to watch the airplanes come and go." He nodded toward the windshield, grimy with dried mud that had been kicked up when they drove through the marsh.

Dimitrios followed Joe-Bob's gaze and saw that what had been a steady stream of arriving and departing airplanes had now petered out to almost nothing. The line of bees flying into and out of the hive had turned into an occasional lonely airplane descending the glide path to the airport or taking off and turning toward some unknown destination.

"I suppose we should get to work," Joe-Bob said languidly. It was clear he was tired and wished for nothing more than to sleep for a while, as Dimitrios had done.

Now, however, there was no time left for a nap. They needed to begin preparing for the critical task they would complete as the sky was brightening over the Atlantic. In roughly ninety minutes, Dimitrios and Joe-Bob, along with the other three members of their little team thirty-five miles away in Merrimack, would change the course of history forever.

They opened the doors of the pickup and plopped down onto the wet ground, instantly sinking six inches into the muck. It was no wonder this area had never been developed. Between the standing water of the marshland and the bustling activity of Logan Airport just a couple of miles away, no one in their right mind would want to live here, even though the view of the sea was breathtaking and oceanfront land a prime commodity.

The two men splashed toward the tailgate in their waterproof boots. Joe-Bob stopped and cocked his head.

"What is it?" Dimitrios asked.

"You hear that?"

Dimitrios shook his head, and as he did, he began to hear a low buzzing, almost like the sound a mosquito would make as it navigated its way to your head to begin munching. It wasn't a mosquito, though, and the two men stared at each other incredulously as it dawned on them both at the same time.

"Somebody's driving out here," Dimitrios said. He couldn't believe his ears. Who the hell would come all the way to the northern tip of the Hull Peninsula in this swampy mess at four o'clock in the morning? His first thought was the police, but that was impossible. No one knew they were here; he was certain of that. If the authorities were aware of their presence, they would have been arrested and taken away hours ago when they first arrived.

The two men hurriedly retreated to the cab of the Dakota.

"Whoever is coming out here, we have to get rid of them," Dimitrios whispered fiercely, as if concerned that the occupants of the four-wheel drive making its way slowly toward them with its lights off might be able to hear him.

They stared at the advancing truck as it materialized out of the darkness. The vehicle was close enough now that they could see it was a Jeep, at least ten years old, and it was filled with young men drinking and partying.

It occurred to Dimitrios that the Jeep's occupants, who were clearly drunk and not paying much attention to their surroundings, might not even have noticed yet that they had company in the marsh. With a little luck, he and Joe-Bob could circle quietly behind them while they were busy carousing and eliminate them easily and quickly.

No sooner had that thought occurred to him than the Jeep slid to a stop in the mud and its headlights blazed on.

It was too late. They had been spotted.

33

Just after 4:00 a.m., Tony, Jackie, and Brian marched through the BCT's two sets of double doors and into the building openly and brazenly, without even a halfhearted attempt at stealth. There was no reason to be overly cautious now, they had eliminated the two men who could reasonably be considered a threat and weren't concerned about a couple of air traffic controllers and a federal government electronics technician.

The men, clad from head to toe in black fatigues and boots, their faces covered with black camouflage greasepaint, moved single file across the terrazzo floor. Their semiautomatic rifles were drawn and held in both hands across their chests.

For the moment the terrorists ignored the wide staircase on the left that led up to the second floor and the operational quarters. Accessing the radar room would come later. First things first. Walking swiftly, they bypassed the staircase and turned left. Tony lifted Morris Stapleton's ID card and waved it in front of the card reader, unlocking the double doors leading to the technicians' workspace.

The card reader issued a loud beep, and the locks disengaged. Tony elbowed his way through the doors, holding his weapon in front of him at the ready. It was highly unlikely that the technician assigned the overnight shift was doing anything other than sleeping, but Tony wasn't taking the chance of running into the guy in the hallway and being caught unprepared.

Tony immediately faced left. Jackie walked in and faced right, ready to eliminate any threat from that direction should there happen to be one.

There wasn't.

A second later Brian entered, too, and the team split up as the doors closed smoothly behind them, Tony moving left along the hallway in front of the equipment room and Jackie and Brian turning right, flanking the room on the other side.

The terrorists were totally at ease inside the BCT building. They were familiar with its layout, having studied blueprints until each man was confident he could navigate the facility with his eyes closed. Getting access to the construction plans and blueprints had been simple—they had been included in the packet of information purchased from Nelson Michaels.

Thanks to Michaels, the terrorist team knew that there were two exterior doors on this side of the building. The hallway they were standing in surrounded the enormous workspace where the technicians stored radar scopes and all the tools necessary to maintain the equipment inside the BCT. After winding around this workspace, the corridors terminated at the north wall, where each one ended at a heavy steel door leading to the outside.

The doors were locked and accessible from the outside only with an ID card like the one Tony had hanging around his neck. From the inside, however, the doors operated as normal. They were fitted with a steel bar stretching across their width at roughly waist height. Use of the key card was not necessary to exit the building.

When Tony reached the terminus of the hallway on his end, he pulled his Glock 9mm, fitted with sound suppressor, from his belt and fired one slug into the handle's mechanism. The only sound was a soft *phht* when the weapon discharged followed a split second later by the sound of grating and smashing metal, but he carefully scanned the hallway behind him for thirty seconds afterward to be sure the electronics technician had not been alerted to his presence.

The hallway stayed quiet, and Andretti decided the technician had not heard the noise. He turned back to the door and tried the handle, shoving hard against it. The door was jammed. Perfect.

Tony retreated back up the hallway and around the corner, stopping in front of the wooden double doors. Within seconds he was joined by the other two terrorists, who nodded simultaneously. They had successfully disabled their door, too.

Only one access point remained besides the front entrance to the BCT. There was a door at the rear of the first-floor foyer on one side of a two-story glass wall. Brian moved back into the foyer to disable the door, while Tony and Jackie began their search for the electronics technician. It was time to disable him as well.

The two men split up when they reached the technicians' cubicles. Undoubtedly the lone tech on duty was sleeping with his head down on his workspace, oblivious to his pending fate. Unless there was an equipment problem during the overnight shift, there would be nothing for the man to do, so why would he bother staying awake?

Tony stepped behind the first row of three cubicles, scanning for a sleeping body. It was empty. Jackie moved to the second row. Also empty.

They were taking their time, moving quietly, but they must have made some small amount of noise because as they walked along the far side of the partitions to check the final row of cubicles, a flash of motion at the far end of the room caught Tony's eye. Above the six-foot-high cubicle walls, Tony glimpsed the top of a man's head moving quickly toward the hallway door.

Tony wasn't worried that they had spooked the tech. The man had nowhere to go, as long as he didn't head for the front entrance, which Tony knew he would not do. That door was the farthest exit away, thus the least likely one he would try to use to escape the threat. When the man entered the hallway, he would sprint straight toward the door just a few tantalizing feet away, which, of course, would not open.

The technician was trapped like a rat in a cage, and the end of his life was rapidly approaching. He just didn't know it yet. Tony looked forward to introducing the concept to him.

34

Nick had always thought there was something a little eerie about the Boston Consolidated TRACON during the midnight shift. The building was huge, so even during the day—with a full complement of staff and administrative personnel and both the Manchester and Boston areas filled with a complete roster of controllers—it was not unusual to walk down one of the many mazelike corridors and not encounter a single soul.

Originally intended to house four or even five New England approach control facilities, only Boston and Manchester had ended up moving into the building. All the other candidates had enlisted the assistance of local senators, representatives, and other political heavyweights to successfully block any proposed move. The powers that be in each of the affected states were none too excited to see dozens of high-paying jobs, not to mention the associated tax receipts from those jobs, leave their states and move to New Hampshire.

The result of all this political maneuvering was a building two or three times bigger than it needed to be for the number of employees who worked in it. It was like Grandma rattling around in her massive old house after everyone else in the family had grown up, moved away, or died off. It struck Nick as a colossal waste of taxpayer money.

Nick strolled into the break room, not bothering to flip on the overhead lights. The glow from the television in one corner playing to an audience of zero provided more than enough illumination for someone who had been working at the BCT as long as Nick. He paused at one of the vending machines lined up along the north wall like soldiers standing at attention and dropped quarters into it.

He grabbed a soft drink and a package of chips—if Lisa was alive, she would have had a fit to see how he was eating—and opened the break room door to take his food back into the TRACON. It was time to give Fitz a break. Stepping through the door, Nick glimpsed what looked like shadows flitting down the long hallway encircling the operations room.

He started in surprise. It was beyond unusual to see anyone outside the ops room at this late hour, and as he focused on the far end of the corridor, he realized with shock that what he was seeing were not some amorphous shadows at all. And it was no one who belonged here, either. Three men dressed head to toe in black combat fatigues were walking in the opposite direction with rifles slung over their shoulders, holding handguns at their sides.

Somehow Nick managed not to cry out; he had no idea how he pulled that one off. He slid sideways, instinctively taking cover in the corner of the hallway across from the break room. In a stroke of luck that had probably saved his life, the three men were facing the other direction when he opened the door and thus remained unaware of his presence.

Had he flipped the lights on when he entered the break room, Nick knew he would likely be dead right now. The intruders must have walked right past the break room seconds ago while he was inside. Why they had not entered the room to investigate it Nick had no idea, but he concluded that since it appeared dark inside, the men had decided not to waste their time.

A surge of adrenaline coursed through Nick's body, instantly bringing him fully awake. It was stronger than any buzz he could have gotten from his soda. He slipped silently back into the darkened break room as the men in combat fatigues disappeared around the corner at the far end of the hallway.

Who the hell were those guys? Something was obviously very wrong, and Nick knew he had to get help.

Crossing the room in five hurried steps, Nick picked up a telephone extension sitting on a table next to one of the plush easy chairs. He lifted it to his ear and was unsurprised to discover that it was dead.

His cell phone was the obvious next choice, but there was only one problem with that option: the FAA did not permit cell phones in the operating quarters. Nick's phone, instead of hanging on his belt at his waist, was lying in his mailbox in the ready room down the hall. It was charged and operational and at the moment totally useless.

He replaced the telephone handset gently on its cradle, almost as if there was a chance one of the unknown intruders might hear the noise and return to investigate. He stood frozen in place, tapping the telephone's hard plastic casing absently with his fingers, lost in thought. What to do? He couldn't stay here forever, cowering in fear in the break room from the guys with the guns. Sooner or later he would be discovered.

Plus, it seemed like a coincidence of the most improbable magnitude that the BCT would be breached by men with automatic weapons on the very same morning that the president of the United States was flying into Boston's airspace.

Nick had no idea what it meant that the guys with guns were here in Merrimack when the leader of the free world would soon be landing nearly forty miles away in Boston, but he was dead certain that it meant something significant.

He had to notify the authorities. Escaping the TRACON and going for help didn't strike Nick as a reasonable plan, since it seemed unlikely in the extreme that the guys with guns (terrorists?) would have stormed the BCT and then left the exits uncovered. Even if he were able to escape the building undetected, and Nick knew he would have to hike for miles just to get anywhere he could tell someone about the situation, and by that time, it would probably be too late.

All of this went through Nick's racing mind in a matter of seconds as he stood next to the useless telephone, feeling helpless and exposed in the shadowy break room. There really was no choice. He had to get to his cell phone in the ready room and use it to call 911, but to do so meant walking fifty feet down the well-lit hallway running adjacent to the operations room. He would be completely exposed the entire time. If anyone should round the corner from either direction while he made the journey he would be toast. And then, assuming he made it all the way to the ready room alive and unharmed, what would he find when he entered it?

Would another terrorist with an automatic weapon be standing sentry, ready to cut him down in a hail of bullets? Nick had no idea how many men with guns had actually entered the TRACON. Maybe the three he glimpsed were just one group of many; there was simply no way of knowing.

One thing he did know, however, was that standing here in the dark was accomplishing nothing, other than to make him more afraid and less sure of his ability to survive the next few minutes. Already a strong sense of impending doom threatened to reduce him to mindless panic. It was an almost physical presence. It was big. And it was growing.

Nick took a deep breath, surprised by how loud the roaring in his ears sounded, and opened the break room door a crack. He leaned forward and peeked through the tiny opening.

No one was there.

He breathed a short prayer to whoever might be listening, then stepped through the doorway and started down the corridor.

35

Dimitrios and Joe-Bob stood in the marshy wetlands of the Hull Peninsula, frozen in the glare of the Jeep's headlights. Their shadows stretched in the opposite direction, fuzzy and indistinct on the muddy ground. They waited calmly to see what would happen next. The situation felt oddly similar to the one last week when the Tucson cop had stumbled onto them as they loaded the Stingers from the Army transport vehicle into their unmarked panel truck.

This time, Tony was not stationed somewhere in the darkness with an automatic weapon, ready to cut these people in half. But on the bright side, the Jeep clearly contained nothing more dangerous than a group of stupid kids looking for a little privacy so they could finish getting drunk and stoned. The chances that they were armed were slim, and even if they were, it seemed highly unlikely they were sober enough to hit anything they were aiming at, anyway.

Dimitrios and Joe-Bob could hear excited babbling coming from the Jeep. It was one of the old CJ models, with the removable canvas top, so the interior was open to the elements. Staring straight into the headlights, the two terrorists were effectively blinded and thus could not tell how many people the vehicle held. It sounded like there might be three separate voices.

It became clear that the kids sitting inside the Jeep had

no idea what to do. They had Dimitrios and Joe-Bob pinned in the glare of their headlights, but they had not spoken a word to them or shut the lights off or done anything at all for close to two minutes.

Fuck it, thought Joe-Bob. *We don't have time for this.* He arranged his face into what he hoped was his most disarming smile and affected his strongest Forrest Gump good ol' boy Southern drawl. "Hey there, fellas, y'all mind turning down them headlights? All that brightness is givin' me a headache, ya know?"

"What the hell are you doing out here?" came the shouted reply from the Jeep. It sounded aggressive and much too loud.

"Same as you, I would imagine. Relaxin'." Joe-Bob kept his voice nice and soft, placating and non-confrontational.

After a moment the Jeep's headlights were extinguished. All Joe-Bob could see now was a slowly fading blue image burned onto his retinas. Not good, but certainly better than before.

"You're in our spot." The tension seemed to have drained from the kid's voice, and the statement was spoken softly rather than shouted. The kids inside the Jeep seemed to have decided that they had the situation well in hand, which was just the way Joe-Bob wanted it.

"Well, I'm sorry about that, boys," Joe-Bob replied. "We'll just be on our way, then. Find us another spot. We didn't mean to step on any toes or nuthin'." He exaggerated his drawl.

There was no reply from the Jeep, so Joe-Bob continued. "As a peace offerin', how 'bout we leave a couple beers with you fellas? No harm, no foul, right?"

"Works for us."

Joe-Bob sloshed over to the cab of their Dakota, reaching in through the door and grabbing two water bottles. He held them against his chest, using one big arm to shield them from view, so that the occupants of the Jeep would not be able to see that they weren't actually beer bottles until it was too late. As he splashed past on his way to the Jeep, Joe-Bob growled softly to Dimitrios, "Grab the duct tape."

By the time he reached the Jeep, Joe-Bob's vision had returned more or less to normal. He could see now that the vehicle held three young men in their late teens, two in front and one in back.

He reached over the Jeep's passenger side door, and as he did, he flung the two half-full water bottles hard into the face of the kid unfortunate enough to be sitting there. He pulled a thirteen-inch tactical combat knife out of its nylon sheath at his waist and in one smooth motion gutted the kid, plunging the razor-sharp CTV2 stainless blade into his belly and pulling up, using its serrated upper edge to slice him jaggedly open between his ribs.

Joe-Bob heard a sharp, surprised intake of breath followed immediately by a weak, watery "Ahhhhhh." The kid's voice sounded bubbly and far away, and he was dying with shocking suddenness.

Blood dripped from the black titanium carbonitride blade, looking almost as inky as the blade itself in the near-total darkness. Joe-Bob lifted his hand to shoulder height, using his massive bulk and the unexpectedly terrifying sight of the knife to intimidate the vehicle's other two stunned occupants. The attack had occurred with such savage swiftness that it seemed neither kid had a chance to grasp what had just happened to their friend. Their reflexes dulled by alcohol and drugs, both young men stared stupidly at Joe-Bob, mouths hanging open in identical displays of shock.

"So, who wants to be next?" Joe-Bob asked quietly with a half grin.

No one answered, so he motioned Dimitrios forward with the knife.

By now the critically injured young man was panting as if he had just sprinted a great distance, his breathing rapid and shallow. Each outward expulsion of breath sounded bubbly and wet, and was accompanied by a low moan, and he had his arms wrapped tightly around the front of his body in an effort to keep his entrails from spilling out of the gaping wound in his belly and chest.

He was mostly failing in that regard. He was also fading fast and would be dead within minutes.

Dimitrios wrapped the duct tape around the driver's head twice before slapping it on the seam. He taped the man's hands to the steering wheel, then shut off the Jeep's engine and pocketed the key. He repeated the procedure with the backseat occupant, taping that man's hands to the driver's side headrest since there was no steering wheel back there.

The wounded man in the front passenger seat slumped sideways against the door, his head lolling out the open window. He was still breathing shallowly but had slipped into unconsciousness.

Joe-Bob used the kid's denim jacket to wipe some of the blood and gore off his knife, which he then slid back into his scabbard. He told Dimitrios matter-of-factly, "Luckily this little misadventure didn't cost us too much time, but we really need to start getting set up. Let's move our asses."

Without looking back, he trudged back to the Dakota. The Forrest Gump good ol' boy accent was almost completely gone.

36

Larry looked at his watch again and sighed. Where the hell was Futz, and what was taking him so long to get his goddamned snack? He should have been back ten minutes ago. It wasn't like Larry minded sitting and staring at a mostly empty radar scope, especially since the federal government was paying him a 10 percent premium on top of an already handsome salary for working in the middle of the night, but he could feel his reflexes slowing and his eyes beginning to droop. He knew he needed a break; even just a few minutes to take a walk and stretch his legs would be enough.

He thought about what had happened to Lisa and wondered how he would react if he had been in Nick's position. Wife brutally murdered and now buried in the ground, without the opportunity to even say good-bye. *Life sucks; then you die.*

Larry had married Sharon a few years before Nick and Lisa tied the knot, and although he and Sharon certainly didn't have the perfect marriage—at least not when you compared it to Nick and Lisa's—Larry knew he would be lost without his wife. He couldn't imagine how Nick was going to cope. He had tried talking to his friend about it once or twice, and Nick had politely but firmly rebuffed him each time. He said he wasn't ready to talk about it yet. Larry supposed he could understand that.

As he was debating whether it was worth making another attempt to raise the subject with Nick, he heard the click of the main TRACON door opening behind him. Larry was a little surprised that Nick would enter from the door at the other end of the ops room rather than the side door he had used when he left, but maybe he had gone to his cubicle in the ready room to grab a book to read while he sat at the scope doing nothing. At least he was finally back, and Larry could get started on his own break.

He sat resting his chin on his hand with his elbow propped on the console in front of the scope, watching the lone target representing ChekPro Flight 112 move steadily toward Logan Airport. In the old days, airplanes running checks were a staple of overnight traffic at facilities all over the country, but with the advent of electronic banking, the check runners were becoming a dying breed. Larry figured within a few years they would be gone entirely. He wondered what the pilot of ChekPro 112 would do then.

Larry felt rather than heard the presence of a person standing behind him. Without turning around, he started a position relief briefing. "Okay, here's what's going on—" He stopped in midsentence as he felt the cold, insistent pressure of a gun barrel being jammed into his neck.

"No, *here* is what is going on," came a deep, unfamiliar voice. Whoever was holding the gun pushed harder until it was all Larry could feel. The barrel was right beneath his ear. It defined his existence. "You will be quiet. You will do exactly as you're told. If you cooperate, you will live. If you do not, you will die an extremely unpleasant and painfully messy death. Do we understand each other?"

Larry swallowed heavily and gave an almost imperceptible nod, afraid that if he moved, the gun would go off and blow his head all over the front of the radar scope.

"Good," came the voice, cold and hard. "Now, where is the other controller?"

Lifting his hand slowly, still staring straight ahead, Larry pointed behind him to the Manchester area, where their midnight controller was sitting.

"I'm not talking about him. He is already being taken care of. See for yourself."

Larry swiveled his head, still moving slowly, aware of the constant pressure of the gun barrel on his neck. He looked across the big, dark room to the Manchester area and saw a man dressed all in black, with black greasepaint covering his face, duct taping Ron Johnson to his chair. Ron's mouth was invisible under a slash of silver tape, and he looked petrified, his wide, panicked eyes staring back at Larry. He wondered if he looked as frightened as Ron and figured he probably did.

"Now, back to my original question, and please bear in mind I am a man blessed with many good qualities, but patience is not one of them. Where is the other controller? I know the Boston area employs two controllers on the midnight shift. Where is your partner?"

These guys hadn't seen Nick yet. Larry hesitated, uncertain how to answer the question, knowing his life was probably hanging in the balance. The intruders were aware that the Boston area used two controllers to cover the mid shift, so they were obviously pretty knowledgeable about the operation, but if Nick hadn't been captured, there was always the possibility he could somehow escape and bring help.

"Answer the question!"

Larry closed his eyes and said a silent prayer before answering. "There is no other controller in my area tonight. He called in sick before the shift started, and the government refuses to pay overtime for a controller just to sit around on the midnight shift, so tonight I'm here alone." He licked his lips nervously and winced, half expecting to see a split second of bright light and hear the beginning of the gunshot roar that would end his life.

Nothing happened.

One second went by and then two. Larry assumed the guy was digesting the information and trying to decide whether to believe him.

"So it is just you and this other man tonight?" The man

gestured with the gun barrel at Ron, who was now completely immobilized in his chair across the room, before returning it to its original spot just under Larry's ear.

"That's right," he answered. It seemed like the man was going to believe him, but who the hell knew what these guys were thinking? Why were they here? What did they want? And where *was* Nick?

A terrifying thought occurred to Larry. If Nick were to walk through the door, the men dressed in black would know he had been lying, and all three of them—Nick, Ron, and Larry—would probably be dead within a matter of seconds. He realized he was holding his breath and tried to force some air out of his lungs. It came out reluctantly and shakier than he would have expected.

Oh, well. There was nothing he could do about it now. He had chosen what seemed like the only viable path with his answer and would now just have to hope that Nick had seen the men and was calling for help from his cell phone or perhaps had escaped and was on his way to alert the police.

Larry took another breath, this one marginally less panicked than the last. "Why are you here? What do you guys want?"

"Shut up. You'll find out when I'm ready to tell you."

"What is Ron going to do if an airplane calls on his frequency while he's got tape over his mouth and he's tied to his chair?"

"I don't care about that sector. If a pilot calls over there and doesn't get an answer, eventually he will call you. When that happens, you will say that the Manchester controller is sick and you will control the plane yourself."

"So you're not going to cover my mouth with duct tape, too?"

"I will if you don't shut your mouth right now."

Larry decided he had asked enough questions for a while. He stopped talking and waited to see what would happen next.

37

Nick had never felt so exposed. He rushed down the empty span of hallway from the break room to the ready room. He stuck close to the concrete wall on the right side of the corridor as he walked, which, when he thought about it, made no sense whatsoever. If the terrorists or whoever they were came around the corner from either direction, they would see him just as easily as if he were marching down the middle of the hallway waving his arms and whistling a happy tune. But somehow it made him feel a little more secure to be close to the wall, so he did it anyway.

In a matter of seconds he arrived at the double doors of the TRACON ready room, which for some unknown reason were always kept propped open. The men had not reappeared yet.

So far, so good.

He paused just outside the doorway, wondering what he would find in the room when he turned the corner. Perhaps the terrorists had left a sentry there. Perhaps the room was filled with men dressed in black fatigues carrying rifles over their shoulders. Perhaps there was a bomb. This whole thing was crazy, and he figured almost anything was possible.

Nick rounded the corner and stepped into the ready room, convinced he would be shot at any moment, but when he got inside, it was empty and quiet. If Nick had not happened to see the men marching down the hallway with his own eyes just minutes ago, he would never have suspected anything was out of the ordinary. He crossed the room in four hurried strides, reaching into his cubicle to grab his cell phone, and pulled out…nothing. The phone was gone.

Shit.

Nick was certain he had left his cell phone in his mailbox; it was what he always did with the stupid thing when he got to work. He was a creature of habit, as were most air traffic controllers. You learned early in your career in ATC that the more things you could do instinctively, the more time you had to plan for the weird stuff that inevitably came up when things started to go sideways on a busy sector. So while he did not specifically remember tossing the phone into his mailbox when he arrived at the facility to start the mid shift, he knew without a doubt he had done exactly that.

The fact that the cell was now gone could mean only one thing: the men had confiscated it. He moved quickly to Fitz's mailbox. If the men had found Nick's phone, they would undoubtedly have searched every mailbox and taken Larry's, too. Still, he didn't know what else to do, so he had to try.

Fitz's mailbox was a mess, even more so than Nick's. Paperwork was crammed haphazardly into it, spilling out of the box at odd angles. There were a couple of books, a pair of winter gloves (in May?), some pens, and a fiftieth anniversary commemorative pin that the FAA had handed out to everyone. Most controllers had immediately thrown them into the trash. Nick hadn't even taken his out of its clear plastic wrapper before shit-canning it.

He was utterly unsurprised to find no cell phone. Either Fitz had not brought a phone to work with him or the terrorists had confiscated his, too.

Nick felt the seconds ticking away and knew the armed men could return at any moment. What should he do now? It seemed that the only option left was to try to slip out of the facility and go for help. He didn't want to leave Fitz and Ron at the mercy of the men, but there was nothing he could do to help them in any meaningful way by staying here. For all he knew, they were already dead.

Nick moved to the door of the ready room and cautiously eased his head out, looking both ways, expecting to be greeted with a gun barrel shoved in his face or perhaps a bullet to the head. Instead, he saw nothing. Making a quick decision, Nick backtracked down the hallway toward the break room.

When he came to the corner where he could either angle right to reenter the break room or turn left and continue down the hallway, Nick made the left turn after first flattening himself against the wall and peeking around the corner to see if anyone was approaching. The ops room was to his left on the other side of the wall, and Nick was beginning to think that was where the men must have gone.

At the end of the corridor was a thick metal door that opened outward, revealing a large, dusty stairwell. A set of wide metal steps wound their way down to the first floor. Nick descended the stairs, wondering whether he would meet a terrorist with an automatic weapon coming the other way. If he did, he would be trapped; there was no escape route out of the stairwell until he reached the bottom.

Halfway between the first and second floor was a small landing where the stairs reversed direction. Nick turned the corner, treading as softly as he could. He still saw no sign of the men.

When he reached the first floor, he paused, trying to recall exactly what was on the other side of the door immediately in front of him. He had worked at the BCT since its opening, but he didn't normally visit the technicians' side of the building, so he was a little hazy about the layout over here. He thought hard, knowing that an accurate recollection of the interior building design might mean the difference between living and dying.

After a moment, Nick shook his head in frustration and mumbled, "Shit" under his breath. He had a foggy notion that the door led into the large room where the techs stored their equipment and worked on radios, radar scopes, etc.

Finally he did what he had known all along he would have to do. He opened the door and stepped through it.

38

The little run-in with the guys in the Jeep had put Joe-Bob and Dimitrios slightly behind schedule, but Joe-Bob wasn't worried. There was still plenty of time to get set up for the president's arrival and prepare his very special welcoming gift. The Jeep was too far away for Joe-Bob to see whether the guys trapped in it were still struggling with their bindings, although he imagined they were. Well, except for the one he had gutted like a deer. Joe-Bob was pretty sure that one was done struggling.

For good.

He kind of regretted having to kill the kid, especially since the poor guy had just had the misfortune of being in the wrong place at the wrong time, but that was the way of the world, wasn't it? Kill or be killed. Do unto others before they do unto you—that was Joe-Bob's motto, and he knew it was probably a pretty satisfactory expression of the worldview of the rest of their little group of misfits too, though they might not readily admit it. If nothing else, Joe-Bob was a realist.

Introspection was not Joe-Bob's strong suit, but every so often he wondered how in the hell he had gotten involved with a homegrown terrorist organization that was preparing to assassinate the president of the United States, not to mention everyone else aboard Air Force One. It wasn't like Joe-Bob had anything in particular against the country in which he had been born and raised; he was just a guy who wanted to raise hell and destroy things.

Joe-Bob had no concrete idea what group he was working for and didn't much care. He knew, as did the rest of the team Tony had recruited, that it was some anonymous Middle Eastern terrorist organization. Not Al Qaeda but something similar. Just the fact that they had been flown to a training camp in the remote mountains of Afghanistan to learn guerrilla tactics proved the group meant business and possessed plenty of resources.

And he also knew that the Tony Andretti alias was so phony it was laughable. Whatever the real name of their mysterious and dangerous leader was, it most definitely was *not* Tony Andretti. He was obviously a born-and-raised raghead, the exact kind of virulent anti-American radical that the United States government had spent nearly ten years, billions of dollars, and thousands of American lives trying to thwart.

Joe-Bob knew all of that, or at least he knew most of it and suspected the rest. He just didn't care. He was a young, disaffected American male who was being used in the most despicable way by the cunning, calculating elements of a faraway radical organization, perhaps even one that was state sponsored. He knew that and didn't care about it, either.

Joe-Bob and the rest of the group were well aware that they didn't fit anywhere in American society, but they weren't deluded enough to think that they belonged in the Muslim world, either. To a man, they knew they were destined to die early, probably violently, so their attitude was that they might as well make a big splash before departing this life for whatever awaited them on the other side, if anything. It was no simpler or more complicated than that.

In the back of the Dodge Dakota, the group had fabricated a support harness out of steel tubing and nylon netting. The homemade harness would supply the shooter, in this case Joe-Bob, with as much support as possible in order to achieve maximum accuracy with the single Stinger missile he would soon fire at Air Force One.

The Stinger, a third-generation shoulder-fired weapon developed more than thirty years ago and popularized by the Soviets during their war in Afghanistan in the 1980s, was utilized for the first time by the U.S. in combat during the short conflict in the Falkland Islands. It combined line-of-sight targeting with a heat-seeking component, and the modern version came equipped with software designed to offer enviable accuracy considering it was a portable, handheld weapon. The Stinger was relatively light at around thirty-five pounds and was quick and easy to assemble and operate once all its components had been procured.

Joe-Bob sat in the cargo bed of the truck, leaning against the cab and assembling the Stinger. He was struggling. He had practiced exhaustively back in the garage in suburban D.C., but the unrelenting inky blackness of the marsh was causing problems. It didn't provide for more than the vaguest visual acquisition of the components.

***

Dimitrios was struggling as well trying to set up the support harness the group had constructed. It probably would have been fine to drive around with the support in place in the back of the truck, but Tony had insisted that they leave it in pieces, covered by a tarp, until they arrived at the marsh and then put it together and bolt it into place. He was taking no chances that some curious policeman would see the contraption and wonder what the hell it was doing in the cargo bed of a rattletrap truck.

***

Joe-Bob slapped his hand in frustration on the steel bed of the truck. It sounded like a gunshot echoing across the heavy air of the marsh. "Fuck it. I know we're supposed to do this in the dark, but I can't see a goddamned thing."

He snapped on a flashlight and smiled. This would make his life a lot easier, and there was almost no chance that anyone would see it from the road. Hell, Ocean Drive was far across the marsh, and, in any event, there was almost no traffic driving by anyway. Even though it was a Saturday night, by now all but the most dedicated of partiers had stumbled home and gone to bed.

***

Dimitrios glanced at Joe-Bob and decided that if his partner was going to reap the benefits of a working flashlight, he might as well do the same, so he snapped his on, too. The men labored without speaking, each concentrating on the task at hand.

***

Forty yards away, the Jeep sat unmoving, a dark vague lump silhouetted against the slightly lighter road far in the distance. Inside it, two terrified young men were immobilized, each wondering if he would survive the night, while a third had already discovered that he would not.

39

Larry took a deep, shuddering breath, feeling the business end of the pistol sink slightly deeper into his neck as he did so. The heat from his body had warmed the gun barrel, so that now instead of feeling cold and frightening against his skin, the gun was warm and in some bizarre way almost soothing. Larry decided he might just be losing his mind.

He was still seated in front of his radar scope, staring blankly at the display showing no traffic inside his airspace. Neither he nor the man keeping the gun pressed to the base of his skull had spoken a word in the last several minutes.

Finally Larry decided to take a chance. What did he have to lose? Very softly, as if by keeping his voice low he could avoid startling the man who controlled his immediate future, he asked, "What are you doing here? Or, I guess to get more to the point, what do you want from me? What do I have to do to survive this night? Or is my fate already determined?"

"To survive," the man mused, "you need to understand a few things."

Larry blinked in surprise when the man answered. It seemed as though he had been waiting for that very question.

"You should be aware that although I am no aviation expert, I *am* a fairly intelligent person. Do you believe me when I tell you this?"

Larry nodded slowly, still trying to keep his body as

motionless as possible.

"Good. So, as a fairly intelligent person who is not an aviation expert, I have studied the subject of air traffic control exhaustively over the last several months in preparation for this mission. I have listened to hundreds of hours of routine communications between pilots and air traffic controllers. The Internet, which your former vice president Al Gore was so generous to invent, is a wonderful supplier of almost any kind of information anyone could desire, including radio communications on air traffic control frequencies. Are you following me so far?"

Larry choked off the reply he wanted to make, "Of course I'm following you; I'm not an idiot." Instead, he simply said, "Yes." His throat felt dry and scratchy. He wished he had some water.

"In my study of those hundreds of hours of radio communications, along with familiarizing myself with much of the equipment you use in this very impressive control room, I feel confident making the statement that I will know immediately if you attempt to alert anyone to our presence or if you say anything even slightly outside the boundaries of what would be considered normal air traffic control phraseology. Do you understand what I am saying?"

"Yes."

"Good. Because I'm sure you are aware that it would be very unhealthy for you to ignore what I have told you. On the other hand, if you approach this situation with the seriousness it deserves and you do exactly as you are instructed, you will not be harmed in any way. You have my word on that."

It took all of Larry's self-control not to laugh at the last statement. The word of a man with a gun pressed scant millimeters away from his brain, with the expressed intention of blasting a bullet into it if his instructions were not followed explicitly, didn't seem to mean much, at least not the way Larry read the situation.

He suspected there was virtually no chance that he would ever leave the BCT alive unless one of two things happened. Either Nick was still alive and had managed to get word out that they needed help, or Larry could find a way to get the drop on this well-spoken but extremely scary and possibly psychopathic dude.

Larry was an outstanding air traffic controller, one of the best in the BCT, but he was no kind of an expert at anything else, especially self-defense or counterterrorism tactics, so he seriously doubted the second option was going to happen. That left him fervently hoping that his buddy Nick was already outside the facility, well on his way to alerting the police, the FBI, the Secret Service, Homeland Security, and any other law enforcement agencies he could think of to the potentially deadly situation developing inside this building.

The president's plane was due to fly into Logan in less than ninety minutes, and Larry didn't have a clue what the intentions of these terrorists were at the BCT, but he knew the two scenarios had to be related in some way, so it was obvious that time was running out. And he had no idea what to do.

He stared straight ahead at his radar scope, which was cluttered with sector maps and final approach courses but lacking in airplanes. One thing he did believe was that this lunatic was telling the truth about understanding the basics of aviation communications. Most of the language was not that difficult to understand; a lot of it was pretty intuitive. If the man had really listened to hundreds of hours of controllers and pilots yakking at each other, he would undoubtedly know if Larry tried to use code words to notify a pilot or anyone else to what was going on here.

The funny thing was Larry had no freaking idea what sort of code he might be able to use even if he thought he could get away with it. He had never received any kind of training for dealing with this situation. As far as he was aware, there was no protocol developed for it, at least not in the Air Traffic Division of the FAA.

He was completely on his own. It was not a comforting thought.

40

Nick eased the door open a few inches, looking first to the right, where the sidewall of the building loomed only a few feet away. A plastic tarp hung from the ceiling, blocking access to approximately the northernmost six feet of the room, which seemed to be in the middle of a construction project. Nick could see through the opaque plastic that no one was in there. It appeared as though work had been halted for the weekend and the area had been sealed up tightly.

As Nick peered cautiously around the heavy door, he could see that he had been right about this being the technicians' equipment room. Half a dozen replacement radar scopes were lined up on the far wall like soldiers ready to be sent into battle. Stacked high on a wire rack running the length of the wall immediately to Nick's left were various electronic components. They were clearly the innards of equipment the technicians worked with all the time—why else would they be here?—but what functions any of them might perform he had no idea.

All these things registered dimly in Nick's consciousness as he scanned the room, looking for anyone or anything that might pose a threat. He saw nothing. Nick was becoming more and more convinced that the three men he had seen must be inside the ops room, since there had been no other sign of them.

In one sense that was good. Nick felt he was in little immediate personal danger, at least for now. That meant that the opposite, however, was true for fellow controllers Larry and Ron. If the men with the rifles and handguns had entered the ops room, then his two coworkers were in big trouble and may already be dead.

With this grim possibility weighing on his mind, Nick pushed the door open wider and stepped through it into the equipment room. As he did so, he tripped over something pliable lying in front of the door. Nick sprawled face-first onto the cool tile floor, trying his best to make as little noise as possible as he fell.

He absorbed most of the fall on his elbows, landing on them hard and bruising both of them, but thankfully he managed to avoid splitting his skull open on the unyielding floor. When he forced himself to his knees and looked back toward the door, he gasped involuntarily, clamping down his jaw firmly to avoid being sick.

Facedown on the ceramic tile floor was electronics technician Harry Tanner. Instantly the pain in Nick's elbows was forgotten. He scrambled on his hands and knees to Harry's side and placed two fingers lightly on the man's neck behind his earlobe, searching desperately for a pulse and finding none. He stared at the puddle of blood that had soaked through Harry's plaid work shirt and pooled on the floor beneath his body. There was a lot. He was amazed he hadn't stepped in it.

He turned Harry over onto his back and gagged again, watching in horror as the blood of the man who had worked for the FAA even longer than he had—Harry was well past minimum retirement age and had planned on leaving next spring—began spreading sluggishly across the floor, no longer trapped under his clothing. It was just beginning to congeal in spots.

Nick slapped Harry's face as if to wake him from a trance and realized the futility of his actions. Harry was dead. Either he had been working in this room when the fuckers with the guns had come in and surprised him, or else he had seen them and made a desperate attempt to outrun them.

Judging by the shocking amount of blood on the floor, it looked as though Harry may have been stabbed to death rather than shot, although Nick was by no means an expert on the subject. Maybe gunshot wounds could cause all that blood, too. But the thought that the men might have come at old Harry with knives rather than the guns they were carrying seemed somehow more horrifying to Nick than if he *had* been shot. The intimacy of the violence implied a level of bloodthirstiness that went beyond just killing the man to further their goals. It almost looked as though the killers had viewed it as sport.

A desperate, high-pitched keening noise filled the room, and Nick realized it was coming from him. He was breathing heavily, almost panting, dangerously close to hyperventilating. His hands were shaking as he knelt over the lifeless body of Harry Tanner. Controllers and technicians didn't normally hang out together at work, but Harry and Nick had had numerous long conversations over the years, and Nick had come to know the man as a gentle soul who loved his wife, his kids and grandkids, and hunting and fishing, in that order.

The initial burst of shock and terror Nick had felt at seeing the armed intruders strolling down the hallway of the BCT as if they owned the joint began morphing into something else. He felt a powerful surge of rage and bitterness and the intense desire to avenge Harry's death, although he had no earthly idea how he might manage to do so.

Nick knew he was reacting not just to the current bewildering and terrifying situation but to the murder of Lisa as well—to the immense jagged hole that had been torn open in his heart with the loss of his wife, a hole he knew he would never be able to close completely. She had been murdered simply because she had stumbled onto something far bigger than she had been prepared to deal with. It was a lot like the situation Nick found himself confronted with now.

He gently eased Harry's eyes closed. Time was of the essence, of course, but if the killers had not found him yet, their main area of concern was obviously not this section of the building, and he was probably relatively safe.

For now.

Nick swore softly that he would not allow these killers to escape; one way or another he would provide some semblance of justice.

He was surprised to discover he was crying softly. Tears dripped down his nose and fell onto Harry's shirt, mixing with all the awful blood that was beginning to darken and thicken into a sludge-like goo. He whispered, "I'm sorry, Harry."

Even in his state of confusion and anger and fear, he knew he was really talking to Lisa, expressing to his dead wife the overwhelming pain and regret he felt, the baseless guilt that ate at him every day, saying it should have been him and not her lying in the ground.

He wasn't sure how long he stayed in that kneeling position, sobbing next to Harry's body. Eventually the tears dried, and Nick knew he was leaving himself horribly exposed, sitting out in the open on the bloody floor of the equipment room. If the men who had butchered Harry returned, he would be a sitting duck, and although by now he didn't particularly care whether he lived or died, he found himself burning with the desire to make a statement to these people to whom human life clearly meant nothing.

Nick concluded that the best statement he could make would be to summon help and stop the murderous fanatics from completing whatever awful task they had broken into the facility to accomplish. He rose silently and padded across the room toward the door. It was time to get help.

41

"Connors 712, cleared visual approach Runway 4 Right, contact Boston Tower 123.7." Larry was sitting ramrod straight at the scope. He had just worked a single arrival into Logan, glad for the momentary distraction from the tangible layer of tension building inside the ops room.

He thought about it and almost chuckled, a surprising and unlikely achievement considering the fact that his nerves were strung tight and he felt like he might puke at any moment. "Tangible layer of tension" was the understatement of the decade, and the clock was ticking. Hopefully Nick had been able to escape the facility and go for help, because the president's plane would be leaving Andrews Air Force Base in less than an hour, and from there it was a short hop to Logan and directly into whatever shit sandwich these lunatics were planning on serving.

The man pointing the gun at him had not said in so many words that Air Force One would be targeted, but what the hell else could it possibly be? And with nothing much else to do except sit and think, Larry suddenly began to feel woozy and ill when he realized what the terrorists' plan might be. Who was to say they didn't have a group of conspirators in or around Logan? It would be simple and perfect.

The gunman lounged next to him in one of the controller chairs, feet propped up on the radar console to Larry's right.

The gun was still pointed steadily in his direction, but at least the barrel was no longer stuck into his neck. He would still be just as dead if the guy pulled the trigger, but somehow it didn't feel quite as terrifying this way.

The man sitting next to Larry was apparently in charge, and earlier he'd had a short, intense conversation with the second terrorist. Larry had been unable to decipher anything that was said, even though they had been standing less than two feet behind him. After the brief conversation, the second terrorist had left the ops room.

Where that man had gone and what he was doing now, Larry couldn't guess. Searching for Nick, maybe? He supposed it all depended upon whether they believed his lie about Nick calling in sick and the FAA not wanting to pay a controller overtime to cover the midnight shift.

That part was mostly true; they wouldn't have wanted to spend the money. But in the current incarnation of the FAA, where the animosity between management and the controller workforce was all-encompassing, they likely would have forced one of the controllers scheduled to work tomorrow's day shift to come in and work the mid instead, then worked one controller short on the day shift.

Allowing the Boston area to be staffed with less than two controllers on a midnight shift was considered a big no-no, although the Manchester area—which did the same job in the same room as Boston, albeit with less traffic—worked every single overnight with just one. Larry had no idea why that was, but it had always been that way. He hoped that this thug so casually waving a gun in his face wasn't aware of that fact, although he certainly seemed to have a thorough knowledge about ATC in general and the Boston Consolidated TRACON specifically.

Suddenly a sickening thought occurred to Larry that was so obvious he wondered why he hadn't had it sooner. He was assuming Nick had seen the terrorists when they entered the building and had been able to avoid them somehow, that even now he had escaped the building and was well on his way to alerting the authorities.

But how likely was that, really? Wouldn't a much more credible scenario be that Nick had been wandering down the hallway on his way back to the TRACON from the break room, bag of corn chips in one hand and coffee or soda in the other, when these Rambo-looking dudes had come around a corner with their fatigues and their black greasepaint and their guns and put a bullet in his brain? The odds that Nick had seen them coming and had been able to avoid being captured or killed were pretty frigging slim.

Larry could almost hear the inexorable tick-tick-ticking of the invisible clock in his head. He wasn't sure precisely what these people were planning, but they had gone to a whole lot of trouble and had risked their lives to storm a secure federal government facility protected 24/7 by armed guards, so it was obviously something major. He wondered whether he would still be alive when the sun rose. He felt queasy and washed-out.

The invisible clock in his head continued to tick.

42

Brian paced back and forth inside the large conference room adjacent to the foyer, located just inside the BCT's main entrance. The side of the room fronting the foyer was constructed of six glass panels, each three feet wide and six feet high, making it the perfect location from which to maintain surveillance on the main entrance, now the only way into or out of the facility.

Brian wasn't clear on exactly why the entrance needed to be watched. The security guards were both dead, and Jackie was sitting in the guard shack at the front gate looking ridiculous in the uniform he had taken off one of the dead guards. Jackie's job was to ambush the FBI agent who would arrive soon to monitor the BCT. The only people inside the building were either being held in the operations room at gunpoint or were already dead.

So the idea of cooling his heels in this glass-walled conference room, guarding the entrance to the facility and waiting for—what, exactly?—seemed more than a little unnecessary to Brian. But this was his assignment from Tony, and one thing Brian had learned early in this little adventure was that you did not deviate from the plan if the plan had been developed by Tony. Their leader seemed perfectly calm and rational, if a little intense for Brian's taste, but behind that calm rationality was a calculating coldness that did not suffer disloyalty.

Ever.

Brian thought about how Tony had dealt with the gang bangers that had tried to disrupt their operation when they had been getting set up in D.C. and shuddered. Tony had matter-of-factly gutted several dangerous men, leaving them for dead, just to send a message. That message had been received loud and clear, and the remaining gang members had steered clear of Tony and his men ever since. Brian had decided right then and there that he would not allow himself to become Tony's message to anyone else if he could help it.

Besides, there were worse things he could be doing than hanging out in this cozy little conference room. A long, highly-polished table ran virtually the entire length of the room, with comfortable leather business chairs orbiting it like satellites. A retractable white screen hanging from the ceiling filled one of the smaller walls of the rectangular office.

If the room had only contained a television, Brian would have been perfectly satisfied to stay here the rest of the night, but unfortunately for him, that particular amenity had not been supplied. He sighed deeply. Nobody said this job would be easy.

In a little while, Jackie would come trudging through the front door, holding at gunpoint whatever unfortunate representative the FBI had sent over to spend the day monitoring the activities of the air traffic controllers who would be working Air Force One into and out of Logan Airport.

Brian had no doubt that Jackie would get the jump on the FBI guy. Jackie was pretty good with weapons, and Brian figured the agent would probably be a low-seniority rookie. The FBI wouldn't bother wasting an experienced field agent on a secure federal facility located nearly forty miles from Boston, where Air Force One was going to be landing and where President Cartwright would be spending the day.

Brian didn't trust Jackie any farther than he could throw him. Under normal circumstances, he doubted whether

Jackie would even bother keeping the agent alive. But Tony had said that the feeb would be coordinating with the rest of the law enforcement monkeys down in Boston after his arrival at the BCT, so killing him would put the whole operation in jeopardy. Brian knew Jackie was just as intimidated by Tony as everyone else on the team was, so he would damn well keep the agent alive. Fear could be a powerful motivator.

But the arrival of the anonymous and doomed FBI agent would not occur for a little while yet, which was why Brian paced restlessly across the soft pile carpeting of the conference room. He was keyed up and had no way of dissipating all his nervous energy. He wished he had something to eat as he stopped and peered through the big plate glass windows at the front entrance.

He didn't expect to see anything moving, and he didn't. He stared at the door for a moment and then continued his relentless pacing.

43

Nick burst into the hallway at almost a dead run. After seeing what had been done to Harry, his only thought was to *do* something. He needed to get to the exterior door and go for help.

He cringed as a barely perceptible snick indicated that the equipment room door's latch had reengaged in the strike plate as it closed automatically behind him. The noise was almost nothing. Normally he would never even have noticed it, but tonight, with three armed-to-the-teeth murderers roaming the halls of the BCT, it sounded like the beeping of an air horn or a thunderbolt crashing over his head.

Sighing softly, he turned and peered down the long hallway as he moved toward the exterior door, half expecting to be greeted by the grinning visage of one of the lunatics training an automatic weapon between his eyes. But the hallway was empty.

Nick tried to calm his nerves but abandoned the effort almost immediately. He was breathing heavily and his hands would not stop shaking. His plan, if you could call it that, was simple. Sneak the few feet to the exterior door, preferably without getting shot in the back, open the door as quietly as possible, and continue into the night, where he would then stick to the shadows, exiting the BCT grounds and going for help.

He hadn't yet decided whether he dared jump in his car, which would be sitting in the parking lot a couple of hundred feet from the door, or if it would be smarter to try to get away on foot. The obvious dilemma was that if he started his car and the terrorists had someone stationed in the guard shack, he would never make it off the property.

On the other hand, if he *was* able to get off the property on foot, it would be a long and difficult hike to any location where he could access a telephone.

He thought about it quickly and supposed he would have to take his chances on foot. His car was equipped with daytime running lights, which would blaze on as soon as the transmission was shifted into Drive, so sneaking past the guard shack in the dark would be out of the question.

But first, Nick had to make it out of the building alive. He took a deep breath and slipped quietly down the remainder of the corridor. Reaching the door in less than two seconds, he pushed hard against the bar running the entire width of it at waist height. Silence now was an impossibility; this door would make noise as it opened no matter how careful Nick was, so he hit it at a fast walk, hoping that if the door made enough clatter to raise the suspicions of the wrong person, he would be long gone by the time that person came to investigate.

The bar didn't move at all, and Nick smashed into the door with a thud. He smacked his forehead and twisted his wrist. "Shit," he muttered.

He looked down at the silver bar and was dismayed to see that the right side was completely destroyed, twisted metal puckering around a jagged hole where a bullet had quite clearly been fired into it. The mechanism had been jammed with the obvious intention of preventing anyone from leaving or entering. If Nick hadn't been so preoccupied, he would have seen the damage as soon as he had burst out of the equipment room; it was that obvious.

He cursed bitterly. He should have expected this. It was a stark testament to how rattled he had been by tripping over

Harry's lifeless body that he thought he was just going to waltz out the door and into the safety of the night. *Of course* the terrorists had disabled the door; otherwise Harry would have run right out of it when he had spotted them. He must have smashed into the disabled door just as Nick had done. He had then turned and tried to escape his pursuers through the equipment room. And he hadn't been quick enough.

Nick backtracked, trotting down the center of the hallway, too rattled to slink along the side wall. He hit the door and disappeared back into the equipment room. Nick tried not to look at Harry's body as he racked his brains in an attempt to figure out what the hell to do next.

He had no luck accomplishing either objective.

44

The ops room felt incredibly quiet to Larry, although in reality the noise created by the scopes, the air-conditioning, and other equipment resulted in a constant low hum—a white noise that was not really noticeable until it wasn't there anymore.

The terrorist with the gun pointed in Larry's direction continued lounging next to him, a situation Larry had come to accept was not going to change until this whole thing was over, and he was beginning to suspect that would be soon. Air Force One would have to depart Andrews Air Force Base for Boston within the next few minutes, Larry guessed, if the president was going to arrive at Logan in time to make his scheduled early morning ceremony.

The terrorist seemed to have no problem with the silence in the room, although it was driving Larry nuts. When Larry had gotten the man talking, it was much easier to pretend the guy was just a visitor, maybe a pilot or someone else with an interest in aviation, rather than a homicidal extremist. But when they sat side by side without talking, Larry could feel panic building inside him, threatening to overwhelm him and make him do something foolish, like bolt for the door or try to attack the man and get control of his gun.

Doing either of those things would be a guaranteed ticket

to an early grave. There was no way he could outrun a bullet to the door, and he knew the man sprawled so casually on the controller chair was paying much more attention to his every move than it appeared. If he took any action that the man interpreted as a threat, Larry had no doubt the guy would simply shoot him right between the eyes.

Finally he could stand the screaming silence no longer. He had to try again. He cleared his throat. "May I ask you a question?" He felt ridiculous speaking so formally to this cold-blooded killer, but he didn't want to appear overly aggressive and get his head blown off as a result.

The man studied him for a moment before answering. Larry was certain he was going to tell him to shut up, so he was surprised when he said, "Of course." The gun never wavered.

"Are you here because of a certain VIP arrival at Logan later this morning?"

The man continued staring at him as a smile spread slowly across his face. Larry knew that was as clear an affirmative response as if he had leapt up and shouted, "Yes, yes, death to the president!"

He pondered how to frame his next question. The faint smell of stale sweat drifted up to his nose, and Larry realized it was coming from him. He wondered for just a moment whether the terrorist could smell it.

Finally Larry spoke again. "You do understand, I assume, that at no time is the VIP's flight ever going to come within thirty miles of this building, right?"

The man laughed boisterously and continued to aim his gun at Larry. It was amazing he could laugh that hard and hold his hand as steady as he did. "We both know we are discussing President Cartwright. Why do you refer to him as VIP?"

Larry felt a flash of irritation. "Okay, then, fine. President Cartwright. But my question remains the same—do you realize Air Force One is not going to fly anywhere near this building?"

The terrorist laughed again, but this time it came out short and bitter, almost a cough of disdain. "Oh yes, I do realize that. But thank you so much for your concern."

Larry waited for him to expand on his answer, and when it became clear he wasn't going to, he pushed on. "If you've researched aviation as extensively as you told me earlier, then you know that with modern advances in safety equipment such as TCAS, the Terminal Collision Avoidance System, which all modern airliners are equipped with, it would be virtually impossible for me to direct the president's plane to crash into another airplane or into the side of a mountain, if that's your intention. Even if you forced me to do that, the equipment in the airplane would tell the pilot that something was not right, and he would have ample time to escape the imminent danger."

The terrorist's feet landed on the floor with a thud. He stood and faced Larry, his eyes black and angry and devoid of any trace of his previous apparent good humor. "Do not presume to understand what is going on here. I do not need or want your advice. Keep your mouth shut and your comments to yourself, and do not make the mistake of assuming that I will not kill you just for the fun of it. I have devoted my entire life to accomplishing what we are going to achieve here soon, so do not treat me like an idiot."

The man sat heavily back down in the controller chair. His hooded eyes regarded Larry steadily. He seemed to have regained control of his emotions, and it suddenly occurred to Larry that this man was feeling the pressure of the situation nearly as much as he was, regardless of how cool and collected he appeared to be. It was not a comforting feeling, considering the other guy was the one holding the lethal weapon.

Larry swallowed hard and felt the click of his dry throat. He returned his attention to the radar scope, which was again devoid of traffic. The situation was hopeless.

45

The old Boston TRACON, which had housed the facility prior to the construction of the brand-new forty-four million dollar BCT building christened in February 2004, had been a dingy little radar room located on the sixth floor of the Logan Airport control tower base building. Compared to the fancy structure now housing the Boston and Manchester controllers, the old facility hadn't been much more than a dusty broom closet.

Everything had been ancient. Radar scopes from the 1950s crammed so closely together that the controllers had practically been sitting in each other's laps; threadbare carpeting; air filtration systems so clogged with dust that controllers tried their damnedest never to turn the lights on for fear they might contract some dread disease just by *looking* at the ceiling.

Naturally, the controllers loved it.

When they arrived at the new facility and began working with their state-of-the-art radar scopes displaying digitally enhanced targets, the place was almost universally despised. It was cold and antiseptic, the equipment wasn't as good, and internal communication was much more difficult thanks to the increased distances between the controllers. The litany of complaints went on and on, some of them legitimate and some not.

The longtime controllers especially—of which Nick was one, despite his relative youth—had a hard time adjusting to the changes. Many of them had been forced to move to New Hampshire from their homes on the Massachusetts South Shore, and most of those with families had bitterly resented being forced to uproot their children.

Nick wasn't one of the people forced to move, since he had already been living in New Hampshire. In fact, his commute had been cut from nearly two hours a day to less than twenty minutes. He had been ecstatic about it, although not too impressed with much of anything else about the BCT.

But right now, he had to admit they had gotten a few things right when they built this place. In the old Boston TRACON, the area directly behind the radar scopes had been a messy tangle of cables and wires and ancient electrical connections, dirty and dusty and often confusing, even to the technicians whose job it had been to keep the stuff working.

However, when the BCT was constructed, the operations room had been placed on the second floor, in an area that was so high above the ground floor that it might as well have been a third story. Under the floor of the ops room was a work area. The wiring and cables for each radar scope were fed through slots in the floor down into the workspace, where it was all organized and easily accessed by the techs for repair and maintenance.

It was a clever bit of engineering, and it was in this area that Nick now stood, listening to the terrifying conversation between one of the terrorists and Larry. Nick was listening through the air ventilation exchanges built into the floor. He stood less than six feet beneath the two men—three if you counted Ron, immobilized and duct taped to his chair at the other end of the room—and could clearly hear everything being said, but he was completely invisible to them.

He wondered if Fitz was buying the terrorist's line of bullshit that cooperation in whatever they were planning would result in his freedom when all was said and done. He doubted it. This wasn't the first time around the block for

Larry Fitzgerald. He had to know something big was going down involving President Cartwright, and whatever it was, the odds of the perpetrators leaving any witnesses alive who could earn them a death sentence were pretty much nil. Of course, Nick had seen the terrorists' handiwork up close and personal, and Fitz presumably had not.

Nick thought again of Lisa, and of the horror of stumbling over Harry Tanner's body, and the anger inside him flared brightly. The same men who had so sadistically sliced up Harry were now holding Fitz and Ron hostage and forcing him to hide like a cowardly mouse in the innards of the BCT. It took all of Nick's willpower not to charge blindly up the stairs and into the ops room to confront the crazy bastards right now.

He forced himself to slow his thoughts. Breathe deeply. Concentrate. Rushing upstairs to a certain death was not something Lisa would have wanted for him, and if there was any kind of afterlife to look forward to, which Nick had always believed to be the case but was now beginning to doubt, he was pretty sure she would be waiting for him with a stern lecture that just might last for the remainder of eternity if he did something stupid.

Think.

There must be something he could do to wrest control of the situation away from the terrorists, but he couldn't imagine what it might be. He had no weapon, no idea where the other two armed men were, no idea how many others might be in the building, no idea even exactly what the terrorists were planning. They were presumably versed in violence and guerrilla tactics; he was not. He was outnumbered at least three to one.

He thought desperately. Nothing came to mind.

Placed high on the walls of the operations room were nine TSDs—Terminal Situation Displays—each one roughly six feet in width by four feet in height. Depicted on two of these plasma monitors was a view of roughly seven hundred miles of airspace immediately surrounding Logan Airport.

Displayed on the screens were tiny airplane icons in several different colors. Each icon's color was representative of a different type of aircraft, the icons symbolizing all the planes currently airborne that were scheduled to arrive at Logan Airport in roughly the next hour. The position of each airplane icon was updated several times per minute, giving the controllers and supervisors in the ops room a real-time picture of how much arrival traffic would be entering the facility's airspace in the immediate future as well as which sectors were going to get the most airplanes, and when.

During a busy day or night shift, these screens would seem almost alive, pulsing with sometimes more than one hundred airplane icons, glowing in colors from white to red to green to yellow. Controllers joked that when the Boston area was busy, the screens looked like their very own electronic Christmas trees.

Right now, though, at just before four thirty in the morning on a Sunday, the screens were practically blank. Traffic at Boston was almost always slow after 1:00 a.m., and that was especially true of the Saturday night into Sunday morning mid shift.

Only three airplane icons graced the huge expanse of northeast airspace depicted on the monitors. Two were inbound on a northern arrival track. The other was inbound to Boston from the south, and this was the one that drew the attention of the man holding the pistol on Larry. It glowed a bright blue, indicating it was a "heavy" jet, or what a layman might consider a jumbo jet. Larry knew immediately that Air Force One had just departed Andrews Air Force Base, carrying President Robert Cartwright on the short hop from D.C. to Boston.

Larry glanced—casually, he hoped—from the TSD display to the terrorist and saw the man gazing back at him steadily. Any hope that the man would not be aware of the significance of that airplane icon glowing blue over Washington was lost. From the look in the man's eyes and his mocking smile, Fitz could see that he was well aware his target was approaching, due to arrive in less than an hour's time.

Larry had not voted for the current occupant of 1600 Pennsylvania Avenue—he disagreed with just about everything the man stood for—but still he could not process the notion that he might soon be partially responsible for the man's impending violent death.

"Well," the gunman said, still smiling, "we have some time yet before the esteemed Mr. Cartwright concludes the final airplane ride of his presidency, so perhaps now would be an appropriate time to discuss the duties you will be performing for me."

"And what would those be?" Larry was surprised at how steady and strong his voice sounded, given how close he felt to a panic attack or maybe even a full-fledged nervous breakdown.

"When Air Force One enters your airspace, you will direct the plane to the final approach course for Runway 33 Left at Logan."

"But we're not landing on 33 Left. We're using Runway 4 Right."

"That's not my problem; it's yours. I want that airplane lined up for Runway 33 Left."

Larry shook his head. "But as soon as the pilot listens to the ATIS, he's going to expect to be vectored to the approach for 4 Right."

The ATIS—Automated Terminal Information Service—was a radio broadcast running on a continuous loop, updated by the control tower at least once per hour. The pilot simply dialed in the appropriate ATIS frequency and was rewarded with a listing of the current weather conditions at the airport, what approach to expect and to what runway, and any other information that might affect the flight, such as airport construction or runway and taxiway closures. As soon as the pilot in command of Air Force One listened to the ATIS, he would immediately question why he was being vectored to a different runway than what was listed on the broadcast.

The man jammed the barrel of his gun under Larry's jaw, his eyes burning with intensity. "Perhaps I have not made myself sufficiently clear. I do not care what you have to say or who you have to say it to, but if you are not successful in getting Air Force One where I want it and when I want it there, you will not draw another breath. Not one."

"Okay, okay, I get it." Larry's voice cracked; no longer strong and steady, it sounded to him like someone else was speaking, someone who was completely terrified and might just piss his pants.

"Take the plane to 33 Left. Okay. I can do that." Larry was panting like he had just run the Boston Marathon and could feel sweat soaking the back of his shirt, even though the temperature in the TRACON was always kept relatively low, more for the sake of all the expensive equipment than for the comfort of the controllers.

The man withdrew the gun from Larry's neck and sat back, once again appearing calm and collected. The swiftness of his mood changes was breathtaking and unsettling. "You will direct the aircraft to intercept the final approach course at least fifteen miles from the airport and as low an altitude as possible without eliciting any suspicion on the part of the pilot."

Larry nodded. "The minimum vectoring altitude southeast of Boston in that particular area is fifteen hundred feet."

The man waved the gun dismissively. "I don't care about your regulations. You will take the plane down to a thousand feet—do you understand?"

Larry did a quick calculation in his head and knew that he could break the MVA by five hundred feet and Air Force One would still be safe—minimum vectoring altitudes were assigned with the intention of allowing plenty of clearance for aircraft over any obstacles on the ground that could be a factor. "All right, a fifteen mile final to 33 Left at a thousand feet. I can do that. But why?"

The man laughed loudly. "Why? I'll tell you why. We have a little gift waiting for your pig president, and he must be in the proper location to receive it. I only wish I could be there to see the wreckage of his airplane sitting at the bottom of a smoking hole in the ground, but unfortunately I will have to make do by visualizing it." He sighed. "We all have our roles to play."

Larry looked back up at the TSD—it was a reflexive action; he couldn't help himself—and saw that the blue icon representing Air Force One had moved a bit closer to Logan Airport. It would be a little while before it arrived in BCT airspace, but it was coming. And there wasn't a damned thing Larry could do to stop it.

47

Nick listened with mounting horror as the words spoken by the terrorist wafted through the air exchange grate loud and clear. The Stinger missiles that had been stolen from the United States Army—the very same weapons that he now knew had gotten Lisa killed—were in the hands of a group of fanatical lunatics and would be used to shoot down the airplane carrying the president of the United States.

The irony of both he and Lisa being affected by the very same crime was not lost on Nick. First, Lisa had stumbled upon the plot to sell the information regarding the missiles to some unknown group and had paid for that with her life. Now, members of the very group that had presumably purchased the information were here in Merrimack at the BCT, forcing Fitz to put the president's plane in the proper location to allow members of the group to shoot it down with those missiles.

That had to be it. There was no other conceivable explanation as to why this man would insist on Air Force One being vectored so far out of position from Runway 4 Right, which was what Logan was utilizing for arrivals tonight. No other reason why he would crow about the "gift" they had waiting for President Cartwright. Nick had done some research on Stinger missiles after his conversation with the FBI agents at his home, and what he learned was terrifying.

Stinger missiles had been around in one incarnation or another for thirty years, maybe even longer, and had been used by the Russians in Afghanistan back in the 1980s as well as by the United States armed forces in various conflicts around the globe, starting with the Falkland Islands over a quarter-century ago.

Normally the missiles were fired by two-man teams, but it was possible for one person to operate the shoulder-fired weapons. They required a minimal amount of training, and modern versions of the Stinger were extremely accurate, combining visual acquisition of the target by the shooter with a heat-seeking component that allowed the missile to track its target even if the aircraft took evasive maneuvers.

Stingers could be used to shoot down targets at altitudes as high as ten thousand feet, but Nick guessed that the man wanted Fitz to get Air Force One to a thousand feet to provide the best possible odds of taking it down. Undoubtedly Air Force One was equipped with the most sophisticated countermeasures available against just such a weapon, but every aircraft, no matter how technologically advanced, eventually reached an altitude on final approach where it was extremely vulnerable.

At one thousand feet, the president's plane would be "low and slow," with flaps extended, traveling at the relatively slow speed of around one hundred thirty miles per hour. At that altitude and speed, Nick knew it would be virtually impossible for the flight crew to take any meaningful evasive action, even if they knew what was coming.

There was no way to avoid it. The president was going to die.

48

Jackie sat in the guard shack on the edge of the BCT grounds, leaning back in the chair that hadn't been splattered with the blood of the dead guard. His feet were propped on the console holding all of the CCTV monitors, and he was bored out of his mind. He had been dozing and was good and pissed off that he had been handed the most uninteresting assignment of all, especially after doing the dangerous and dirty work with the two guards.

Thanks, Jackie. You did a great job taking out the only two guys who could stop us from infiltrating this highly secure government facility. Now go and sit in the outhouse doing nothing while we get nice and comfy inside and prepare to assassinate the president. Oh, and don't worry. We'll be sure to let you know if we need you to handle something really distasteful again.

Assholes. Sometimes Jackie wondered why in the hell he ever listened to Tony anyway. Everyone else in the dysfunctional little group was scared to death of the guy because he came from the Middle East and wasn't afraid to send people to their Maker. Well, *he* wasn't afraid of Tony. The fucker pulled his pants on one leg at a time, just like everyone else, and Jackie knew that he could be as brutal as Tony if he wanted to. Hadn't he already proven that by killing those two guards single-handedly?

So, fuck him. Jackie had half a mind to walk in the front door of the BCT and tell Tony to send Brian outside to sit in the guard shack and jerk off. That sissy kid had done nothing to earn his spot on the team anyway, and it was really beginning to irk Jackie. Not that he wasn't going to enjoy fucking with the FBI dude when the time came, but until then he had nothing to do, and the time was dragging. There wasn't even a real frigging television out here for Chrissakes, just these stupid tiny monitors.

He sat with his feet on the security console, mud dripping from his boots all over the closed circuit monitors, eyes slowly closing, when a car turned into the entrance. The glare from its headlights hit Jackie square in the face, blinding him for a second. The driver of the car flipped off his high beams, then shut off the vehicle's headlights entirely, per the nighttime protocol posted outside the guard shack. This allowed the security personnel to get a good look at the occupants of the vehicle before they stopped in front of the gate.

Procedure dictated that everyone entering the BCT stop at the gate to show his or her ID to the guard. When satisfied, the guard would wave his own ID in front of the reader installed next to the security building, raising the gate and allowing the vehicle to access the parking lot. The gate would then automatically lower behind the vehicle.

A large, dark sedan approached the building slowly, coasting to a stop next to the side door of the security shack, the same door Jackie had stood in when he gunned down Jim Shay a little while earlier.

Jackie strolled outside in his ill-fitting uniform to see two middle-aged men sitting in the front seat of the car, each holding a Styrofoam cup of steaming coffee, a box of donuts placed on the seat between them. Tony had briefed Jackie that an ATC supervisor as well as an operations manager—the supervisor's supervisor—would be arriving shortly before 5:00 a.m. to oversee the facility and feign importance while the president was inside Boston's airspace.

This car obviously contained those two men, who had apparently decided to carpool to work. Jackie decided that had been very thoughtful of them, because now he didn't have to worry about one of them driving up to the gate while he was eliminating the other. It was like a two-for-one special.

The driver's side window rolled smoothly down with a barely discernible whir. Peering out the window at him was a man with silver hair and glasses, holding a federal government ID out for inspection. It was obvious he was familiar with the routine. He blinked owlishly up at Jackie and said, "Hey, buddy, haven't seen you before. New on the job?"

Jackie ignored the question and the ID the man was persistently waving in his face, instead sticking his head through the open window and asking, "Do either of you drink your coffee black?"

The two men looked at each other, confusion evident on their faces, and the man on the far side of the car said, "Well, yeah, mine's black. Why do you ask?"

"Just curious, I guess. And to answer your question, yes, it's my first day. Only been here for an hour or so. I gotta tell ya, I think this is going to be my last day, too, because this is one boring fucking job." Then he raised his pistol and fired point-blank into the driver's face.

The man's head exploded, spraying bright crimson blood—interspersed with chunks of bone and brain matter—onto his passenger, who was so shocked he didn't react at all. He just sat there, caught in a sudden downpour of blood and human tissue without an umbrella.

Jackie flicked the barrel of his gun a fraction to the right, and it suddenly dawned on the passenger that he was in danger. He dropped his coffee and scrabbled for the door handle in a desperate attempt to flee. His hand slipped on the blood coating the car's interior, and instead of yanking the door open, his hand flew up and he nearly punched himself in the face. Jackie shook his head sadly—that was one pathetic display—and fired again.

The passenger's head exploded just like the driver's.

Jackie opened the driver's side door and reached across the driver's dead body, plucking the passenger's coffee cup off the bench seat where it had fallen when he had made his abortive escape attempt. Hardly any coffee had leaked out through the tightly sealed plastic lid, and although the outside of the cup was soaked in blood and unidentifiable gore, Jackie was undeterred. He had never been what anyone would consider a picky eater. He wiped the cup as clean as possible with the sleeve of Morris Stapleton's grimy uniform and drank deeply, savoring the rich brew.

Planting his left foot on the tarmac outside the car door, Jackie used his right combat boot to shove the driver's body into the corpse of the passenger, slumped against the door. Then he pushed both of them to the floor. Blood was everywhere; the interior of the car looked exactly like what it was—the scene of a brutal double homicide—but that wouldn't matter. By the time anyone saw the carnage, this job would be over and Tony and his team would be dead like these two or well on their way to safety. Jackie was laying two to one odds on dead over escaped, but he didn't much care either way.

Now that he took a good look at the car, Jackie could see that it was dark blue. Midnight blue, he thought they called it, which in his opinion was stupid. He figured if you were going to name a color midnight, it should be black, not blue.

He slid into the car and closed the door. Blood soaked into the seat of his uniform trousers immediately. He reached out through the window and waved Jim Shay's ID in front of the card reader. The gate rose, and Jackie eased the big car straight past the guard shack and into the employee parking lot, where he parked the vehicle off by itself on the west side of the lot.

The passenger side window had shattered, apparently from the force of the second victim's skull smashing into it when he had been shot, so Jackie didn't bother to lock the car. With a broken front window, what would be the point?

Instead, he simply closed the door and walked away.

He took another deep pull on the coffee. It was still hot and strong, containing only the tiniest hint of that distinctive coppery blood taste. Jackie walked leisurely back toward the guard shack, now fully awake, his senses tingling. It was good to be alive.

Maybe that crazy towelhead Andretti had known what he was doing after all when he gave this assignment to Jackie. There was no way Brian could have managed it, the weak-assed surfer dude pussy, and besides, Jackie had enjoyed it far too much to allow anyone else to handle it.

Now all he had left to do was hang out at the guard shack for a few more minutes. The next victim would be cruising up to the gate anytime now.

49

Nick was reluctant to leave the relative safety of the small space underneath the floor of the ops room. It was highly unlikely the terrorists were aware of its existence, and even if they were, their minds were on other things, so the likelihood of Nick being discovered was slim. The problem, of course, was that as long as Nick remained here, hidden out of sight, he would be neutralized, unable to do anything to stop the impending tragedy that was gathering momentum like an out-of-control freight train.

He moved cautiously back through the equipment room where Harry's body lay face down in a pool of his own blood. Nick passed Harry purposefully, telling himself to avoid looking at the murdered technician but not managing to do so. Harry's blood was congealing where it contacted his clothing or the floor like thick maroon water gradually freezing and hardening into black ice.

After arriving at the first-floor hallway and the damaged exit door, Nick crossed quickly, paying no attention to the useless exit. Instead, he opened another heavy metal door on the opposite side of the hallway and started up a flight of stairs. These stairs were identical to the ones he had descended earlier after first seeing the men in the black fatigues; they were simply located on the opposite side of the building.

The stairs and handrails were metal, and there were metal pipes running along the ceiling and down the side walls. All this metal combined to form an acoustic nightmare, an enclosed area where the slightest noises echoed and boomed. One man climbing the stairs might sound like an army, and that was something Nick wanted to avoid at all costs—unless, of course, he could actually *find* an army to climb the stairs with him.

He reached the second floor without incident and opened the door leading to the carpeted hallway running adjacent to the ETG lab, a small radar training room consisting of five scopes. Inside this room, new controller trainees, called developmentals, were given computer-generated scenarios to run involving the airspace and procedures peculiar to Boston, allowing the controllers to become as familiar with them as possible before beginning their training on live traffic.

Nick slipped into the cubicles across the hallway from the lab where the contractors who performed briefings and conducted training for the FAA were stationed during administrative hours. He gazed across the hallway, trying to decide how he could access the lab without being seen or heard by someone carrying a gun who might want to use it on him.

The ETG lab, like most areas inside the BCT, was accessible only by swiping an employee's ID card in front of one of the ubiquitous card readers. Nick's ID would get him into the lab; that would not be a problem. The problem would be the annoyingly loud beep that accompanied the reader's recognition of an ID and the associated unlocking of the door. If one of the terrorists was anywhere in the vicinity, he could not help but hear the sound and would undoubtedly come running.

If the men had somehow gotten their hands on an ID and had been able to access the BCT—and Nick assumed they had; the very fact that they were here in the building seemed to prove it—they would also be able to enter the ETG lab, and then the game would be up. Nick would be trapped. He would be captured or killed and, worse, whatever slim chance he had of somehow stopping the assassination of President Cartwright would vanish.

Nick checked his watch, frustrated. Air Force One had departed Andrews and was in the air, and the minutes were passing by with astonishing speed. If he was going to put his hastily contrived plan into effect, he had to get into that lab *now*. He took a deep breath, then walked across the hall.

50

At a franchise donut shop a mile from the BCT, Kristin Cunningham stirred her usual three creams and five sugars into her coffee, breathing deeply, enjoying the rich aroma she hoped would help wake her up. She was nearly ten years into her law enforcement career, with the last five spent as an FBI Special Agent, so working odd hours was nothing new to her, nor were uninteresting assignments like the one she had drawn today.

Her entire workday would consist of hanging out at the Boston Consolidated TRACON. It was standard procedure for at least one agent to be present inside every affected ATC facility when the president was flying, so of course another agent would be monitoring the situation inside the control tower at Logan Airport as well. The controllers in the tower had jurisdiction over the actual pavement on the ground at Logan and the airspace immediately surrounding the field, out to a distance of five miles.

Normally, United States Secret Service agents were assigned this duty, and in fact there would be a Secret Service presence in the tower at Logan, but, as with government agencies everywhere, money was tight, so the bureaucrats in charge had elected to use their own people to patrol the area immediately surrounding the president in Boston, farming out the chore of monitoring the BCT to their brethren at the FBI.

As an agent with relatively low seniority, Kristin had inherited this duty, meaning she would spend the next twelve hours or more drinking coffee, eating way too much food that was way too unhealthy, and fending off the advances of air traffic controllers. It must be the temperament required to control airplanes, she thought—being responsible for giant aluminum tubes hurtling at each other at dizzying speeds all day, each with hundreds of people on board. Her limited experience with male controllers had been enough to convince her that they all thought they were God's gift to women.

The exception, she thought as she took a tentative sip of her coffee and was pleased to discover it tasted perfect – she felt better already – seemed to be Nick Jensen.

Although they had talked for only a few minutes and the conversation had been all business, Nick seemed more humble than the typical controller, which she thought was strange because she had been told he was one of the best. But then again, finding out your wife had been murdered would certainly shake you, so maybe he was still in shock from that tragedy.

Kristin walked out of the donut shop and slid into the front seat of her car. She started toward the facility and found herself looking forward to seeing Nick again. She had reviewed the roster of controllers who would be working at the BCT when she arrived and noticed his name.

Jeez, she thought, *what does it say about me that I'm looking forward to seeing the poor bastard whose wife just got killed?* She shook her head in disgust but couldn't help how she felt. *Doesn't matter anyway. It's going to be all business for both of us. Maybe sometime when he's gotten over the trauma of losing his wife, we might be able to see each other socially. Who knows?*

She swung off the access road and headed toward the security building at the edge of the BCT property. The guard shack was constructed from the same puke yellow bricks that had been used to erect the facility itself. She wondered whether the federal government had gotten a discount on the masonry because of its hideous color. Based on her personal experience with government service, it seemed unlikely since they never seemed to buy anything at a discount, but why else would anyone have intentionally used such a nasty shade of mustard? It was off-putting, the architectural equivalent of a grimace.

As she questioned the mental acuity of the BCT's designer, she pulled up to the gate in her seven-year-old Monte Carlo and waited for the security guard.

Finally the rent-a-cop slouched through the door, his uniform wrinkled and filthy, with what looked like a big piece of fabric ripped off the sleeve and hanging down at his elbow.

Very strange.

Kristin had been here several times in the past, and each time previously the guard had been waiting at the door to the security building when she arrived, uniform creased and shoes shined, standing erect in an almost military fashion.

It was a big deal to these security guys to have the FBI or the Secret Service on the premises, and normally they responded in a manner very much *un*like the way this guy was acting. Kristin began to feel uneasy. Something smelled wrong.

She reached slowly under her light jacket for her service weapon, concealed in a small shoulder holster resting against the side of her breast under her left arm, but as she did so, the guard drew his own gun and jammed it into her left cheek, stopping her hand's progress immediately.

"At least you have a little bit of sense," the man said not unkindly, "but you definitely don't want to put your hand anywhere near that peashooter you have under there, or I'll be forced to blow your pretty face into a thousand tiny pieces. I guess I don't have to tell you it won't be so pretty then."

"Who are you?" Kristin asked evenly.

The man smiled. "What makes you think I'm not the

security dude?"

"Oh, I don't know. Maybe the fact that you look like a goddamned slob and handle yourself like the town drunk on a Friday night."

The smile disappeared, and he shoved the gun into her face again. The pain blossomed. "Move your cute little ass over," he barked.

She slid across to the passenger seat while he lowered his bulky frame into the driver's side, his weapon never leaving its target.

He relieved her of her gun, waved an ID in front of the card reader to raise the gate, and drove into the parking lot.

Kristin watched the man warily, waiting for a chance to grab his weapon or shove open her door and roll out of the slowmoving car. "Maybe you're unaware of this, but you're interfering with a federal law enforcement official in the performance of her duties. What you're doing will earn you a long stretch in prison with some very unpleasant people. It's not too late to stop and avoid any really major problems. I suggest you give that some serious thought."

The man laughed good-naturedly, not exactly the response Kristin had been going for. "Interfering. That's a good one. If I blow your fucking head off right here where you sit, would that be considered interfering, too?"

Kristin said nothing, just glared at the man as he wheeled her car into a slot next to a large dark vehicle, the two cars looking lonely and lost in the huge, mostly empty lot. Far across the pavement, much nearer to the BCT entrance, four other vehicles sat in a neat row, presumably the cars belonging to the employees working the Saturday night mid shift. One of them was probably Nick Jensen's.

The man shut down the engine and pocketed Kristin's keys. "Get out," he commanded, so she did. Then he walked Kristin across the lot and into the BCT, his gun pressed firmly against her spine the entire way, as if she might forget he was holding it.

She didn't forget.

51

The beeping noise signifying that Nick's ID card had successfully unlocked the door to the ETG lab was even louder than he had feared. It was magnified a bit by the fact that the big building was almost completely empty. It sounded like someone had depressed the trigger on an air horn. He knew if any of the terrorists had heard it he would likely be dead within the next five minutes.

Maybe less than five.

Maybe a lot less.

He crept into the dark room and closed the door behind him, being careful to make as little noise as possible. The irony of trying to close a door silently after the loud electronic wail was not lost on Nick, but he figured there was no point in taking unnecessary chances. Even if the intruders had heard the short burst of noise, maybe they wouldn't be able to track down where it had come from when they came to investigate.

Nick shuffled backward in the dark until the backs of his legs came in contact with the console in front of the training scopes. The room was long and narrow, maybe thirty feet by eight feet, so he didn't have far to go. He stood motionless and counted to one hundred, listening to his heart thudding in his ears. It sounded so loud that he figured they might be able to find him based on that noise alone.

After two or three minutes, when no one came bursting through the door with guns blazing, Nick began to relax. He decided they had not heard the buzzing of the card reader after all. He risked turning on the interior light; there was no point in sneaking in here if he was just going to cower like a cornered rabbit. He had work to do.

The plan—Nick knew calling his idea a plan was giving it a lot more credibility than it deserved, since it was really not much more than a vague notion forged out of desperation—was to reprogram the radar scopes out in the ops room to show computer-generated traffic rather than actual live traffic. He would run a training scenario on the TRACON scopes in hopes of confusing the gunman.

Nick knew there were plenty of holes in his so-called plan. The biggest one was that although it was technically possible to run an ETG feed onto the ops room scopes, he didn't have the slightest clue how to do it. He was no computer genius; in fact, Lisa had handled all of the routine maintenance on their desktop at home as well as both of their laptops.

Then, if he even figured out how to force the fake targets on to the live scopes, he had to find a way to let Fitz know the plan, so his friend could transmit on radio frequencies that weren't in use. There was no point in forcing the phony traffic onto Fitz's scope if Air Force One was going to call on the actual radio frequency and ask what the hell was going on.

And *then*, even if he managed to figure a way around all of those problems, there was the small issue of what would happen to the president's plane if the BCT was suddenly off-line. The Boston Air Route Traffic Control Center—the facility controlling the high-altitude traffic throughout New England that would be handing Air Force One over to the BCT—could not simply give up the airplane without having accomplished a radar handoff.

A *radar handoff* was the term used when one controller told a controller working a different sector, either via automated methods or over a landline, that the airplane in question had been radar identified, and the receiving controller was prepared to accept separation responsibility for that aircraft. Until a handoff had been achieved, which would obviously never happen if the radar scopes at the BCT were no longer displaying live traffic, Boston Center would not be able to permit Air Force One to enter BCT's airspace.

Under Nick's hastily conceived scenario, the president's plane would get diverted to another airport if Boston Center could not accomplish a handoff and if they were unable to raise the BCT on any of the available landlines to transfer control of Air Force One. There would be hell to pay until everyone figured out what had happened, but at least the president, not to mention everyone else on board Air Force One, would still be alive.

There was another glaring drawback to Nick's desperate plan, too. It didn't necessarily ensure that anyone inside the BCT would survive—quite the opposite in all probability. But if nothing else, at least the terrorists' assassination plan would be thwarted. That was the best-case scenario, the result Nick was hoping for if everything proceeded smoothly. He tried not to think about the fate of himself and Fitz and Ron.

Now, though, standing inside the ETG lab, fearing that an armed lunatic might come smashing through the door at any moment and shoot him, Nick reached the conclusion that even his minimal level of optimism had been groundless. The plan was falling apart before he could even get it rolling.

Nick had no idea how to reprogram the ETG scopes.

He desperately tried to remember the layout of the room. Fully certified controllers, unless they suffered an operational error—a situation where two airplanes were permitted to get closer to each other than standard separation allowed, known in controller parlance as a "deal"—only visited this room for refresher training on various emergency scenarios, none of which had ever involved trying to prevent a group of ruthless terrorists from blowing up Air Force One.

Nick had never been charged with an operational error,

so he had not had occasion to spend very much time at all in this strangely shaped room. In fact, he could not even remember the last time he had been in here, but he was quite certain he had merely sat back and half dozed while the controller with the lowest seniority in the group ran the emergency scenario.

Nick had a vague notion that there was a set of operator manuals stored in a small bookcase on the far left side of the room. He hoped the set of books included a programming guide that would walk him through the steps to necessary accomplish his task.

He searched frantically through the detritus of dozens of training sessions, finding discarded partially written training sheets, a couple of pens, even a half-full cup of old coffee with a chunk of greenish brown mold floating in the middle like a tiny island. There was a computer—you couldn't go anywhere in the modern world without running across a computer, Nick thought—but the manuals he thought he remembered were nowhere to be seen.

Nick swore under his breath and felt a bead of sweat trickle down the back of his neck. Time was rapidly running out, and he was no closer to putting a stop to the president's assassination than he had been when the terrorists had first stormed the BCT, an event that felt like it had taken place days ago, rather than the hour or so it had actually been.

He had been dreaming anyway if he thought he could piece together some sort of MacGyver-like phony traffic scenario that would fool the guy holding the gun to Fitz's head. He had heard the man tell Fitz that he was more than a little familiar with ATC procedures and phraseology. He probably would have seen through the ruse immediately, and then things would have been worse than they were right now. If that was even possible.

He paced up and down the little room, the second hand sweeping around the face of his watch with frightening speed. He couldn't even turn the ETG scopes on, never mind reprogram them, without a manual to follow. And there was nothing here.

Nick wondered where Air Force One was now. The president's plane was getting close to Boston's airspace. They were truly screwed.

Kristin Cunningham was not exactly what she appeared to be on the surface. Petite and pretty, with a face framed by wavy hair falling almost to her shoulders, Kristin had been defying the expectations of others ever since graduating high school in Manchester, New Hampshire, a decade ago. Her parents, not to mention her teachers and even her closest friends, had fully expected Kristin to go off to college after graduation and study something esoteric, like art history, or the rise and fall of the Roman empire.

It was a natural expectation. Kristin had earned outstanding grades in school her entire life; she loved reading and studying. Although she had played and been reasonably successful at a number of different sports, she was nobody's idea of a tomboy and had always seemed more comfortable sitting in a study carrel than cavorting on a playing field.

This personal history made it all the more surprising when immediately upon graduating high school—during her graduation dinner, in fact—Kristin announced that she would not be attending college after all. A career in law enforcement was what she wanted to pursue, and she would begin working toward that goal right away. To say her parents were shocked would be an understatement, but Kristin was undeterred and eventually turned even her father's skepticism into enthusiastic support with her hard work and unflagging energy.

She attended the police academy and was hired by the Manchester Police Department upon graduating and had never looked back. After spending five years on the force, the FBI came calling, prizing her for her independence and ability to think on her feet, two traits not always in abundant supply in government service, as well as for her fearlessness and spotless record.

Working out of the Southern New Hampshire field office, Kristin was able to live near her parents in the area she loved, while performing work that she knew was important and occasionally even made a difference. She never once regretted the decision to pursue a career path that diverged wildly from the one her friends and family had expected of her.

Now, with the barrel of a semiautomatic pistol pressed into her back, being pushed as a captive into the air traffic control facility she had been assigned to monitor, Kristin felt ashamed. She had allowed this moron to get the drop on her, and what had she been doing at the time? Mooning like some love-struck junior high girl about this Nick Jensen character. And now that lapse of attentiveness was probably going to cost both her and Nick their lives, assuming he wasn't dead already.

She shook her head and mumbled, "Goddamn it" through clenched teeth.

The guy shoved her in the back with the gun. "Shut up."

They approached the double doors, and the man reached around her to wave his stolen ID in front of the card reader. As his hand hovered momentarily in front of the reader, Kristin considered stomping on his foot or grabbing his hand and twisting it, hopefully taking the man to the ground and wrestling his gun away from him.

The only problem was, the man still had the gun pressed firmly into the middle of her back, and she knew there was no possible way she would be able to knock him down fast enough to disable him before he could fire at least one shot, which would probably kill or paralyze her, and what would that accomplish?

She took a deep breath and blew it out in frustration as the big reinforced glass door swung open and the pair entered the BCT. Kristin knew the ops room was on the second floor.

The man with the gun, though, steered her toward a glass-fronted conference room that looked out of place, like it had been lifted out of a decent-sized private corporation and plunked down in the middle of this federal government building.

Kristin could see a man pacing back and forth inside it. He was dressed in black from his watch cap to his combat boots, with dark greasepaint on his face. It was jarring and seemed almost surreal: these comfortable surroundings, about as nice as you could expect in government service, overtaken by armed thugs.

The man pushed Kristin through the door.

The moment they entered, the guy dressed in black said, "Are you kidding me? A chick? Are you sure this is the right person?"

"Christ. Of course it's the right person," the other man said dismissively, his voice dripping sarcasm. "I know what a fucking FBI ID looks like, okay? Besides, the back of her jacket has three letters on it. Care to guess what they might be?"

The other man looked unconvinced.

"What? You don't think there are any lady FBI agents? Don't you watch TV? They're everywhere on the tube. It's the latest thing."

"I suppose. It's just that she looks so . . ."

"Small?"

"Well, yeah."

"Who gives a shit about that?" the man answered, his gun still poking Kristin in the back. "It'll make her that much easier to control."

Kristin could see immediately that the man stationed inside the conference room was the one she was going to have to work on to get out of this mess. He was barely older than a kid, and he seemed much less sure of himself, less hardened, than the other guy.

She turned to him and said quietly, "It's not too late to put a stop to whatever it is you're doing here. No one has gotten hurt yet—"

The man standing behind her laughed. "Oh, really? That's a good one. Tell that to the two dead security guards or the two FAA guys who rolled up to the gate just before you and died about ten seconds later. Tell that to the electronics technician cooling in a pool of his own blood right now. You have no fucking clue what's going on here, missy, so just shut your friggin' mouth before I blow your pretty head off. One more dead asshole makes no difference to me whatsoever."

Kristin's blood ran cold. The man was dressed in a torn and filthy – and bloody – security uniform, which he had undoubtedly taken off one of the guards he had killed, so presumably he was telling the truth about the other dead as well. That meant these people had murdered at least five innocent men tonight. This changed everything. They had nothing to lose and thus could not be reasoned with. What could you offer a person like that?

Nothing.

She decided to try a different tactic: to gather a little information that she might be able to use to her advantage later, assuming she lived that long. "How many of you guys are in here? Is it just the two of you?"

The man behind her said, "Shut up. You're not in charge here; we are. The only reason you're still alive is because we can use you, but if you piss me off, I'll shoot you in the back of the head right where you stand. One shot. End of pretty FBI agent. We can do what we need to do without you, so don't go getting the idea that you're going to stay alive just because you're a cute little thing wearing a Windbreaker that says FBI on the back."

Kristin swallowed hard and said nothing.

"That's better, baby," the man said mockingly. "Now, let's

do a little business, shall we?"

She didn't answer, so he continued. "We know that you need to coordinate with your superiors and notify them that everything is hunky-dory up here in the sticks before President Cartwright's plane enters Boston's airspace. Do that now."

With mounting horror, it dawned on Kristin that the armed invasion had nothing to do with this facility, at least not specifically. It was all about Air Force One. These men were part of a much bigger plot involving the president.

Shaking her head, Kristin said, "Come on, guys. Be reasonable. You know I can't do that." She smiled at the man in black and then turned the same reassuring, high-wattage smile on the man standing behind her.

He stepped around her and moved to the conference table, his gun never wavering. It was now pointed directly at her chest. With the pistol, he gestured at the cell phone hanging in a leather holster at her hip. "Make the call."

She locked eyes with him. "I can't do that."

He nodded, taking two steps forward and then stopping. He was now standing directly in front of her, invading her personal space. He smelled of sweat and blood and death.

Kristin refused to look away. "I can't do it," she repeated.

Without another word, the man lowered his gun and shot her in the knee.

53

Nick was back in the technicians' equipment room, searching with increasing desperation for something to use as a weapon against the man holding Larry hostage in the ops room. He had abandoned the ETG training room is disgust and backtracked, not knowing what else to do.

As he dug through the stockpile of tools and equipment, his gaze fell on a soldering gun, propped in its stand with the metal tip used to melt lead sticking straight up in the air. If Nick could get close enough, maybe he could use it to burn the man, but although it would certainly be painful to the guy, the soldering iron would not even come close to providing the kind of knockout blow Nick needed. If anything, it would probably just piss the man off, and he'd kill Nick slowly and painfully, instead of shooting him between the eyes.

He shook his head. The soldering gun was definitely out.

A pile of screwdrivers lay heaped in two big bins, one containing the standard, slotted kind and the other filled with Phillips head models. These looked a little more promising. Nick found several of both types of screwdrivers that were heavy and at least twelve inches long, clearly designed to allow the technician access to hard-to-reach areas. Maybe he could use one of these.

Still, Nick knew that the odds of him taking down an

armed terrorist with a screwdriver were slim. Even if he was able to get close enough to bury the tool in the man's head or neck, a possibility that seemed unlikely, what were the chances he could hit the exact spot he needed to incapacitate the man? Especially since he didn't have any idea where that spot might be.

The basic problem was the same as it was with the soldering iron—he could probably inflict some damage on the man, but it would likely not be enough. Nick knew he would get only one chance. Once the advantage of surprise was lost, the fight would be over quickly.

A utility knife lay open on a workspace, its one-inch blade exposed. Whoever had been using the tool had never retracted the blade when he was finished with it.

He closed his eyes and pictured himself plunging the razor-sharp blade into the neck of the terrorist and realized that as tempting as the utility knife appeared to be as a potential weapon, it suffered from the identical problem as that of the screwdrivers: he would have to be much more precise than he was capable of in order to have any chance of success.

In the hands of a competent fighter, the utility knife or any of the other tools he had considered may have been able to subdue the terrorist in the TRACON, especially when combined with the element of surprise. But Nick knew he was far from a competent fighter. The last time he had even been involved in a physical altercation was in fifth grade when he had been thoroughly whipped on the playground. By a fourth grader.

Frustrated and afraid, Nick's temper boiled over. He thumbed the metal switch to retract the blade on the knife, then turned and threw it as hard as he could at the back wall. It thumped into the opaque tarp hanging from ceiling to floor that was being used to segregate the construction zone from the rest of the room and fell harmlessly to the floor. The knife clattered onto the ceramic tile a couple of feet from Harry's lifeless body.

Nick stared at Harry, overwhelmed by a feeling of desolate hopelessness. What had been done to the older man was horrific, brutal, the ultimate violation. Suddenly it seemed of utmost importance to cover him, to take some action to lessen the obscenity that had been perpetrated upon him. Eventually his body would be found, and the thought of countless investigators, all of them disinterested strangers, seeing this quiet, kind man lying on the floor where he had been brutally hacked to death, so horribly exposed, dried blood crusting the tile around him, seemed like an insult to the man's memory. He deserved at least a little dignity.

Nick knew that he had bigger issues to worry about, things that at the moment were far more critical than some lame attempt at preserving the dignity of a man who was beyond caring about his appearance. Maybe this suddenly seemed so important because Nick was exhausted and the situation taking place just one floor above him seemed so utterly bleak. He was fresh out of ideas about how to handle the terrorist, so perhaps this was just a way for him to avoid dealing with the terrifying reality of the president's plane being shot down, with the corresponding likelihood that he would also be a casualty, another lifeless corpse leaking blood all over the federal government's property.

Regardless, whatever the reason, Nick could not ignore the growing feeling, the compulsion really, that he needed to cover Harry. It was risky, sure, because if a terrorist were to reenter this room and see Harry's body covered with a shroud, it would be clear that someone was here, that there was a person running around the building unaccounted for. The terrorists would undoubtedly begin searching for him and would find him easily. The only reason he had avoided capture this long was due to the simple fact that they were unaware of his presence.

Still, what was the likelihood that they would return to this unimportant room tucked away on the ground floor? As far as the terrorists were concerned, they had eliminated the only potential threat: the technician who had been working down here. There was no one else alive in the building that they were aware of, and their focus was going to be on the radar room, especially now that Air Force One had to be getting very close to Boston's airspace.

The risk seemed relatively small, and Nick could not shake the feeling that it was critical he take care of Harry. He looked over at the tarp hanging just a few feet from the body. It would be perfect to drape over Harry, so he would not be on display like some gruesome Halloween decoration for everyone who came through here to gawk at when this nightmare was over.

Time was of the essence. He should not be wasting what precious little of it he had left by worrying about Harry, who was beyond help. But to Nick, that lifeless, desecrated body represented every horrifying second that had passed since he saw the three men walking down the hall.

His mind was made up. Nick grabbed the utility knife and walked two steps to the tarp. Reaching as high as he could above his head, he sliced the heavy plastic in a horizontal line, stopping and sawing through the reinforced seam at each edge. The large piece of plastic drifted down, momentarily covering Nick and making him look like a poorly conceived Halloween ghost.

He turned and draped the tarp over Harry's body, choking off a sob as he did so. It was more than big enough to cover the entire area, including the puddle of blood that had worked its way a couple of feet in every direction from Harry's chest.

Nick knelt beside the body, now fuzzy and indistinct under the makeshift shroud, a shapeless lump on the floor. "I'm so sorry," he whispered, knowing the words were hopelessly insufficient but unable to stop himself from saying them.

For some reason, Nick felt better, more at ease, which was crazy. His situation was no different than it had been a few moments ago; it was worse, in fact, because as he had been caring for Harry's body, the clock continued to tick. The president was now a little bit closer to Boston and a date with a Stinger missile, and Nick, Larry, and Ron were undoubtedly a few minutes closer to being massacred themselves.

Still, Nick felt irrationally calm and clearheaded. He stood and turned toward the door, and as he did so, his gaze swept across the construction site that had been cordoned off and concealed by the plastic tarp.

He stopped in his tracks and did a double take, then stood perfectly still and stared, frozen in wonder. Among the tools and supplies stored neatly on a rudimentary table made up of a two-by-eight plank placed across a pair of sawhorses was the weapon Nick had been searching for.

54

Larry's hands were shaking so badly he wasn't sure he would physically be capable of taking the handoff Boston Center was attempting to give him on Air Force One. As the high-altitude facility controlling traffic over all of New England, plus a portion of New York State, Boston Center was the last link before the BCT—Boston Approach Control—in the air traffic control chain that had begun working the giant Boeing 747 from the time it began taxiing for departure at Andrews Air Force Base.

Giving and taking handoffs on airplanes in the NAS—the National Airspace System—was almost entirely an automated affair, especially at busy, high-density facilities. In order to transfer control of an aircraft to another facility, or to another sector within his own facility, the controller simply made a keystroke entry and then manipulated what was known as a "slewball," similar in design and purpose to a computer-game controller, to move a cursor across the radar scope to the target representing that airplane. Then he would simply punch a button on the keyboard, initiating the radar handoff.

The target would begin flashing on the receiving controller's radar scope and would continue flashing until the receiving controller used his own slewball to move his cursor to the target and press the button on his own console. The target would stop flashing on the receiving controller's scope and would *begin* flashing on the scope of the controller initiating the handoff, indicating that the receiving controller was now prepared to accept separation responsibility for that airplane. The handoff was then considered complete, and the airplane would be permitted to enter the receiving controller's airspace. Communications transfer would follow.

It was a simple automated procedure that controllers performed hundreds of times during the typical workday, so ordinary that to seasoned radar controllers it was as natural as taking a breath of air. See a flashing data block, observe the digitized radar target and recognize the airplane, and take the handoff.

The controller initiating the handoff would instruct the pilot to contact the receiving controller on his or her specific radio frequency. When the pilot checked in on that frequency, the controller would issue specific instructions to ensure the separation and sequencing necessary for that airplane to depart, land, or transit the airspace.

Taking a handoff. Simple.

But not for Larry, not today. Operations Manager Don Trent, First-Line Supervisor Dean Winters, and at least one representative of the FBI or the U.S. Secret Service were supposed to have arrived in the facility by now to oversee the operation. None of them had shown up, which could mean only one thing—they had been stopped by the other terrorist, the one who had duct taped Ron to his chair and then left the room. It was inconceivable to think it could be a coincidence; that they had all run into traffic or overslept. Not with Air Force One flying into Boston. Screwing up in that way was a career ender in the FAA and undoubtedly even more so in the FBI or Secret Service.

Larry wondered if any of them were still alive or if they had simply been murdered and disposed of, and his hand began shaking even more. He could feel the irresistible force and sheer brutal power of the gun pressed against his neck just under his ear. The terrorist stood behind him now and seemed nearly as tense as Larry, although Larry didn't see how that could possibly be the case.

He heard the man whip a cell phone out of a pocket and punch a key. Moments later he said, "It's time . . . Yes. Ten minutes."

It would take approximately ten minutes for Air Force One to reach the point in Boston's airspace where the terrorist with the gun was insisting Larry vector it. The president of the United States had roughly ten minutes to live.

Larry rolled his cursor out to the target representing the president's airplane. Normally the data tag corresponding to an airplane read something like ABC123, which represented aviation shorthand for ABC Airlines Flight 123. Air Force One was represented in air traffic control facilities everywhere simply as AF1.

The cursor reached the target, still flashing patiently as the data block moved steadily toward Boston's airspace, and Larry stabbed at the button that would alert the Boston Center controller that Boston Approach Control was accepting the handoff on Air Force One. He missed the button entirely. He tried again and managed to strike the button, but this time the cursor wasn't placed directly over the target, so nothing happened.

"Damn it," Larry muttered softly.

The man rapped the gun against the side of his skull.

Bright colored lights exploded in Larry's head. It felt as though he had been clubbed with a baseball bat.

"Do it," the man commanded, his voice a harsh rasp.

"I'm trying," Larry answered desperately, wondering what it would feel like when the bullet crashed into his skull and began making scrambled eggs out of his brain. Sweat flowed freely down his face, and he vaguely registered the sound of heavy, ragged breathing, realizing dully that it was his own. He thought of his wife and two children and wondered if he would ever see them again, and if they could ever forgive him for contributing to the assassination of President Cartwright.

One more attempt at taking the handoff. This time the

cursor reached its intended destination and the flashing stopped.

Air Force One entered Boston Approach Control's airspace.

55

The floor rushed up to greet Kristin, and she could feel blood staining the leg of her new dark blue pants, which had set her back nearly a hundred bucks. *Now these pants are ruined,* she thought crazily for a second, before a rolling wave of intense pain overwhelmed her, blotting out everything else, beginning at her right knee and radiating outward.

Kristin was childless, but she had it on very good authority that the worst pain a human being would ever endure was that of childbirth. If that was really the case and bearing children was even worse than this, then she decided she was definitely out.

When the terrorist demanded she call her team at Logan and tell them everything was okay here, she had known immediately that refusing to do so would earn her some sort of negative reinforcement—you didn't have to be an FBI agent to figure that one out—but this was much more than she ever expected.

She gasped and sucked in a breath through clenched teeth, trying to maintain consciousness in the face of her body's rebellion against the sudden trauma inflicted upon it. She looked up from the floor and saw a man looming above her. It was the man who had shot her, and he was telling her something she could not make out, in a voice that seemed unnaturally reedy.

She shook her head and blinked to clear her fuzzy vision and tried to focus on what the man was saying, but it was so difficult. She couldn't get past the unbelievable fiery agony burning through her leg.

Call.

He was saying something about a telephone call. He wanted her to make the call to her superiors.

The man fished her cell phone out of the holster on her hip and placed it on the floor in front of her. Behind it, in front of the absurdly large plate-glass windows of the conference room, a thin grey cord ran out the back of a telephone's base like a rat's tail and snaked its way along the floor, disappearing behind a table. From this angle, Kristin could see dust bunnies and a sprinkling of crumbs that had gathered on the carpet under the table; it was clear the janitorial service contracted to clean the BCT had not been doing a thorough job.

Kristin reached out to pick up her cell. It seemed as though her hand stretched out for ten or twelve feet before it reached the phone, like she was looking at it through the wrong end of a telescope. She was surprised to see how much her hand was shaking. It occurred to her that she was going into shock, and she wondered in a detached way if she was dying.

The man told her again to dial her supervisor. It sounded like he was talking underwater.

The man kneeled down and placed his gun at her temple. He leaned close to her ear and whispered. "I'm going to scatter your few simple brains all over this beautiful conference room if you don't make that fucking call right now."

Kristin believed him. She punched the speed dial with her trembling hands.

On the first ring a voice said, "Watkins."

"This is Cunningham," she said in a voice that sounded like someone else's. Someone she didn't know. Someone who was dying.

"Hey, how's life up in the wilds of New Hamster?"

"Great," she said, concentrating on remaining conscious and keeping her voice steady. She felt increasingly woozy and thought she might throw up at any moment. The pain was immense.

"Are you okay?"

"Just . . . just not feeling very well," she mumbled, feeling sick and scared and ashamed of herself. She knew she should be trying to pass a message to Lieutenant Watkins, but she could barely think at all.

"Everything's all right up there?"

"Yeah, sure. Everything's fine."

"Okay, thanks for checking in. We'll give you a call as soon as the president's motorcade is moving into the city. Talk to you soon."

"Yes, soon," Kristin repeated hollowly, her leg feeling like it was being blasted by a blowtorch.

"Take care of yourself; you don't sound too good," Watkins told her.

For some reason she found that very funny. "I will," she said with a high-pitched laugh that sounded just short of hysterical, even to her.

The connection broke, and the terrorist removed the gun from her head as he rose. "See? That wasn't so hard, was it?"

The room was spinning now, twisting around and around like the antigravity wheel she used to love to ride every fall when the county fair passed through her tiny town. Kristin guessed she had spent easily a couple hundred dollars on that ride when she was a teenager. Who knew you could get the same effect without spending any money at all?

Of course, there was the small matter of being shot, of having a chunk of lead traveling at near supersonic speed blast your knee apart. But what the hell. There's no such thing as a free ride in this world, as her old man liked to say.

She tried to focus on the man with the gun, but he was spinning just like the room, and now Kristin knew she was going to be sick. He was saying something else that she could not make out. He was so damned far away.

He must have gotten tired of trying to make her understand because he prodded her right leg with the toe of his combat boot.

Instantly the world exploded in an atomic blast of pain, and then everything went black.

56

Nick stood just inside the door on the west side of the TRACON ops room, holding his weapon in both hands and watching, sick with fear, as the terrorist held a pistol steadfastly against the side of Larry's head.

It had been a stroke of good fortune—probably his first since this whole nightmare began unfolding—finding the fully charged, battery-operated nail gun lying in the first-floor construction site. The thing was filled with heavy-gauge nails, maybe tenpenny?

Nick had seen a video once of the injuries a roofer had suffered when he fell off a house and reflexively squeezed the trigger of his nail gun on the way down to the ground, firing three nails into his skull. The damage had been extensive, with X-rays depicting the spikes protruding well into the man's brain after punching holes right through the thick protective plate of the skull. Nick was hopeful that if he could fire even one shot into the guy's head, the man would be incapacitated and maybe even killed; he certainly would be unable to hold his gun on Fitz as he was crashing to the floor with a thick nail stabbing into his brain.

Larry was seated in his controller chair, facing his scope. The terrorist stood behind him, facing the scope as well. They had their backs turned toward Nick, and he could see the flashing data tag displayed on Larry's scope that must surely represent Air Force One. Nick was too far away to read the information contained in the tag, but judging from the intensity with which the terrorist was watching the radar display, he knew there was no other possibility.

Far off on the other side of the big room, Ron sat duct taped to his chair. His eyes were closed, and Nick hoped he was simply dozing. There was no obvious sign of a gunshot wound or any other kind of wound for that matter, nothing resembling the damage that had been done to Harry, but Nick knew these men were cold-blooded fanatics and would not be above killing another defenseless man.

He noticed Larry struggling to accept the automated handoff on Air Force One. Larry's hands were shaking so badly he could barely control the slewball. Nick felt sorry for him and for the fact that he had a loaded weapon aimed at him. Then he looked down at his own hands and realized they were shaking just as badly as Fitz's, maybe worse.

He tried to calm himself. The next couple of minutes were critical, literally life-and-death. He would get one chance to take the terrorist by surprise, and he knew he had to make the most of it if he wanted to put the man down. Desperately he tried to control his fear and focus on the task in front of him. What would be the best approach to take—speed or stealth?

The edge of the console currently providing cover for Nick was only about fifteen feet from where the terrorist stood. He could step clear of the console in three long strides. The obvious problem, though, was that if he made even the slightest noise during that time—a scrape of his shoe on the carpet, a rustle of clothing, anything—there would be more than ample time for the man to fire his gun into Fitz's head and blow his brains all over the TRACON.

On the other hand, if he moved slowly and deliberately, Nick was reasonably sure he could quiet his approach enough so that the man would not hear him coming until it was too late for him to react. But what if he was wrong? What if he couldn't sneak up on the man? What if the terrorist saw a shadow or turned at the wrong time or just *felt* Nick's presence? What then? This scenario would doubtless end the same way, with Fitz's dying body slumping out of his chair onto the floor.

He thought about Lisa and wondered whether she had been aware of what was happening to her as she was being murdered. Did she have any idea why she had been targeted? Was she aware that the man who ended her life was taking it from her just because she had been unlucky enough to stumble across the wrong information in the course of trying to do her job?

Nick pictured his wife, with her warm brown eyes, her angelic smile, and her determination to always do the right thing, and he felt a surge of calm confidence. He could do this. With a little luck and a little determination of his own, this could all be over in just a few minutes.

57

"Boston Approach, Air Force One is with you, leveling at one-one thousand, with ATIS Information Charlie."

Larry keyed up his mike, unsure how in the hell he was going to keep President Cartwright out of harm's way and also continue breathing for more than the next couple of minutes. The barrel of the terrorist's gun pressed relentlessly into his neck just below his ear. "Air Force One, this is Boston Approach. Fly heading zero-six-zero. That's your vector for the ILS Runway 33 Left approach. Boston altimeter two-niner-niner-seven."

There was a short delay while the flight crew forty-five miles south of Boston, flying over Providence, Rhode Island at eleven thousand feet, digested the information they had been given. Then the call came back. "Uh, Approach, on the ATIS broadcast the tower is advertising Runway 4 Right as the active. Did we miss something?"

Larry had known the pilot would question the assignment of a landing runway that was not being broadcast as the active runway on the ATIS. It was a basic tenet of aviation everywhere that airplanes perform their best when they are landing and departing on the runway that is most closely aligned with the wind direction, and on the latest weather sequence, it was showing out of the northeast, zero-three-zero at eight knots. The flight crew of Air Force One wanted and expected to land on Runway 4 Right.

The terrorist forced the gun up under Larry's ear and said softly, "You *will* take that airplane to Runway 33 Left. Say whatever you must to convince him to accept it, but that *is* where that airplane is going to go." Although spoken quietly, the words were filled with an implied menace that Larry did not miss. He supposed that was the point.

"Air Force One, sorry about that, but Runway 4 Right will be closing momentarily and will not be available for at least an hour. We had an aircraft incident, and there is debris on 4 Right that needs to be removed. The winds are light enough where the decision was made by the tower supervisor to go with Runway 33 Left. The ATIS will be updated shortly to reflect the change. Sorry to spring it on you like that, but we didn't get any advance notice, either."

Larry was taking a calculated risk. If the crew of Air Force One were to call down to Massport—the Massachusetts Port Authority, the state-run agency responsible for the operation of Logan Airport—they would discover in short order that there was no closure planned for Runway 4 Right and there had been no aircraft incident.

If that happened, Larry had no idea what he would do. He was banking on the fact that the winds were relatively light and that 33 Left was a longer runway than 4 Right anyway, so it wouldn't be a big deal to them. He also hoped that since they were on a tight schedule, they wouldn't want to waste time arguing about a landing runway when it didn't really matter.

Seconds ticked by. The AF1 target moved closer to the middle of the scope, where the depiction of Logan Airport was scribed on the digital map. The terrorist and Larry waited in silence for the response.

"Okay, then, 33 Left will be fine. We'll fly a zero-six-zero heading. Did you give us lower?"

"Not yet," Larry replied, "but now you can descend and maintain three thousand." He wondered if his shaking voice was as noticeable to the pilot as it was to him; he guessed not, since the man didn't seem to recognize anything was wrong.

The Boeing 747 turning and starting its descent toward Boston was actually one of two identical customized airplanes traditionally considered by the public to be Air Force One, although in reality that designator was used to refer to any airplane occupied by the president of the United States if that plane was under the command of the U.S. Air Force. Normally that plane was one of the two customized Boeing 747s. Sometimes the president was ferried on a Marine helicopter if, for example, using an airplane would be inconvenient or unwieldy. In that case, the helicopter would be known as Marine One as long as the president was aboard.

The terrorist spoke softly, almost casually. "I thought I made myself clear when I told you that I wanted you to get the president's plane as low as possible. I know you can do better than three thousand feet."

Larry closed his eyes and nodded, hoping he wouldn't accidentally jar the man's finger on the trigger and blow his own head off. "I understand, but if I issue a descent clearance to an altitude of, say, fifteen hundred feet when they are still that far away from the airport, the crew will get suspicious. It's not something they would be expecting to hear. I'm assuming you don't want them to be suspicious, right?"

The answer seemed to satisfy the man, although Larry knew he could have issued the descent clearance. He just didn't know where the terrorists were planning to strike, so his goal was to keep Air Force One at a reasonable altitude for as long as possible. He couldn't imagine what difference it would make, but he needed to feel like he was doing something to try to delay the inevitable.

He wondered about Nick. Had he been captured or killed, or was there any chance at all that he had escaped and was even now on his way back to the BCT with help? Larry didn't know how many terrorists were involved in this plot; he knew there were at least two, because he had seen them. Maybe there were many more. If that was the case, the odds of Nick even being alive, much less rushing back with the cavalry to save the day, were pretty much nonexistent.

If he *had* lived, though, and he *was* bringing help, he damned well better hurry up about it, because the clock was winding down.

Just cling to that hope, he told himself. Nick was bringing the state police, the Merrimack police, the FBI, the Secret Service, the Department of Homeland Security, and the freaking CIA and the NSA. The U.S. Marines and a few Navy SEALs would be okay, too.

That thought gave him a moment's hope, but then he refocused on the digitized target representing Air Force One, now less than twenty miles from the airport and approaching three thousand feet in altitude. Soon the pilot would expect a turn onto the final approach course, and the zealot standing right behind his chair holding a gun to his head would be expecting him to issue a further descent clearance to the airplane.

Jesus Christ, Nick, hurry up. Please.

58

Nick moved quickly to close the distance between himself and the man pressing the gun to Larry's head. The terrorist appeared completely engrossed in what was happening on the radar scope.

Saying a silent, hurried prayer of thanks to the God he had always believed in but most recently had been castigating for taking his wife away from him, Nick was surprised to discover he made it nearly the entire fifteen feet without tripping over a chair or scuffing his feet on the floor or alerting the man to his impending attack. He was going to make it!

As he rushed forward, Nick saw Air Force One on the radar scope turning northwest, dangerously close to Logan. He feared he had cut it too close and that the worst-case scenario would be played out. He could see it all clearly in his head. He would disarm the terrorist, taking him down and thinking he had saved the day, and then the huge Boeing 747 jumbo jet would be blown out of the sky anyway. One moment the target would be there on the radar scope, and the next it would simply have disappeared.

Who knew where the coconspirators with the missiles were actually located? They had to be fairly close to the airport, but that was exactly the problem—Air Force One was even now fairly close to the airport.

Nick reached a point roughly three feet behind Fitz and the terrorist, the two of them clumped together watching the scope like it held the secret to life. Nick supposed that at the moment it did. He raised the heavy nail gun to his shoulder, holding it exactly like he had seen hundreds of movie and television heroes hold their guns: with both hands, aiming it under his right eye with his left eye squeezed shut.

Nick fired, but as he did, the terrorist dropped to the floor and rolled. Somehow the man sensed his presence and at the last second performed an evasive maneuver more rapidly than Nick would have ever dreamed possible. Maybe Nick made some almost imperceptible noise; maybe he caused some minute change in the air currents. Maybe it was nothing more than sheer dumb luck on the part of the terrorist. Whatever it was, the man had felt him coming and reacted like a gazelle.

Vaguely aware of a *humph* noise coming from the man as he hit the thinly carpeted floor and jarred the air out of his lungs, Nick heard the heavy nail strike the screen of the radar scope located to the right of Larry. He knew then he had missed the terrorist. The scope imploded with a loud pop, and instantly the acrid metallic smell of frying electronic circuitry filled the air.

Everything was going to shit, and even worse, it was happening way too fast. Desperately trying to readjust his aim and fire another nail at the terrorist, Nick could see plainly that he was going to be too late. He felt like he was trying to maneuver under water while the other man was moving with the grace and speed of an elite athlete. Before Nick could squeeze off another shot, the man rolled over, sprang up into a shooter's crouch, and aimed his weapon at Nick. The gun was big and black and terrifying.

Nick heard a scream, and he realized it was coming from him. He barely registered Fitz diving out of the way, hitting the floor to his left, as he pulled the trigger on the nail gun before he could even take proper aim. He simply turned it in the general direction of the terrorist and squeezed, panic coursing through his body as he waited to die.

The terrorist's bullet slammed into Nick's shoulder and spun him to the floor, and as he fell, he heard another scream, a high-pitched one that he was almost certain was not coming from him. Was it Fitz? Had Fitz been hit, too? Was it possible that the terrorist had shot both of them with one bullet, or had Nick been so freaked out he had missed the sound of the man pulling the trigger on his weapon more than once?

Nick had failed. He waited for the end, for the man to put him away with a second bullet, this time between the eyes. One second passed. Another. Nothing happened. Nick realized he had squeezed his eyes tightly shut in anticipation of the kill shot that had never come.

He opened his eyes and saw the terrorist stretched out on the floor six feet away, unmoving. The man was lying flat on his back with a thick nail protruding from the middle of his forehead like the top half of an exclamation point. An inch and a half of the nail was visible under his shock of unruly black hair; the remainder was buried in his skull. Blood flowed freely and heavily from the wound, already forming a near-perfect circle around his head as it pooled on the carpet.

Nick leapt to his feet, barely noticing his own warm, sticky blood oozing down his chest and soaking his shirt. He trained the nail gun on the terrorist and approached slowly, and when he was close enough, he kicked the man's pistol out of reach. It was surprisingly heavy, and it skittered and bounced across the floor, eventually coming to rest against the back of the supervisor's console in the inner ring. The man still hadn't moved.

Somewhere in the recesses of his consciousness, Nick heard Larry keying his microphone. "Air Force One, climb *immediately* and maintain one-four thousand! I say again, max climb to fourteen thousand feet; do it now! Turn right *immediately* to a heading of one-three-zero degrees! An *immediate* right turn! Again, do it right now!"

Still focusing on the prone, unmoving body of the terrorist, Nick knelt and placed one shaking hand on the man's neck, feeling for a pulse. He was irrationally afraid that the man would do what villains in horror movies always did—grab his hand and begin fighting again. Even though he knew it only happened in Hollywood, he couldn't shake the feeling that the man's eyes would spring open and he would close one viselike hand around Nick's wrist and then somehow rise like a zombie, or like Glenn Close splashing out of the bathtub at the end of *Fatal Attraction,* and come after him again.

Nothing happened.

Nick pressed two trembling fingers to the man's neck where the carotid artery was located and where there should have been the steady throb of a pulse. He was both relieved and sickened to discover there was none. Nick Jensen, who had not so much as been involved in a fistfight in twenty-five years, had just killed a man.

In the background, Nick could hear the pilot of Air Force One shouting, "What the hell is going on down there?"

But Nick knew the pilot would be comply with the urgent instructions he had been given. He was angry but alive.

They had done it.

They had saved the president.

59

It all went down so fast that it was nearly over before Larry even realized what was happening. The radar scope to his right imploded, its surface disappearing in an impressive shower of glass into the machine's circuitry followed immediately by a sizzling noise as the components were zapped and destroyed, and his survival instinct kicked in.

He half felt, half saw a blur on his right and registered it as the terrorist diving to the floor to escape the bullets being fired by whoever had come to save them. Or maybe he had been hit by one of them; he couldn't say for sure. All Larry was certain of was that he had to get out of the line of fire—*now!*

He pivoted left and dived onto the carpeting like an Olympic swimmer hitting the pool. His left arm struck the floor and scraped across it as his body followed, skidding along the carpet and instantly raising an ugly red rash from his wrist to his shoulder. His head smashed into the floor, and for a second, he had the absurd vision of tweeting birds circling his head like they always did in cartoons when the characters fell off a cliff, got run over by a truck, or were held hostage by crazy, fanatical terrorists fighting a gun battle in the middle of someone's supposedly secure workplace.

Then his head cleared, and he struggled up onto his hands and knees, prepared to take cover behind the cops or

FBI agents or SWAT teams that had come to rescue them. He looked up and froze, his jaw nearly hitting the floor again, so unbelievable was the sight that greeted him. It was Nick, good old Futz, and he was taking on this terrorist, this professional killer, with what looked like...a nail gun.

Larry watched, openmouthed, seeing everything in what seemed like the Super Slo-Mo that the networks sometimes featured during football games. The terrorist tumbled onto his back and flipped right over his shoulder, landing on his hands and knees. It looked like something you might see in the circus. The man got up into a shooter's crouch with a speed and dexterity that Larry found almost impossible to believe, bringing his pistol to shoulder height and opening fire.

Nick went down in a heap, spinning almost one full revolution from the force of the bullet that struck him somewhere in his upper body. A gush of blood blossomed, soaking through Nick's shirt almost instantaneously.

Horrified, Larry watched as Nick fell to the floor, and then he turned his head to see who the terrorist was going to finish off first. What he saw he almost could not believe. The terrorist lay on his back on the floor, a shiny silver nail protruding from his forehead.

Somehow Nick had managed to fire a nail—a fucking nail!—dead center into the man's head as he had been preparing to kill them both. The man remained unmoving as Nick leapt off the floor, walked over to him, and kicked his gun away.

Larry only then remembered Air Force One and rushed to his handset, frantically calling off the approach of the Boeing 747 and telling the flight crew to climb and turn as rapidly as possible. The next few minutes were a blur as he called Boston Center and handed the president's airplane off to them. He didn't realize he was shouting into the landline until he terminated the call. The poor controller at Boston Center probably thought he was dealing with a raving lunatic. At that point, maybe he was.

Air Force One and President Cartwright would be returning to Andrews Air Force Base. There would be no ceremony in Boston today. The crew had filed no flight plan to return to Andrews, but that was Boston Center's problem. They could clear Air Force One to its destination and give the flight whatever route they chose; at least the pilot would be alive to fly it.

After that, working almost in a daze, Larry called the controllers inside Logan Tower and told them that Boston TRACON was not accepting any traffic; they were closed and out of business until someone much higher up in the FAA food chain than he could decide how to proceed from here. One thing Larry knew for sure was that he was in no condition to separate airplanes. Neither was Ron or Nick, who was bleeding from the shoulder where he had been shot.

Larry looked at Nick, who was grimly shoving the terrorist's pistol into the waistband of his jeans, and suddenly remembered that this man lying on the floor had not been working alone; this nightmare wasn't over yet.

"This guy's dead," Nick muttered hollowly.

Larry didn't answer because there was nothing to say.

Nick fished a small handgun out of an ankle holster just above the terrorist's combat boot and handed it to Larry. "If any more of these fuckers come waltzing through the door, send them straight to hell. Don't forget to take off the safety."

Larry couldn't believe this was Nick, the man he had known and worked with for so long. He seemed more like Rambo. Only skinnier and a lot paler.

"You've been shot," Larry said, shoving the gun into his waistband like Nick had done. It was a stupid thing to say. Undoubtedly Nick knew he had been shot; the leaking blood was a dead giveaway. The pain undoubtedly was, too.

"I'm fine," he replied, shaking his head slowly, although he was clearly not fine. "I'm going to see if I can find the other guys and maybe take them by surprise. You cut Ron free and call the cavalry—start with the FBI and Secret Service. Don't forget to notify facility management when you can. I've got a real bad feeling about Don Trent and Dean Winters."

Larry nodded. Even now, the speed with which everything had happened was hard to conceive of. "Good luck."

Nick gave him a quick, distracted smile and dragged himself to the front entrance of the ops room, dripping blood onto the floor behind him. He opened the door, glancing left and right, then disappeared into the hallway.

60

The first thing Kristin became aware of as she willed herself slowly back from the murky depths of unconsciousness was the pain. It started out as a vague throbbing, a notion of extreme discomfort that her body recognized was a problem before her conscious mind did. She struggled like a drowning person to break through the surface and regain consciousness, and as soon as she did, the full agony of her shattered right knee struck her with the force of a speeding freight train.

She gasped as the nerves in and around her knee screamed at her. It felt like someone was holding an exposed live wire against her leg, the electric current pulsing and blasting. Or perhaps like someone was firing bullet after bullet into the knee, mercilessly holding down the trigger of a lethal weapon with a limitless supply of ammunition.

A wave of nausea rolled over Kristin, and she swallowed hard, holding her breath, knowing that if she threw up, the retching action would jar her leg and the pain would escalate exponentially. She couldn't imagine how it could get any worse but didn't want to find out. Misshapen black clouds roiled at the edges of her vision as her brain threatened to shut down again. Kristin longed for the relief that passing out would bring but feared that she would never reawaken if she gave in this time.

Struggling to focus as the black clouds sent scouting

parties of small dots blooming across her line of sight, Kristin concentrated on the tiny flecks of gold scattered throughout the wine-colored carpet. They were easy to see from her vantage point, lying on the floor of the BCT conference room in exactly the same spot where she had been shot.

Grudgingly—and probably temporarily—the black clouds receded, and her vision improved to where Kristin felt she could move her head and look around without sending herself right back into unconsciousness.

She turned her head gingerly, wondering if that motion, seemingly unrelated in any way to her knee, would cause the pain level to shoot up again. It didn't. She looked around the room and spotted a man in combat boots pacing from the west door to the east door and back again.

The other guy was seated at the head of the conference table. What he was doing, Kristin could not tell. This terrorist seemed much less sure of himself than the man who had shot her. He might simply be awaiting instructions, since he didn't strike her as the type who would take a lot of initiative. She found it odd that neither of them had gone back outside to the security building at the front gate to deal with any early-arriving employees.

The thought crossed her mind that perhaps these men were not concerned about arriving employees because they expected to finish whatever they were planning and be long gone before any of them began arriving. That meant they would be exiting the building soon but undoubtedly not before slaughtering anyone still alive. It didn't seem likely they would want to leave any witnesses. She shuddered, and a bright flash of pain seared up and down her leg.

Kristin tried to force her brain to work, but her thoughts were muddled and slow. It was a Sunday morning, so no administrative or support personnel would be working today, but still, a full complement of controllers and technicians would arrive soon to start their eight-hour tours of duty. Dozens of people could potentially lose their lives if these gun-wielding terrorists were still in the building when they got here. On the other hand, if the terrorists had departed by then, it would mean the president was dead, not to mention Kristin herself. She had to figure out a way to stop these people.

Her service weapon had been taken away, and she had no doubt that the man who shot her in the knee had checked her over for other weapons. Undoubtedly the backup revolver she always carried strapped to her ankle was long gone. Even if it wasn't, how did she expect to access it? Pulling the gun out of its holster would require sitting up and bending her knee slightly, something she knew she could not accomplish without forcing a new wave of fire through the ruined limb. She was certain that just the attempt would send her crashing back into unconsciousness, maybe for good.

She eased her head back and was amazed to catch sight of her 9mm Glock. Was this really possible? Or was it some bizarre, pain-induced hallucination? Kristin closed her eyes and forced herself to get past the searing pain in her leg and concentrate on the task at hand. When she reopened her eyes, the gun was still there, not six feet away, tossed carelessly into the corner of the room by the door.

Clearly the men holding her had assumed she would not regain consciousness. Maybe they even thought she was dead; Kristin had no idea how much attention they had paid to her after she collapsed.

Something else was clear, too: the men weren't watching her very carefully now.

It was time for a little experiment. Gritting her teeth, Kristin planted her elbows into the plush carpet with as much force as she could muster given her awkward position on the floor. She was terrified that the man on the other side of the room would see her and open fire again. If he did, he would surely kill her this time. The terrorists didn't need her any longer; there was nothing to stop him from doing exactly that. The fact that she was obscured from his vision by the long conference table did little to quell her rising hysteria.

Still, she knew that giving up and lying on the floor like a victim—something she refused to be—would only serve to get her, and probably many other people, killed. Because of her weakness, the president was already dead or would be soon; she could not bear the thought of dying without at least trying to take one of these bastards with her.

She had to do something.

The thick carpet fibers provided at least a measure of traction under her elbows, but Kristin was unsure whether it would be enough to allow her to drag her body along the floor. There was only one way to find out. She bit her lip in hopes of preventing herself from crying out when the inevitable wave of pain struck, clamping down with such force she drew blood.

She dragged her body forward a couple of inches, and the invisible man firing the flamethrower at her leg ratcheted up the weapon until the blast furnace agony constituted her entire existence. The black clouds loitering at the edge of her vision blossomed like out-of-control thunderheads, growing with a speed and intensity she could scarcely comprehend.

She felt the acidic burn of the coffee she drank earlier this morning as it rushed up her throat, and she puked all over the carpet. Her head smashed down on the floor, and a bright new blossom of pain confirmed for Kristin that she had just broken her nose. She let out an involuntary gasp that was choked off as her consciousness slipped away.

61

Nick wrapped his sweaty hand around the grip of the semiautomatic pistol he had taken off the dead terrorist. The weapon felt bulky and heavy, frighteningly lethal. It seemed as though he could feel the gun's deadly power radiating from it like a physical presence. It was a power he did not want and a presence he feared.

His shoulder throbbed and burned from the gunshot wound. At the time, he had barely registered the impact of the bullet; his entire focus had been on swinging that heavy nail gun around and getting off another desperate shot before being taken down for good by the terrorist.

He had been aware, of course, that he was shot—how do you miss something like that?—but between adrenaline and sheer terror, Nick had been temporarily able to compartmentalize his body's response to the physical trauma.

Now, however, as he crouched at the top of the wide staircase leading to the ground level foyer, he wondered how badly he had been injured. He wasn't sure he really wanted to know.

The initial gush of blood had slowed to a thick but constant dribble. That was the good news. The bad news was that it was next to impossible for Nick to raise his left hand above his waist, and he was feeling weak and faint. He knew he was slipping into shock and hoped he would be able to find the strength necessary to see this nightmare through, however it was to end.

From his vantage point, he could see most of the glass-fronted conference room on the first floor known as the fishbowl. The room was located diagonally across the wide foyer from the staircase, and the gigantic windows that made it such a convenient spot for the terrorists to monitor the front entrance made it just as easy for Nick to monitor them.

Inside the fishbowl, two men dressed in camouflage fatigues and combat boots restlessly cooled their heels. No sooner did one check his watch than the other would mimic him exactly. It was clear they knew Air Force One should be getting blown out of the sky anytime now and were apparently awaiting notification from the dead guy in the TRACON that their mission had been accomplished.

There was no way of knowing whether these two men were the only terrorists still inside the BCT. Nick fervently hoped there were no others, because the thought of another gunman coming up behind him and shooting him in the back of the head was horrifying.

Something else inside the fishbowl grabbed his attention. Across the room from the two anxious terrorists, a young woman lay motionless on the floor. Nick could not be certain from this angle, but he thought she looked an awful lot like the FBI agent who had come to his house last week to discuss the binder of information he had found hidden amongst Lisa's things in their closet.

Special Agent Kristin Cunningham.

He wondered if she was dead. As he watched, though, the downed agent appeared to move her arms, just a little and for only a second. It looked as though she was attempting to drag herself forward. She tried to lift her head; then it slammed down to the carpeting and she was still.

Add that scary sight to the list of reasons why I've got to do something—and fast, Nick thought. He may have just watched that young FBI agent die. But even if she was still alive, it was clear she wouldn't be for very much longer.

The problem was he couldn't imagine how he was going to go up against two terrorists—neither of whom was as distracted as the guy in the radar room had been—and have any chance of taking them down.

On the bright side, he finally had a real weapon to rely on as opposed to a rechargeable pneumatic power tool, but the other side of that particular coin was that he had never fired a handgun in his life and had no clue whether he could actually hit anything with it.

Didn't matter. By now Larry would certainly have notified the authorities. Undoubtedly the cavalry would be arriving en masse in just a few minutes, which normally would be a good thing.

But Nick had no doubt that every exit had been disabled by the terrorists, meaning that the only way into the building was via the front door—the entrance that the two heavily armed terrorists were currently covering from their spot in the fishbowl. A protracted standoff would be inevitable after the first responders got cut down in a hail of bullets.

Plus, there was no way of knowing whether these lunatics had booby-trapped the entrance with explosives. Maybe the entryway would blow sky-high as soon as the good guys tried to storm the BCT. For that matter, who was to say the whole building wasn't rigged to explode at any moment? Who really knew *what* these guys were thinking?

So there was no benefit in crouching up here at the top of the stairs, waiting for help to arrive and for someone else to handle the situation. Nick decided he must be completely out of his mind, because he had just talked himself into another armed confrontation, his second in a matter of minutes.

But how should he approach it? He thought about trying to pick the two men off from here, only to quickly discard that idea. He was easily sixty feet away and would be shooting at a downward angle through thick plate glass with a handgun. A weapon he had never fired before. The odds of hitting anything under those circumstances were infinitesimal, and that was for someone who knew what he was doing. Hell, from up here there was just as good a chance he would end up shooting Agent Cunningham as either of the two men he was aiming at.

Even if he hit one of them, the other guy would have ample time to take cover, and then they were back to the drawing board—a standoff that would likely cost the FBI agent her life.

Nick shuddered involuntarily, the sudden motion sending a wake-up call through his injured shoulder. *How appropriate. I get shot, and I actually get a shooting pain at the site of the injury.*

He chuckled and the pain intensified.

Sweat rolled down his face and he felt queasy.

His vision blurred and then cleared.

He got off his knees and moved carefully along the catwalk suspended high above the foyer and the fishbowl below.

62

Nearly fifteen minutes had elapsed since Joe-Bob answered the call from Tony at the BCT, telling him Air Force One would be within missile range inside of ten minutes. When the call came in, he and Dimitrios scrambled into the back of the truck and made final preparations, readying the Stinger to fire the shot that would make history.

Ninety seconds after that they were ready. Since then they had stood, tense and silent, in the Dakota's cargo bed, waiting to get a visual on the Boeing 747 carrying President Cartwright and his staff. The plane would lumber overhead as it approached the airport, flying low and slow in preparation for landing, making it an inviting target that was nearly impossible to miss. It would be like shooting fish in a barrel.

Joe-Bob was strapped in, harnessed to the homemade support rigging the group had fashioned out of scrap iron, steel, and nylon netting when the plane came into view. Its landing lights were shining brightly in the southeast sky as it popped suddenly out of the bases of the clouds, appearing in a completely different location than he and Dimitrios had seen the arrivals show up all night. There was no question about it; this was the right airplane. This was Air Force One.

Joe-Bob and Dimitrios watched the plane approach with mounting excitement. It seemed to hang unmoving in the sky, a trick of perspective caused by the fact that it was flying so slowly and directly toward them.

The plan was for Joe-Bob to wait as long as possible before firing the shot that would take down the leader of the free world, ideally pulling the trigger when the jumbo jet was maybe a quarter mile away, slightly to the side and still approaching. The Stinger would then take a path straight into the belly of the behemoth, impacting the airplane before the sophisticated countermeasures built into Air Force One could do more than perhaps sound an alarm on the flight deck. The crew would know they were about to get hit but would be unable to do anything to avoid it.

The tension was palpable. Joe-Bob tried to calm his nerves and slow his breathing, glancing to the north over the Atlantic Ocean where the airplanes had been descending all night long. The sky was devoid of any landing lights. Either there was no other traffic destined for Boston this early in the morning, or the controllers had stopped all the other airplanes in anticipation of the president's arrival. Joe-Bob didn't know which it was and didn't care.

He turned his attention back toward the three bright yellow lights in the sky, expecting to see that they had grown a bit in size as the Boeing 747 approached.

He gasped.

The lights had disappeared. Scanning frantically from the horizon upward, Joe-Bob finally spotted a single strobe. He spat a curse. Air Force One was banking sharply east in a steep climb, gaining speed and altitude, already in a position that made it virtually impossible to hit with the Stinger.

What the hell had happened? He had diverted his attention for only a few seconds, and in that time, the crew flying the airplane must have been alerted to the danger that awaited them below. Air Force One was clearly climbing up and away, perhaps leaving Boston entirely but definitely climbing out of danger.

Joe-Bob cursed again and smashed his fist into the brace that had been meant to provide support for the missile shot that would make history. All their planning had gone to waste in the blink of an eye. Tony was going to be pissed. Joe-Bob watched as the strobe from the retreating Air Force One, already difficult to see, faded into the grey shroud of gradually brightening sky northeast of Boston and disappeared. His fist was throbbing, and he wondered absently how many knuckles he had just broken.

"Help me out of this fucking harness," Joe-Bob snarled to Dimitrios, who was still staring at the spot where they had last seen Air Force One as if perhaps the plane was going to suddenly reappear. But they had already missed their chance, and Joe-Bob was determined to find out why.

Within seconds he disentangled himself from the support harness and yanked his cell phone out of his pocket. He punched the only number stored in the memory of the disposable phone and waited for the call to go through to Tony, the man who had come up with this "perfect plan" and who had convinced him and the rest of the group that they could change the world.

He held the phone to his ear and waited. Nothing. Tony wasn't answering, which could mean only one thing—somehow the entire plan had unraveled within the last few minutes and Tony was dead. Killing him was the only way he could have been stopped because he certainly would not have given up now, not when he was literally seconds away from achieving his goal.

Joe-Bob looked at Dimitrios, who was staring back at him with almost comically wide eyes. At that moment Dimitrios looked like a scared little kid. Joe-Bob flipped his phone shut and said, "We've got to get out of here. Right now."

"What are you talking about? What about shooting down the plane?"

"The fucking plane is gone, you moron! And if it's gone, it's not coming back. Something has gone seriously wrong. Tony's not answering his phone, and the only explanation for why he wouldn't pick up is that everything's gone to shit. If that's the case, how long do you think it'll be before the cops find us and we take the fall for this whole cluster fuck?"

Dimitrios shrugged. "I don't know. Soon, I guess." He still didn't seem to grasp the significance of what had just happened. Or maybe he was even dumber than Joe-Bob had thought.

"You're damn right it will be soon, and in case you've forgotten, there's a Jeep sitting sixty feet away right now with a dead guy *you* helped kill inside it."

"I didn't kill anybody," Dimitrios protested.

"Bullshit," Joe-Bob replied. "You were right here, and you're just as guilty as I am. You're a fucking *accomplice to murder*. If you want to avoid spending the rest of your life behind bars or maybe even taking a lethal injection, you had better get in this goddamn truck right now, because if you don't, I'm leaving without you."

"What about Tony?"

"Fuck Tony. If he survives, which I doubt, he'll make his way back to D.C. when he can, and we'll meet up with him there. I hope he does, because I'd love to kick his sorry ass all over the East Coast about now. In the meantime, though, we've got to worry about our own sorry asses. It's going to be daylight soon, and we can't hang around this frigging mud puddle much longer."

Joe-Bob tossed the still assembled Stinger into the cargo bed of the pickup, where it landed with a crash. Then he leapt over the side, landing in the watery mud with a splash that peppered the side of the already filthy vehicle. The two men clambered into the Dakota, and Joe-Bob fired it up, four-wheeling to the road, the slipping, sliding tires spraying dirty water and brownish vegetation in all directions.

They hit Ocean Drive at thirty miles per hour and turned south, tires screeching, planning to head straight to Interstate 95. Tony big plan had turned to shit, but they were still alive and still free, and Joe-Bob aimed to keep it that way.

63

There was almost no chance of Nick being spotted by the men pacing anxiously back and forth inside the fishbowl. For one thing, their focus was on the BCT entrance exactly opposite the second-floor catwalk. And for another, the walkway holding Nick had been constructed with four-foot-high walls of the same blond wood panels used on all the interior walls in the foyer and the office areas.

The very bottom portion of the wall on either side of the catwalk consisted of a one-foot-high steel mesh screen running the length of it underneath the wood solid panels. That mesh, which allowed an astute observer to see the feet of anyone crossing the walkway even if they had ducked under the protection of the panels, constituted the only possible vulnerability. Nick decided he was willing to take that minimal risk. The terrorists were unlikely to suddenly crane their necks and peer across the lobby toward the second floor for no reason, especially while so preoccupied with other issues.

At least that was Nick's fervent hope.

In the end, he had no other choice, since it was imperative that he get to the south side of the building, where the fishbowl was located. Nick scuttled along the catwalk, drawing no gunfire and no apparent notice from below. The far end of the walkway was almost directly above the east wall of the fishbowl, meaning any risk of being seen by the men downstairs vanished as he disappeared from view into the corridor leading to the administrative wing.

After passing the restrooms on the left side of the hallway, Nick opened a heavy steel door at the southeasternmost corner of the building, turning left at the point where the corridor went right, and disappearing into a stairwell identical to the one he had climbed up thirty minutes ago in his failed attempt to confuse the terrorist in the radar room by reconfiguring the radar scopes inside the ETG lab.

He moved quickly now. He felt increasingly woozy and faint as the pain from the gunshot wound in his shoulder came and went in sickening waves. His blood-soaked T-shirt stuck to his chest and back, and he shivered violently. If he didn't complete his task soon, he might simply pass out and collapse where he stood.

At the bottom of the stairwell, Nick paused and cracked the door a couple of inches, peering out into the first-floor nest of offices that housed the BCT big shots. None of these empty offices concerned Nick. Their doors were all closed and presumably locked. He stood in the doorway and focused on the short hallway to the right. This corridor led to the foyer and was located under the catwalk he had just crossed to reach the stairwell. The end of the fifteen-foot corridor on the left made up the east wall of the fishbowl.

The fishbowl was wide open on the side facing the foyer, allowing the armed men a virtually unobstructed view of the main entrance to the BCT as well as of the entire foyer.

What the fishbowl didn't provide for the terrorists, however, was a window on any of the other three sides, including the east side, where Nick was now creeping along the hallway with his back against the wall. He paused at a gigantic support pillar just outside the conference room's east entrance. The pillar ran from the floor of the foyer to the ceiling of the BCT, towering three stories above. Its circumference was easily three feet and provided perfect cover. Nick leaned against it, trying to catch his breath.

He was still shaking violently, and every time he did, more of the lightning bolts of pain ripped through his shoulder and down his left arm, which was now almost totally useless and hanging limply at his side. He was sweating profusely but nevertheless felt freezing cold, like someone had turned the building's thermostat down to twenty degrees.

A few feet away, on the other side of the pillar and through the door, were the two men Nick needed to neutralize. He squeezed the terrorist's gun in his right hand.

These men knew what time Air Force One was supposed to have arrived at Logan Airport; therefore, they would know that their missile should have knocked the Boeing 747 out of the sky by now. Nick was afraid that one or both of them would leave the conference room at any moment to check on the progress of their operation, although with their seemingly extensive knowledge of the facility, he figured there was a good chance they would just call the ops room extension.

He guessed they hadn't done so yet. If they had, it stood to reason that at least one of them would have sprinted upstairs immediately when the call was answered by Larry or Ron rather than by their fellow lunatic. Nick shuddered to think what would happen then. Even though Fitz was armed with the dead terrorist's backup weapon, he figured the two controllers in the ops room would be no match for either of these men in a shoot-out, particularly given the ordeal they had just gone through.

Of course, neither would he, but he did his best to push that disturbing thought to the back of his mind as he rested against the support pillar and tried to decide how to proceed from here.

64

Officer Ray Reid rolled slowly down Ocean Drive in Hull, Massachusetts, on routine patrol. Working the overnight shift for the Hull Police Department wasn't exactly what he had envisioned himself doing after mustering out of the Army, where he had served two tours of duty as an MP in Iraq, but what the hell. At least he had a job, which was more than a lot of guys who had spent time in the godforsaken blast furnace of the Middle East could say, and as an added bonus he was actually doing what he wanted to do: earning a living in the field of law enforcement.

So even though he would much rather have been sleeping in the arms of his wife, Melissa, getting up in the middle of the night to change their daughter Margaret's diaper for the third or fourth time, Ray wasn't about to complain. He would spend a couple of years building his résumé here, then move on to a better job somewhere else, maybe in a bigger town, maybe with the Staties, or maybe he would even try to catch on with the FBI.

That was all in the future, though. For now, Ray was a small-town cop, and that was good enough for him. For as long as he could remember, his goal had been to serve as a peace officer. As a little boy he had become enthralled with the sharply creased dark blue uniform police officers wore, the shiny black sidearm that dangled on their hips, and the way everyone seemed to treat them with awe and respect and maybe even a little bit of fear.

He was a good cop, too. He didn't push people around and try to intimidate regular citizens like some of the guys he knew, who seemed to be drawn to the job because they wanted the chance to swagger and bust people over the head with their nightsticks. Not that he wouldn't do exactly that if necessary. But Ray wanted to help people, plain and simple. And at six foot three, two hundred sixty pounds, Ray Reid was physically imposing enough that he rarely needed more than his considerable bulk to convince obstinate people that his way was the right way.

The sky was beginning to lighten over the water, gradually changing from pitch-black to a fuzzy gunmetal grey, as he maneuvered his cruiser down the deserted thoroughfare. This was one of Ray's favorite places in the world, and he liked to patrol it close to the end of his shift whenever possible. If he rolled his window down and really listened carefully, he felt he could almost hear the waves lapping against the shore, which was impossible at this distance but still a pleasant thought.

His shift ended in less than two hours. Melissa wouldn't be up yet unless Margaret was being unusually fussy, so there was no reason to rush home. Maybe he would stop at the diner downtown for an omelet before going home to bed, and then there would be no question about being able to sleep. With a full stomach, Ray would be out like a light for hours.

He was trying to decide whether to risk a cup of coffee with his omelet. Would it keep him awake and defeat the point of eating in the first place? Lost in his reverie, Ray started in surprise as an old Dodge Dakota, dented and caked in mud, barreled out of the marsh and shot onto the road about forty feet ahead of him. The truck roared off toward the center of Hull, tires squealing and mud flying off the undercarriage.

Ray blinked, almost unable to believe what he was seeing. What the hell these idiots had been doing out in the flats at this time of the early morning he didn't know, but it was pretty clear what they were doing now—driving recklessly. He flipped the switch on his dashboard, illuminating the flashing blue light bar on the roof, and goosed the big engine.

As he sped down Ocean Drive, Ray radioed dispatch of his location and that he was in pursuit of a speeding truck. It was obvious to him that the people inside the Dakota were trying to run, only pulling to the side of the road when it became clear their vehicle, while perfectly suited for mucking around in the marshy flats, was no match in power or speed for the Hull PD cruiser rapidly gaining on them.

After the truck pulled to the side of the road, emergency hazard lights dutifully flashing, Ray followed procedure, calling the plates in to the dispatcher but being told, as he had known he would, that there would be a delay in getting any information back regarding the Virginia tags on the truck. Sometimes information moved slowly in a small police department.

Ray sighed and stepped out of his cruiser. Moving with routine caution but not too much concern, he had gotten almost all the way to the truck's window, sticking close to the side of the vehicle to present as small a target as possible in the event something went wrong, when he saw someone lean way out of the window and turn to face him. It was a man, and a wooden smile was plastered on his face as he looked at the approaching officer. The smile stopped well short of the man's eyes.

Ray instinctively knew that something was wrong. He hadn't survived two tours in Iraq by wandering blindly into danger, and he stopped in his tracks, freezing a second too late as the driver held out a semiautomatic pistol. As Ray dropped into a crouch and attempted to draw his service weapon, the man fired three shots in rapid succession, two of them hitting Ray and slamming him to the cold pavement.

The driver's head disappeared into the vehicle, and seconds later the old Dakota took off again, black smoke rising from its tires, peppering Ray with gravel and dirt. He thought of Iraq and the absurdity of the notion that he had survived that madhouse only to be gunned down in the tiny town of Hull, Massachusetts, where nothing ever happened to anyone, especially not to police officers patrolling the streets in the wee hours of a Sunday morning.

Operating on adrenaline and instinct, not even feeling any pain yet, although he knew that was coming, Ray shielded his face with his hands, protecting it from the worst of the flying debris. Then he opened fire on the rapidly retreating truck. He knew he was injured, maybe badly, but in those first few moments, he could think of nothing besides returning fire. He grunted in satisfaction as one of his shots blew out the fat left rear tire of the pickup, then he watched it careen off the road and back into the marsh.

The Dakota landed with a loud muddy splash, steam rising from the engine compartment as the hot motor impacted the dirty standing water.

Ray keyed the mike pinned to his collar, advising dispatcher Amanda Lewis that he had been shot and needed immediate assistance, all without taking his eyes off the disabled truck.

He was pretty sure he had seen at least one other occupant inside the vehicle besides the driver, and he figured that the men inside would be attempting to flee any second now. Whatever they had been up to, it was serious enough that they were willing to shoot a police officer to facilitate their escape, so they certainly wouldn't be waiting docilely inside their vehicle for even more cops to arrive.

It didn't take long. Both doors in the Dakota flew open at the same time, and a man tumbled out of each. They hit the muddy ground running as fast as possible given the lack of traction, using the bulk of the truck as a barrier so that Ray was unable to manage a clear shot at either of them. This meant they were headed deeper into the marsh and away from the road and their only viable escape route, so after about a hundred feet, both men made a sharp turn and splashed back toward Ocean Drive.

By now they were too far away for Ray to have any reasonable expectation of hitting either of them, so he simply held his fire, cursing like the ex-Army grunt he was and feeling weaker by the second. He knew help would arrive soon; Hull was a small town, area wise as well as in terms of population, so it wouldn't take long for John McDonald in Cruiser Two to come screaming up Ocean Drive. He crawled to the gravel shoulder of the road and waited.

Ray hoped the ambulance wouldn't be too far behind John. He thought about his beautiful Melissa and little baby Margaret and prayed that Mel wouldn't freak out too badly when she heard he had been shot. Maybe he could get treated at the hospital on an outpatient basis and go home before she ever woke up; she would still be pissed, but at least she wouldn't worry. He pictured her face as he slipped into unconsciousness, the darkness overwhelming him as the dim wail of approaching sirens sounded in the distance.

65

Brian sat at the head of the conference room table and wondered how badly all of this was going to end. They had killed half a dozen or so people already—he had lost track of the exact number—and by now the total probably included the president, not to mention everyone else aboard the president's airplane. He tried to imagine how many people that might be. Fifteen? Twenty? He had no clue.

Brian knew that Tony had planned an escape, but he had expected all along that they would die in this operation, regardless of how it turned out. It just didn't seem possible to Brian that they could manage to assassinate a sitting U.S. president and escape with their lives. They were never going to get out of this building, and if they did, the five of them would be hunted relentlessly until they were all either captured or killed, most likely the latter.

He didn't care about dying. He didn't have anything to live for, anyway. He felt kind of bad about the FBI chick lying on the floor, moaning occasionally as the life slipped out of her, but he couldn't say anything to that bastard Jackie. He knew Jackie didn't care if she lived or died. In fact, he undoubtedly preferred that she die so there would be one less witness to worry about. He was probably going to kill her soon anyway if she kept gasping and groaning.

The way Brian saw it, Jackie was just one stress-triggering

event away from snapping and killing everyone around him. Brian had no difficulty whatsoever picturing Jackie as one of those crazy fuckers who goes into his old high school armed with a couple of automatic rifles, taking out as many people as possible before turning the gun on himself.

But even though Brian knew he was probably not going to make it out of here alive, he still didn't want to tempt fate by suggesting they try to save that tiny young woman bleeding out a few feet away.

Looking up at Jackie, who was still pacing back and forth, wearing a pathway in the carpet like he thought he was General Patton or something, Brian said, "How long should we wait before calling Tony? It should be all over by now—don't you think? Shouldn't we be getting the fuck out of Dodge?"

Jackie jumped, almost as if he had forgotten Brian was still in the room.

If that was the case, Brian wished he had not spoken at all, since he had no desire to remind Jackie of his presence. It looked like his partner was pondering the question, like Brian had asked him the meaning of life or his recipe for Kung Pao chicken or something. Smoke from his cigarette wreathed his head in an indistinct halo, which Brian found ironic because Jackie was about as far removed from an angel as you could get.

"Yeah, probably," he answered and continued pacing.

Brian wondered if Jackie had taken speed or something. It sure looked like he had. Or maybe he had just gone so far around the bend that he couldn't sit still or else the voices in his head would get to him. Brian chuckled, but the sound died in his throat when he saw the black look Jackie leveled at him. For just a second, he had the insane notion that Jackie knew what he was thinking.

Brian reached for the telephone to call Tony, and that was when all hell broke loose.

66

Nick was more tired than he had ever felt in his entire life. Hell, exhausted was more like it. He wondered if he had suffered nerve damage because his left shoulder throbbed continuously where he had been shot and every now and then sent a sharp zing of tightly focused pain racing down his arm and into his hand, which was by now hanging limply at his side, useless. He was freezing and couldn't stop shaking and felt like he might hurl at any moment. Time to proceed.

He was crouched in the tiny space between the thick, circular support pillar and the open door on the east side of the fishbowl. Nick had been watching for a few minutes from here, and it was clear that something was going to happen soon. The two terrorists—one seated at the head of the conference table with his back to Nick, the other pacing restlessly—were in the middle of a terse conversation.

Nick kept a constant eye on Special Agent Cunningham, who appeared to be unconscious but still clinging to life. She had let out a low moan once or twice, and Nick was actually close enough to her to see her eyelids twitch. It looked like she was dreaming or perhaps trying to wake herself up.

He realized he needed to get help for her immediately. The man sitting at the table glanced at the agent occasionally but was doing nothing to help her, and the other one paid no attention to her at all, not even when she moaned. It was as if she didn't even exist to him.

Nick knew he had zero chance of catching these two terrorists off guard, especially with one of them walking back and forth, turning to face Nick every few seconds. Still, he had to try. What other choice did he have?

He needed a diversion, something that would buy him an extra second or two, enough time to get two accurate shots away—one per terrorist—before he got his head blown off by one of the men. With his left arm and hand useless, Nick was forced to set his gun on the floor to fish out his key ring. He felt terribly exposed while he did so, but he couldn't think of any other reasonable method of creating the diversion he needed.

Reaching into his pocket, Nick withdrew his car keys, careful to keep his fist wrapped around them so they wouldn't jingle and give his position away. Along with the key to his car, the ring contained two house keys and the key to Lisa's car. Her car was now a total loss, impounded by the police following the accident, but Nick had been unable to get rid of the key. Keeping it was pointless and stupid, but tossing it would be like throwing one more piece of his dead wife away, and he was not prepared to do that.

In addition to the four keys, the ring contained a souvenir one dollar gaming token from one of the casinos the couple had visited on their honeymoon in Las Vegas five years ago, as well as a bronze medallion Lisa had given him for Christmas three years ago that was supposed to keep him safe under any circumstance. Nick had laughed like it was the most ridiculous thing he ever heard, but he had never been without it since that day. Now he wished Lisa had bought one for herself.

Hefting the key ring in his hand, Nick decided it was not quite as heavy as he would have liked, but it would have to do the trick. It wasn't like he had a lot of other options.

He lifted the handgun off the floor and placed it in his left hand, wincing as the muscles in his arm spasmed from the effort it took to wrap his hand around the black matte grip.

The throbbing intensified, and Nick could hear a faraway roaring sound in his ears. Slowly he rose from his crouching position until he was standing fully erect behind the corner of the open door. His knees cracked and he froze, praying neither of the men heard the noise, which sounded as loud as a thunderclap to him.

Nick held his breath and waited for the surprised shouts from inside the fishbowl that would tell him he had been spotted, followed immediately by the automatic rifle fire that would rip his body to shreds.

When it became obvious that his position was not compromised, he placed his eyes squarely against the inch-and-a-half opening between the hinged edge of the open door and the jamb. The terrorist sitting at the conference table would pose no immediate threat—his back was to Nick—but the other one continued to pace like a caged lion. Nick knew he had to time it perfectly, waiting to act until the man turned to march in the opposite direction. Nick figured this would give him maybe three seconds to clear the door and take down the two men. Maybe. If everything went according to plan.

For the third time this morning, Nick said a quick prayer to whatever gods were supposed to protect people locked in a life-and-death struggle with armed revolutionaries.

When the terrorist turned to start pacing in the other direction, Nick rushed into the fishbowl. He took one giant step forward and then flung his key ring as hard as he could at the opposite wall.

67

Shudders racked Kristin's body, rousing her reluctantly from her state of unconsciousness. The first thing she noticed was the pain in her mangled leg. She hadn't thought it could get any worse, but she had been wrong. White-hot agony constituted her entire existence and was now joined by a traveling companion—the relatively pedestrian pain of a broken nose. Dried blood crusted her face, and every pulse beat caused her nose to throb in perfect timing with her ruined knee.

Her head was resting on the floor facing left, and at that angle she could see the combat boots of the man who had shot her. He was walking back and forth on the far side of the long conference table and talking to the other man, who was seated at the table behind her. She wondered how long she had been out and decided that it must not have been too long if they were still here.

The two terrorists were trying to decide whether to call upstairs to the radar room. They wanted to know whether Air Force One had been blown out of the sky yet, which meant there was at least the slimmest possibility that it had not. The president might still be alive. Kristin knew this would be her last chance to try to save him.

She twisted her head in the other direction, ignoring the pain in her broken nose, and searched along the base of the wall fronting the foyer, finding what she was looking for on the carpet by the door. Her stomach clenched as she thought about trying to move, remembering the debilitating pain that had ripped through her body the last time she attempted it, a pain so strong she had vomited and then passed out. She could still taste the sour puke in her mouth.

Kristin knew the terrorist pacing on the far side of the table could not see her. The angle was wrong; the table blocked his view. The other man she was not so sure about. It was entirely possible that he *could* see her, but from the intensity of the conversation and the fact that she was so gravely injured, Kristin felt the chances were fairly good that they had forgotten all about her. They no longer considered her a threat, if they ever had.

Once again, Kristin planted her elbows into the plush carpeting and prepared to move. This time she knew what to expect, so hopefully she could steel herself against the onslaught of pain. She closed her eyes tightly, preparing to fight off the roiling black clouds that were even now threatening to impinge on her vision and drag her down into unconsciousness again.

She had to stay conscious. If Kristin passed out this time, she would never wake up again. She didn't know how she knew this, only that she did. When she reopened her eyes, she discovered that the clouds had diminished a bit.

It was time. Kristin balled her hands into fists, digging her fingernails into her palms until they threatened to draw blood, and dragged herself forward. One inch. Two.

She was still awake, although between the fire coursing through her leg and the sharp pain in her throbbing nose she felt as though she would get sick again at any moment. The terrorists didn't seem to have noticed her yet. She kept going. Another inch. Her useless leg dragged behind her, trailing drying blood along the carpet. She felt woozy and ill. She gritted her teeth and kept going.

68

Brian reached for the telephone on the conference table. It was amazing how many phones were inside this building. In this small conference room alone there were two. He had tried to figure out approximately how many telephones the building contained while sitting here bored out of his mind and discovered he couldn't even hazard a guess. It was a lot; that was for sure.

Jackie was still doing his goddamned marching drill, and it was driving Brian crazy. He couldn't wait for Tony to tell him that the guys were finished down at Logan Airport so they could make their escape. Brian had to admit it was starting to look like maybe they would actually get out of here alive, but either way, at least he wouldn't have to put up with that lunatic Jackie anymore.

Brian picked up the phone, and as he did, a jangling silver blur whizzed past his head a couple of inches to his right. It smashed into a strange-looking modern art print hung on the far wall with a metallic crash, making him jump and cringe. He dropped the phone in surprise, and it bounced off the polished surface of the long table and fell to the floor.

Jackie ducked and spun around to face the threat, sliding the rifle off his shoulder where it hung from a leather strap. The cigarette dropped out of his mouth and fell to the floor. Instantly it began smoldering on the flame-resistant carpet.

Thick black smoke of surprising intensity started to fill the room.

For one second everything was still; then the sudden silence was broken by the unmistakable staccato bark of a pistol shot. Brian reached for his weapon, the telephone forgotten on the floor.

As soon as he threw his keys, Nick pulled the gun out of his unresponsive and numb left hand. It was a miracle he hadn't dropped it in the short time it took to whip the keys against the fishbowl wall.

He aimed at the pacing terrorist, who was pivoting and bringing his rifle to bear on Nick. He squeezed the trigger, and the resulting blast was unbelievably loud, echoing off the walls of the small room and ringing in his ears. It was almost disorienting.

The gun bucked wildly and the shot missed, blasting a fist-sized hole in the far wall. Chunks of drywall and pieces of two-by-four stud flew everywhere, tiny missiles peppering the room but incredibly not hitting the terrorist. Or if they had, he didn't react. Fine white dust blew out of the hole and coated the man's arm. The art print Nick had ruined with the keys fell to the floor, jarred off the wall by the concussive pistol blast.

Nick couldn't believe his eyes. The man was still standing. He was less than ten feet away, and the bullet had missed him. Even though he had never fired a pistol before, even though he was shaking and slipping into shock, even though he was blasting away at a moving target while on the move himself, Nick had fully expected to put the man down.

Now he was in big trouble. Nick squeezed the trigger

again. This time the sound of the bullet being fired was muffled, like he was hearing it underwater as his ears were still ringing from the first shot.

The terrorist tumbled backward, crashing into the corner of the conference room with a force that surprised Nick. Blood sprayed out of a hole the slug had punched in the man's chest, forming a delicate crimson arc that flew through the air and splashed onto the conference table, reminding Nick of the famous fountains at one of the resort hotels in Vegas that he and Lisa had visited a lifetime ago on their honeymoon.

The length of the bloody arcs immediately began to shorten as the dying terrorist's heart weakened. The second one barely reached the edge of the table, the one after that only made it halfway.

Nick frantically tried to sight the pistol in his badly shaking hand to take out the other man. But the missed first shot had cost him. When Nick located the man, he knew right away that he was too late. The terrorist had his weapon aimed at Nick's chest. Unlike Nick's gun, this man's weapon was held firmly and steadily in two hands. A look of grim determination spread across the man's face. He was not rushing; he was moving at a measured, almost leisurely pace.

It was over. Nick could not escape.

70

Nick waited for the end, seeing everything in slow motion. It felt as though he had been inside the fishbowl for hours, bullets flying everywhere, but in reality it had been no more than a few seconds. Powdery white drywall dust continued to fly, riding the air currents, slowly making its way across the room to where Nick was standing. The last of the chunks of plaster and wood chips blasted out of the wall by his first errant shot—the missed shot that had condemned Nick to death—were touching down at destinations all over the room.

The terrorist Nick had actually hit was still bleeding, but the initial gush of arterial blood from his chest had slowed to a trickle and was now dribbling down what was left of the man's shirt. His eyes were open but unfocused. He was dying.

Nick knew he would be joining the man in death in a second. He was still fighting, still desperately trying to get his weapon to do what his brain was telling it to do, but he felt slow and off balance, lopsided somehow. The gun refused to point at the second terrorist. It refused to do anything at all. It was stuttering in his shaking hand, and he knew he would never hit anything he was aiming at. The ironic thought occurred to him that he might actually shoot himself.

Nick watched as the second man took forever to aim at his chest. He was going to be shot in the heart as he watched it happen. In a corner of his mind, he wondered if Lisa had watched the knife slit her throat open while she was trapped in her car. He hoped not.

The pistol was now incredibly heavy in his hand and completely useless. It felt like he was holding a brick. His shoulder was burning, his left hand numb. Nerve damage, he figured; it had to be. He wondered how it would feel to die, whether there would be a lot of pain or maybe none at all. He thought about Lisa and hoped she would be waiting to greet him, wherever he ended up after this.

He finally heard the shot that would end his life, the sound fuzzy and strange thanks to the damage the other shots had done to his ears. The sound of the bullet being fired seemed strangely insignificant considering it was to be the instrument of his death. Nick waited to be blasted across the room and into the wall like the man he had shot. He waited for the blood to spurt out of him in rapidly diminishing arcs.

It didn't happen.

Nothing happened.

Instead, he watched in slack-jawed amazement as the man who was going to kill him jerked like he had been hit with a baseball bat and then smashed down onto the conference table, struck in the side of the head by a bullet. Shards of bone and grey brain matter splattered the wall to Nick's left as the man's blood sprayed onto the off-white background, completing a Dali-esque tableau of blood-red destruction inside the fishbowl.

The terrorist's body flopped on the table as comprehension dawned in his dimming eyes. His hands opened and closed like he was reaching for something with which to pull himself upright and he gasped for air. The left side of his skull was gone, replaced by a jagged, gaping hole. He twitched twice and finally was still.

Nick glanced right in time to see Special Agent Cunningham, eyes wide, face bone white, nose mashed grotesquely to the right side of her face, standing on one leg in a modified shooter's stance, leaning back against the far corner of the room for support.

She was shaking as badly as Nick was, maybe more so. She looked at Nick with haunted eyes and opened her mouth to say something, but no words came out. Nick heard an unintelligible croaking noise that morphed into a whimper as the gun fell from her hand. She stumbled toward him, her weight shifting to her mangled right leg, and crumpled to the floor.

71

Nick clutched a bouquet of yellow roses in his good hand as he paused in front of the open hospital door. He felt foolish. He was sweating and just as nervous as he had been before facing off against the terrorist known as Tony Andretti—authorities were still trying, thus far to no avail, to determine his real name and country of origin, not that Nick really cared—armed only with a rechargeable pneumatic nail gun.

"Jeez, asshole, get a grip," he muttered to himself, pushing through the doorway and into the hospital room before he could lose his nerve. Inside, Agent Cunningham stared listlessly at a television bolted into a metal stand in the upper left corner of the room. She looked impossibly tiny and helpless in the bed, surrounded by beeping machines and what appeared to be shiny metallic and chrome torture devices. Her right leg was immobilized, suspended above the bed by a system of pulleys and cables that looked to Nick like they should be used to hoist a building.

One of the network news shows was broadcasting on the television's snowy screen, treating the story of the attempted assassination of President Cartwright with the usual overblown media hysteria.

Agent Cunningham finally noticed Nick after a moment and muted the TV with a remote. "Can I help you?"

He smiled in amusement. "You already did. You saved my life yesterday, Agent Cunningham. It would be pretty hard to top that—don't you think?"

Recognition dawned in her eyes, and she grinned sheepishly. Nick thought she looked beautiful, even with the two puffy black eyes she would be sporting for a while and her grossly misshapen broken nose. "Sorry about that; I should have recognized you. And please call me Kristin." She shrugged and shook her head. "It must be all these drugs they're pumping into me; they've made me a little groggy."

"No problem, Kristin. I'm not exactly at my best right now, either." He placed the flowers on a small table next to the bed and extended his hand, grimacing as the motion pulled at the bandages wrapped tightly around his shoulder.

Kristin watched him and winced. "Are you all right? They told me you got shot but that you really *nailed* that Andretti character." She smiled wickedly.

"I'm fine," he answered. "It's just a flesh wound. Isn't that what all those Hollywood hero types are supposed to say?"

This time she giggled. It sounded nasally thanks to the cotton wadding stuffed into her rebuilt nose.

"Anyway, I'm not really sure what the protocol is for dealing with getting shot in the shoulder by a fanatical terrorist. In my line of work, people don't generally come after me with guns. Actually," he whispered conspiratorially, "it hurts like hell. Some hero, huh?"

"You *are* a hero. You saved my life just as much as I saved yours. The doctors tell me I wouldn't have lasted much longer inside that conference room, considering how much blood I had lost. If you hadn't acted when you did, we wouldn't be having this conversation right now, so I would say you deserve some flowers, too." She looked ruefully at her immobilized leg. "I guess I'll have to owe you."

Changing the subject, she said, "They caught the two guys who were camped out by the airport waiting to shoot down the president's plane. They were parked in a marsh, and when it became clear that something had gone wrong, they tried to escape, but they got into a gun battle with a local cop. He was wounded but managed to shoot out one of their tires. The idiots escaped on foot but were apprehended before they made it two miles. I hear the cop they shot is doing well and is expected to recover fully."

She examined her fingernails. "They killed someone in another car that stumbled on to them. He was just a kid."

"I heard. It seems they killed a lot of people."

"I'm sorry about your coworkers."

"Thank you."

An awkward silence descended over the room, and Nick mumbled, "Well, I guess I should be going. The doctors said you need your rest and that I could only have a couple of minutes. Thanks again—"

"Your wife was a hero too, you know."

Nick stared at the floor. "I can't help but wonder what would have happened if she had reported what she discovered sooner. Even just a day or two earlier, instead of holding on to the binder. Maybe if she had acted a little more decisively, the whole mess could have been avoided before it ever got started."

Kristin shook her head emphatically. "You can't look at it like that. She didn't realize the significance of what she discovered. You better believe that if she'd had any idea how serious it was, she would have taken action immediately. Either way, it's not her fault she didn't live long enough to tell anyone about it."

Nick sighed. "Yeah, I know. But thanks anyway for saying so. I really appreciate it. That means a lot."

"Hey," Kristin said, "when I get out of this prison and can get around again, maybe we could do dinner and fill each other in on what exactly happened in that building. It's one thing to get a debriefing from the officious administrative types; it's another thing entirely to go over it with the one person who was heavily involved. Plus, I make a mean pot roast. Are you game?"

Nick smiled at her and said, "Sounds great. I haven't had

a real meal since . . . well . . . you know." He scuffed his shoe absently on the institutional grey tile. "Anyway, I'll be back to check on you in a couple of days. Maybe even bring some more flowers."

He lifted the bouquet off the table and placed it in her arms, then turned once again to go. It was time to get back to work. The airplanes were waiting.

ACKNOWLEDGMENTS

FINAL VECTOR represents both my first and most recent book to be published. The first edition was released in February 2011 by Medallion Press, and this second edition is the same book, with the only real exception being a brand-new chapter leading things off. The original Chapter One was removed during editing prior to the book's release by Medallion, and I've reinstalled it because I believe it establishes the tone of the story right off the bat. Aside from that change, I've tinkered with some of the phrasing and description with the goal of making the narrative flow a little more naturally.

That said, I cannot thank enough the folks at Medallion Press enough for believing in a largely unknown author with a slightly different take on the typical aviation thriller. I have nothing but admiration for everyone at Medallion, including Helen Rosburg, Paul Ohlson, Jim Tampa, and especially Editorial Director Lorie Popp, whose professionalism and editing skill added immensely to the first edition final product.

As a long-time air traffic controller in the real world, I would be remiss if I didn't mention the contributions of Brian Hansen, Joe Serafino, Tony Serino, Jeff Zarella and Dan Gravelle, friends and co-workers all. My fellow professionals at NATCA, the National Air Traffic Controllers Association, have been working toward the dual goals of aviation safety and the betterment of the controllers' lot in life for virtually my entire career, and to them I owe a debt of gratitude as well.

My wife, Sue, and my entire family have been the best, most vocal supporters of my work anyone could ever ask for, and to them I say thank you, although I know that could never be enough.

The print edition formatting, interior and exterior, was done by Robert Shane Wilson, a tech wiz and damned fine writer in his own regard. Huge thanks to Bob for doing a job I couldn't handle on the best day I ever had.

The visually stunning cover art comes from Scott Carpenter, who was so successful executing my vision for the cover that I just couldn't narrow my choices down to one. This explains why the print edition you hold in your hands looks a little different on the outside than does the ebook edition. Thanks so much to a great guy and a great designer.

Finally, thanks to you, the reader who parted with your hard earned cash to check out my book. There are plenty of other outstanding authors you could be reading right now. The fact that you chose FINAL VECTOR is humbling and gratifying, and I will never take your support for granted.

29231161R00172

Made in the USA
Charleston, SC
05 May 2014